SEASIDE MAGIC

VIANLIX-CHRISTINE SCHNEIDER

To my grandma, Abu. Love you.

Prologue
1943

Dilandro picked up toys that had been left on the floor in his four-year-old daughter's room. To take his mind off his dreadful day, he had joined Caroline at the tea party she was having with her stuffed animals.

Soon after joining, she had rushed off to get snacks and got distracted by her mother. He could hear them working together in the kitchen, rolling out dough to make bread for dinner. His little girl had forgotten all about him.

Once the floor was clear of all toys, the smell of bread baking in the oven filled the house, making his mouth water.

He looked at the window, spotting some handprints from his daughter low on the glass. He made a mental note to clean it later. His eyes moved toward the front yard. A cold winter had just ended, and spring was among them. Most of the trees held buds, promising colorful flowers. The sun shined down on the lush, green grass. His eyes then shifted toward the woods that stood a few hundred feet away from the house. Just as he was about to turn to leave the room, a shadow stood out against the trees like a sore thumb, making him freeze. He squinted, trying to make out what he was seeing.

A man dressed in all black stood with half his body hidden by a tree. As if he didn't want to be seen. A black mask covered his face.

Dilandro stumbled back with a dry mouth as he realized who stood in the woods. Swallowing, he wondered how long it had taken him to finally find him. With a chill, he thought, *how long has he been watching?* Had the masked man seen him with his daughter? Like a fool, he had never believed the legend of the masked man. Of the man who had caused his family so much pain. Dilandro had been only a baby when they had lost their parents to the masked man. He had grown up in hiding with his three older brothers but never held the fear for the masked man that they held. They had explained who he was and what he could do, but Dilandro had brushed it off as a work of fiction.

Once he was old enough to live on his own, he left and started a family—the masked man nothing but a distant memory from his childhood. But now, as he stared at the mysterious man standing on his property, he wished he had stayed hidden and listened to his brothers.

He pushed that thought aside. "Lucy!" he called, not taking his eyes off the man. "He's here!"

In a matter of seconds, the house's mood changed from blissful to tense.

Heading toward the kitchen, he ignored the painful way his heart beat. Lucy rushed out of the kitchen and met him in the hallway. Her pale skin was dusted in baking flour, along with her green dress.

Her voice shook. "Are you sure?"

He took hold of her arms. "He's here."

Caroline stood in the kitchen doorway and looked up at her parents, her eyebrows together in thought. Her blue dress that stopped above her knees was covered in baking flour. Her black Mary Janes were also dotted with it. One sock was rolled down at her ankle.

"Hide her." Without another word, he moved to shut the curtains.

As Lucy picked up Caroline, he moved to ensure the front door was locked. He then peeked out the window, moving the curtain slightly out of the way. The masked man was walking toward their house, making his way across the bright yard. His fists were down by his side.

"Lucy, hurry!" Dilandro roared.

Caroline needed to stay out of sight. The masked man could not know he had a child. He looked back as Lucy opened the coat closet by the stairs. Caroline held a curious expression in Lucy's arms.

"Stay here, love," Lucy said as she placed her down with the coats. Her green eyes were bright with worry.

"What about bread?" Caroline asked in a small voice.

"We're going to play hide-and-seek, sweetie," Dilandro said as he moved to her. "Don't come out, all right?" He lowered himself to her level and kissed her forehead. "I love you."

She smiled as he stood. "You count. I hide here."

He closed the closet door, moved over to his desk in the living room, and pulled his wand out from one of the drawers. As he picked it up, hope and fear engulfed him.

"I want to help," Lucy said.

I can't lose Lucy. He turned toward the front door as she grabbed his wrist. Before she could add anything, he turned to face her. Their lips locked with desperation. *Please let me see her again.*

He pulled away. "You have to stay here and keep her safe." He pointed at where their child, who was pure enough to think they were still playing, hid.

Lucy glanced at the closed door. Her eyes watered as she pushed a lock of her light brown hair from her face.

"Do not come out for anything. Do you understand?" he asked with tears in his brown eyes.

He worried—with all his heart—that the man standing outside would hurt his girls if something went wrong. He wouldn't know what to do with himself if something happened to either of them.

"Be careful," she whispered as her arms wrapped around him.

He kissed her forehead. "Please keep her safe." His voice was nothing but a shaky whisper. "I love you."

"I love you too."

Dilandro walked outside. His hands shook as he held his wand out in front of him. Failing to hide his fear. He hoped his powers were still strong like when he was young, but he doubted it. Years ago, like a fool, he had stopped using magic, thinking he would never need it.

"Well," the masked man said in a calm voice as his purple eyes locked on Dilandro, "I finally found you."

Chills covered Dilandro's body. *I should have stayed in hiding.* "It took you long enough," he said, fear in his voice.

The masked man laughed under his breath. "You seem scared."

Dilandro didn't want to have small talk with this man. To let him toy with him. The masked man would die here.

He pointed his wand. "This will end today!" His voice was weaker than he would have liked.

His enemy laughed. The sound was like a hiss. Clutching a wand of his own, the masked man pointed it at him. "This will end today. Just not the way you think it will."

Dilandro flicked his wrist, yelling out the first spell that came to mind. "Gepsic!" Power rushed through his body and out his wand. To his delight, his magic still held the power it had in his youth.

The spell hit the masked man's face. With a loud shout, he took a step back, cradling his face. His mask broke in half, one half dropping to his feet while the other stayed on.

He looked up at Dilandro, full of rage and hate. Slowly, he removed his bloodstained hand from his face. Dilandro swallowed at the sight. A deep cut started in the middle of his forehead and reached across his nose and to his cheek. So much dark red blood ran down his face.

With great force, the masked man flicked his wand at Dilandro.

The power came fast, forcing Dilandro to think even faster. He moved his wand in a circle, and the spell disappeared before reaching him. "Gunfoly!"

With a small step to his left, the masked man avoided the spell.

Winded, Dilandro flicked his wand once more. "Gepsic!"

The masked man flicked his wand, sending his own spell back to him. Pain zapped his body. The masked man flicked his wand again, hitting him.

Dilandro froze. He couldn't move at all—except for his fearful eyes—even if he tried. His short brown hair stood frozen. A wave of panic ran over him as the masked man walked over.

"You've lost," he hissed, making direct eye contact with Dilandro.

Dilandro tried to move with all his might, but it was pointless. His eyes moved frantically. *This can't be it!* The masked man lifted his wand to his face with wicked eyes. He could smell the blood from the masked man's face.

The masked man's eyes then glanced over Dilandro's

shoulder. Chills spread through Dilandro's body as a familiar voice filled his ears.

"NO!" Lucy screamed from somewhere behind him.

He tried to yell, but not a sound came out. *Lucy, please no!* This was his war, not hers. He never wanted her to get involved in this part of his life. No matter how fake he had thought it was.

He looked at the masked man before him with pleading eyes. *Please don't touch her!*

The masked man walked past him and toward Lucy.

No!

"Oh." The masked man laughed. "I didn't know you were home, Lucy. If I knew, I would have invited you to say goodbye to your pathetic husband."

Dilandro tried to calm himself. She also knew how to use magic and was quite gifted; she could handle this masked man. But his mind still shouted for her to go inside. To go away from this man. A part of him knew she would never go back inside, even if he begged her to. Which made his anxiety grow.

The masked man's voice filled his ears. "Let's let your husband watch while I kill you!" Using his magic, he forced Dilandro's frozen body to turn toward his wife.

She stood on the porch, her wand in her hand. She locked eyes with him as a light breeze blew by, making the moment feel frozen in time.

Please! Go inside!

She swallowed hard as the masked man pointed his wand toward Dilandro with a wicked smile.

"Ready to die?" he asked Dilandro.

She flicked her wand at him. "Freezenone!"

With the spell removed, Dilandro dropped to the ground. The masked man flicked his wand at her.

"No!" he roared as he tackled the masked man to the ground.

Their bodies jolted with the impact. He slammed his fist down over the cut on the masked man's face. The masked man cried out and dropped his wand from his hold. Lucy was at his side in a second, picking up the wand. Standing, he took the wand from her and snapped it in two.

The masked man's eyes widened for a beat before anger twisted his face. "You will regret that!" He seemed to reach toward Dilandro, his fingers stiff. Yellow power emerged from his fingertips and went into Dilandro's chest.

Lucy cried out as Dilandro took a few steps back. A hand went to his chest as desperation grew within him, and the pain intensified. He looked over at his wife with agony. Sorrow in his eyes. He mouthed, "I love you."

Then he vanished.

****

"NO!" Lucy shouted.

Time slowed as she stared at where her husband had just been. He was gone. Because of the masked man who stood with a smile. Anger bubbled in her, pushing away the pain of her loss.

"Where is the girl?" the masked man asked in a calm voice.

Her body shook with rage. She wanted to fight him. *But he can't find Caroline.*

Flicking her wand, she teleported back into the house. Her eyes fell on the mantel by the sofa. Pictures of the three of them smiled at her, showing the life the man outside had stolen from her. She sobbed and kicked the ottoman. It moved, making a loud scratching sound against the wood floors.

"Mama?"

Caroline's small voice snapped her back to the problem.

Her daughter seemed so innocent, not knowing what had just happened. A doll was in her hands.

"Caroline!" Lucy picked her up and noticed tears in her daughter's brown eyes.

"What happening?" she asked as Lucy held her tight. Tears soaked her cheeks.

Lucy needed to move fast. The masked man outside would come in soon. Why he hadn't yet only made her fear stronger.

"Where Dada? I heard yelling." More tears streamed down Caroline's face as Lucy moved to her bedroom.

Her heart was broken, but she knew what had to be done. "Caroline, your father will always be with you." Once in the bedroom she would never share with Dilandro again, she sat Caroline down on the bed.

Movement sounded from within the house.

He's inside! She shut the door.

When they had Caroline, Dilandro's oldest brother— George—had made a plan for if the masked man found them. It was simple. She just had to teleport them to her sister's house. Together.

But how could she just leave the man who killed Dilandro? How could she not make him pay for everything he'd taken from her?

"Where Dada?" Caroline asked again.

Lucy kissed her forehead. Her decision made. "I need you to be brave," she said as she held her daughter's arms and looked her in the eyes. She noticed how much she looked like her father. Their brown eyes were identical. Her brown hair held the same soft waves his hair held when it grew too long.

"Mama!"

A loud sound echoed through the house.

"I love you so much," Lucy said. "I hope one day you can understand what I had to do." She pushed a lock of her daughter's hair behind her ear.

Caroline sobbed. "I'm scared!"

She pulled her to her chest. *Me too.* "We'll be together again someday. I promise!" she whispered as she backed away from her.

The masked man teleported into the room. Caroline screamed, and Lucy quickly waved her wand.

"Teleportsheam!"

Caroline no longer sat in front of her. All that was left was the doll she had been holding.

She was safe.

"You fool!" the masked man yelled as he slapped her across the face.

She gasped as she dropped to the floor.

"You can't hide her from me!" he hissed. He grabbed the collar of her dress and yanked her to her feet. His bloody face was inches from hers. "Where's the child?"

"She's safe!"

"I'll find her," he hissed. He raised his free hand up, his fingers stiff like before.

For a beat, she regretted staying, regretted leaving Caroline. "She's gone! You'll never find her. You—"

She screamed out in pain as yellow power traveled from his hand and into her chest. She glanced at the doll on the bed with tears in her eyes before she was gone, much like Dilandro.

****

As Lucy disappeared from his hold, the masked man took in a rage-filled breath. "This was not what I had planned!" he yelled.

He had come to kill Dilandro and the child, the only two in the house who had Smith blood. He hadn't come for the mess he had made.

Why was I not fast enough? There were so many places that Lucy could have sent the girl.

His eyes fell on the bed, where a Raggedy Ann doll lay abandoned. He picked it up gently.

It had a small tag on its leg. *If lost, please return to Caroline Smith.*

He smiled.

Now, he had a name.

Chapter 1
1953

Caroline Smith pulled her knees up to her chest as she tried to find a comfortable position to sit in. She had been sitting in the same hard wooden train seats for the past five days. The seats dug into her back no matter how she moved. It had gotten so bad during one of the days—she didn't remember which one—that she had tried standing for a while, but it had just made her dizzy.

She looked out the window, trying to take her mind off her back pain and the fact the cart smelled like mold.

A bright red farm sat in the middle of the greenest field she had ever seen. Cows chewed on grass as it dangled from their mouths. A farmer rode a lovely white horse in the distance with his small dog running next to him. She smiled as she watched them before the train window showed endless trees once more.

The sun flashed through the branches and into the train, adding a headache to the list of her problems.

She looked back down into her lap, closing her eyes in hopes it would help her head. Around her, faint conversations were held by the other passengers stuck on this hell on rails with her. Someone's baby laughed far behind her, and the tapping of someone knitting came from a few seats ahead of her.

"Where are you traveling to?" the young man in the seat behind her asked the young woman beside him.

Caroline sighed. She didn't care where the woman was going or where she would get off. She only knew where the train would stop for herself, and that was all she cared about.

She was moving in with her grandmother, the only one still alive. She lived in North Carolina. A whole 2,991 miles away from where she had lived her whole life.

Nervs gawked in her stomach. She didn't know her grandmother. The only memory she had of her was at her parents' funeral after they had accidently drowned ten years ago. *As long as she's not like Uncle George.* A chill brushed up her spine.

With a shake of her head, she pushed that thought away. She just got out of there; she would not waste a thought more on him.

"I'm on my way to my best friend's wedding," the woman behind her said. Her voice was so happy. Too happy to be sitting in the same uncomfortable chairs as Caroline.

The man's smooth voice made Caroline open her eyes to hear his answer. "Do you want a plus one?"

Caroline bit her lip to keep from laughing. *Is it really that easy to get a significant other?*

Reaching down into her only bag, she pulled out a small bag of peanuts. She took a few into her hand as she leaned her back on the window. The dusty green curtains held a strange smell. But it made her back feel a little better.

A little.

Caroline poured the handful into her mouth and pulled her bag up to her lap. She took out the wallet she had stolen from her Aunt Mia—George's bitter wife—and saw she still had enough to get on a bus to the town where her grandma lived. As long as she didn't buy anything else to eat.

A weak smile formed as she thought of how angry her aunt would be once she learned what she had done.

But she was halfway across the country. Too far for Mia to hit her. George now had her full attention, someone else she could yell at. Caroline didn't feel sorry at all. In fact, she hoped they fought often and wouldn't know a day of happiness.

His voice came to her head.

You're such a fool. I'll be surprised if you make it to North Carolina.

She shook her head as if to get rid of his voice. She was doing just fine. In fact, despite everything, she was happy.

Glancing over her shoulder and out the window, she was not sure where she was. Trees where the only things zipping passed the window. Wherever she was at, there was only a day left. And despite what her uncle thought of her, she would find her way to her grandma. It had been George and Mia's idea to send her away anyway, and she had never been so happy to move.

Pain shot through her back and her neck. With every bump, the train moved her just enough to send pain throughout her body. *You got this. One more night.*

She grabbed one more handful of nuts before sliding what was left into her bag and putting her bag under her seat. She needed them to last. With her head pounding, she closed her eyes. She hoped that when she woke, she was at her stop, and nothing hurt.

North Carolina, here I come.

Chapter 2

As the sun rose over the mountains, it shined into the train. Caroline covered her eyes with her hair to go back to sleep. The train was uncomfortable, but nights made everything worse. Once the sun would go down, only a few flickering lights hung in the dark space, not enough to read or distract oneself with.

She hadn't slept well, up against the window just like all the nights that had come before. She couldn't wait till she was in a good bed again. *Soon.* She ran her hand down the oversized shorts of her jumper, making them lay flat against her legs. Looking around the cart, she found that most people were still sleeping or doing some light reading now that the sun shined in.

With today being the last day on the train, she wanted to be ready, to know where she was going the second she got off. She bent over and reached under her seat for her bag. Leaning over it, she dug around for the letter.

George had sent word to her grandmother, saying that Caroline wanted to move in with her. He had written the letter as if Caroline had sent it, but she wouldn't have. Even with how much she hated living with him and Mia, she would never have thought of moving so far from where she had grown up. So far away from Uncle Edmund.

She wanted to look over the address, to know what town she would travel to once she got off the train. With the letter in hand, she leaned back in the seat. Her eyes read over the unfamiliar handwriting.

Caroline,

I have never been so happy to read a letter in my life. It's so nice to hear from you! How are you? I would love to have you come here to Duck, NC! The sooner the better. Most of the summer fun is about to start, so I know you'll love it here. I already have a room that you are welcome to take. The house has felt so empty since my girls moved out. It would be nice to have someone to share it with.

I can't wait to give you a big hug. Sending all my love and praying for a safe trip. See you soon!

Lots of love,
Julia (Jewel or Grandma)
XOXO
165 Seasons Lane, Duck

Caroline mouthed the address.

She had waited night and day for that letter. George and Mia had made it very clear what would happen if her grandma didn't want her. No one ever talked about Julia, making her a bit surprised when she not only responded but *agreed* for her to live with her. She had always found it strange that no one talked about her. Almost as if she didn't exist.

But maybe her grandmother was just as misunderstood as she was. She seemed nice enough in her letter.

A small smile came to Caroline at the idea of there being

a room picked out for her. A place her grandmother had picked especially for her.

She sent a silent prayer that she would be happy and that living with her would be like when she had lived with Uncle Edmund—her father's second oldest brother. Her heart then dropped at the thought of the man she had seen as a father. The man who moved her out of his house after seven years.

She sighed. She didn't want to think about him.

The train raddled, bringing her back to the space she was in. The uncomfortable seats.

It then slowed for its stop in a few miles. The last stop!

One of the railroad workers walked into the cart and stood by the door she would be exiting through soon. He was tall and skinny, reminding her of a baby giraffe. "Next stop is Asheville, North Carolina! If you are getting off at this stop, please have your bags ready. Also, have your ticket in hand to show a member once you deboard."

Caroline put the letter in her bag and looked for her ticket.

"We thank you for riding with us." He smiled, turning on his heels before going to the other carts to repeat the message.

At last, she would get off this train! Have her feet back on solid ground. With each bump, she was further away from the Smith brothers and closer to her grandma.

A smile formed on her face.

****

As Caroline stepped off the train, she took a deep breath of fresh air. The train had been stuffy, making the air heavy. Her window had only cracked open, not giving her much air throughout her trip. But here, the air was crisp and refreshing.

The sun was bright, making everything around her seem whiter. The heat welcomed her like an unwanted hug.

She got in a line of people she had ridden with and held her ticket to show it to the worker at the end of the line.

"Next!" the worker called out, his face bright red. He looked hot under the summer sun.

The train's steam was hot on her legs as she approached him. "Here you go!" Excitement jumped into her voice.

He looked down at her ticket without saying a word. His face formed a frown.

She didn't know what he was looking for, but he took his time. Her mouth grew dry at the thought he would send her back.

After a while, he wrote something over it with a marker and handed it back to her. "Have a nice day, kid."

"You as well!"

As she stepped out of the line, Caroline held her bag with both hands and looked up at the few signs that indicated when the buses would come and where they were going. Everyone moved around her with purpose, while some hugged family members who had greeted them at the station. Swallowing, she read over the signs and spotted Duck. She smiled, seeing that the bus she needed was written to pick her up in two minutes. *I can wait two minutes in this sun.*

A worker walked up and erased the time. Her smile dropped as he wrote down an hour and a half.

"Great," she puffed out.

She sat on the curb at her bus stop. A few buses drove by, but they were all going elsewhere. The sun beat down on her as she waited and waited. Her legs baked in the heat. She feared getting a sunburn before even arriving at the beach. A few other people showed up, waiting with her, but no one spoke. She pulled out her grandma's letter and fanned herself, but that didn't help much.

Two hours later, a bus showed up, making the loudest squeak as it came to a stop.

Caroline sighed. "Thank goodness." *I'm melting out here.* She picked up her bag and waited for the bus door to open.

"You going to Duck?" the bus driver asked as the door opened. He stood, cracking his back with three loud pops.

"Yes."

"That will be ten cents," he said, pointing down at a small box filled with money.

"Oh, right." She dug for Mia's wallet as people pushed past her to get in and drop their ten cents into the box. After grabbing the last of her money, she dropped the change into the box and took the ticket the man handed her.

The door slammed shut behind her.

Only five other people sat on the bus. They all watched her as she walked toward an empty seat. After she sat, she looked out the window, her back pain returning. These seats were harder than the train's. And held mysterious stains. If the trip could go any faster, she would be happy. All she wanted to do was shower off the week in the train and the heat from waiting for the bus.

She put her bag under her legs like before and felt someone staring at her. She looked up. A boy—no older than four—watched her as he sat across from her.

She tried not to look back at him as the bus started moving.

Not even a minute into the drive, Caroline clutched her chair. The bus driver changed lanes for no reason, cut people off, and drove over the speed limit. She closed her eyes a few times and hoped they didn't hit anything or drive off the road.

They stopped twice to use the bathroom throughout the six-hour drive. For most of the ride, no one talked to each other. The only sounds that echoed throughout the bus were the boy coughing and the bus driver cursing.

A lifetime later, Caroline watched as the forest view from the window opened. The scenery changed to a large body of water as they drove over a tall, thin bridge. White caps danced with the water's movement as huge seagulls cried out and flew over the water and the bridge.

The sky added to everything around her. Light pink and orange mixed at the horizon, and an odd shade of blue made the rest of the sky. It seemed as if God had come down and painted the lovely colors. The water mirrored the sunset.

The bridge itself seemed to last forever, but Caroline didn't mind. The view was perfect. She could even smell the salty ocean from inside the bus.

Putting the side of her face against the glass, she saw the long peninsula that her grandma lived on. Where she would live. She noticed a few houses by the water with some dots—people—out fishing. The land that lay far away also seemed so green and inviting. Like the trees hid something amazing behind them.

Duck was somewhere within the trees, waiting for her.

A seagull rode the small waves. She felt peace as she looked at the water. It was all so breathtaking that she almost forgot the anxiety of meeting her grandma. That was until the bus driver sharply changed lanes, making another driver honk their horn.

Her chest went cold as she grabbed her chair once more. Her fingertips found gum under the chair. *I'm going to end up in the water! And drown like mom and—*

She pushed that thought away and laughed under her breath. Of course, fate would have her bus crash off a bridge while so close to paradise.

Once safely over the bridge, the bus stopped dramatically.

She looked out the window, not recognizing the town she was now in.

The bus driver opened the bus door, stood, and stretched his back. Four cracks this time.

Caroline grabbed her bag and walked off the bus before anyone else moved. After she jumped off, she took a deep breath. She had never been happier to be on solid ground. No more trains and no more buses with drivers who should never have gotten their license.

"Wow," she said, looking at the lovely town in front of her.

Even though the sun was lowering, people filled the small town, walking and laughing. The beach added to the charm. Every building looked different with beautiful colors that matched the sky.

So many little shops lined the street; she didn't know where to look first. A donut shop had a strong divine smell coming from it. Her mouth watered. One shop sold beach toys for children. Three young boys stood outside of the shop, showing off their new toys to each other.

One white building with large columns stood at the end of the main street, the road curving around it. She didn't know what the building was, but it looked important.

Young women walked by with their puffy skirts and their hair done in the latest fashion. The poodle hairstyle curled to perfection. Some women walked by with parasols to protect them from the lowering sun. The men wore white shirts and shiny shoes. Some people enjoyed ice cream as they walked. Some cars drove by, mostly Ford convertibles with soft music coming from them. The drivers smiled while they drove with their families.

Never had she seen such a sight. Something so charming and so captivating.

Caroline giggled. The people seemed so happy and relaxed here. It was so different from her hometown back in Washington. She closed her eyes and tried to see if she could hear the ocean from where she stood. It was faint, but she could hear the waves breaking on the sand.

The bus cried out, making her jump as her eyes shot open. Her bag dropped to her feet, and she turned, watching the bus drive out of the town. It almost hit a very good-looking teenager with sandy hair on a bike. He looked a bit fearful as he kept riding. When he passed her, she couldn't help but linger on him a bit.

Turning back to her bag, she picked it up. The sun was almost fully set now; it was time to find the street her grandma lived in.

She mumbled the address, looking for any clues about where it might be. "165 Seasons Lane, Duck."

She walked around, trying to see if she could find her grandmother's neighborhood. But she also knew she would get lost the minute she walked out of town. Her stomach twisted. *Maybe George was right. I'm too foolish to do this on my own.*

"Excuse me," Caroline called to an older lady as she walked by.

The older lady stopped with a kind smile. She wore a white dress that reached low on her knees. "Yes, dear?"

"Do you know where this neighborhood is?" She pulled the letter's envelope from her bag.

The older lady grabbed her reading glasses from her breast pocket.

"I'm lost. I have no idea where this is."

She laughed once she had her glasses on. Her blue eyes seemed larger with her eyewear. "I live in that neighborhood!"

Caroline smiled. "Really?! What are the odds."

The lady took her glasses off and pointed down the road. "It's right down that street. It's the only neighborhood on the left."

Caroline looked the way she had pointed. The town seemed to simply end there. Plenty of trees and a few roads led off into the unknown. "Thank you…" She paused, waiting for a name.

"Patti Clark."

"Thank you, Mrs. Clark. I'm Caroline Smith, by the way."

Mrs. Clark nodded with a smile. "Oh, you're the Caroline girl your grandma has been talking about!"

Caroline felt her cheeks heat. "Really?"

Her grandma had been talking about her? Something in her lit up with joy.

"Oh yes, my dear," Mrs. Clark said with a laugh. "Go find her. She'll be so happy to know you've made it safely."

"Thanks again."

They both went their own ways, Caroline walking the way Mrs. Clark had sent her. She smiled again, letting herself get excited about the change her life had taken.

Chapter 3

Caroline saw the street Mrs. Clark had pointed to. The old lady had been right. It was the only street on her left. Her grandmother's neighborhood.

As she walked, she held her bag with one hand and whispered the address once more. She hoped the colorful sky would give her enough light to see the numbers on the houses, still worried she would get lost.

A beautiful island filled with different brightly colored flowers sat at the entrance of the neighborhood. There was a path with a roof of trees overhead that led her straight to the neighborhood.

As she turned to head in, a woman, who was maybe in her fifties, walked past her. They both held eye contact for a moment. The world seemed to slow. The stranger looked at her in a familiar way, like she had known her due to an unknown connection. As she continued to walk, leaving the stranger behind, the woman called out.

"Are you Caroline?"

Caroline stopped and turned to look at the woman. Now that she got a better look, the woman looked like someone she had known once.

"You are Caroline!" the woman said, smiling.

"So, are you my… Are you…Julia?" she asked, not wanting to call her grandmother. Not yet.

The woman's smile stretched from ear to ear. "Yes! I'm Julia!"

The woman took a step closer. Her brown curly hair was pulled out of her face in a loose ponytail. She was dressed in the most refreshing outfit Caroline had ever seen. Her white blouse was sleeveless with two small bows on her shoulders. Her soft pink and white plaid skirt reached her knees. Small white heels put everything together.

Caroline hoped living here would make her look as breezy as she did. She imagined she looked awful in her blue jumper that she had worn for days on end.

"You look just like my daughter!" Julia sighed with watery eyes.

Caroline smiled, enjoying the compliment. She didn't know what to do or say.

Julia looked like her mother was well but older. But she didn't voice the thought.

"Everyone tells me I look like my dad," she said instead.

"You do." Julia laughed after a beat. "Oh, my goodness! I can't believe you finally made it!"

Caroline smiled. "If you saw how bad the bus driver was, you would be even more shocked I lived." She had said it as a joke, but Julia didn't laugh.

"Are you all right?" Julia asked as her smile fell.

"Oh yeah. I mean, I made it."

Her eyes lingered on the ring of faint bruises around her arm. "What happened?" she asked.

Caroline smiled awkwardly. Mia had happened. The night before she had left, Mia had grabbed her so tightly that her fingers had left dark purple marks. The bruises were mostly yellow now, but she still didn't want to share how she got them. "I walked into something."

Julia nodded, and an awkward silence fell over them. The silence was so heavy that Caroline could in fact hear the ocean.

Julia looked just like Caroline's mother. She had her same green eyes, along with a smile that could light the world. A few freckles ran across her nose and cheeks. She also had Lucy's round face, but her jaw was a bit more noticeable than her mother's. Or at least from what Caroline had seen in pictures.

Her sun-kissed skin showed that she lived by the beach. She was not tall but not short either, just like the photos of Caroline's mother. She was taller than Caroline for sure though. Caroline stood about her shoulder.

"Can I hug you?" she asked.

Caroline laughed. "Sure." She put her bag down and wrapped her arms around her grandma. It was such a strange thought. *I am hugging my grandma.* Her grandma smelled good, like a candle with a silly name.

"You can call me Jewel if you want. Everyone does."

Caroline pulled away, thankful for the nickname. As she backed away, she opened her mouth to speak, but nothing came to mind. *What do I tell someone I haven't seen in ten years?*

Luckily, Jewel took the wheel. "So, you had a long journey?" She picked up Caroline's bag for her.

"Yeah. Very long," Caroline said.

"Where is your Aunt Mia? Or George?" She looked around for them as if they would pop up at any moment.

"I came alone."

"*What?* You did that trip all by yourself?"

Caroline nodded.

Jewel put a hand to her chest. "Well, you are a lot braver than I am. I thought they were coming."

"Nope. Just me."

"If I would've known you were coming by yourself, I would've gone to get you."

Caroline waved her hand, dismissing her worries. "They didn't even take me to the train station. I had to walk there. It was only a two-mile walk. No problem."

Jewel looked mortified. "I don't know what to say. The rules are not to leave you alone like that."

Her eyebrows came together. "Rules?"

Jewel's face switched back to her smile. "That doesn't matter anymore. You're here, and you're safe. That is that."

Caroline nodded.

Silence fell over the pair once more. She smiled as she glanced around her. Large trees held a few birds that looked down on her. Her eyes fell on Jewel, who smiled back. It felt like someone should be talking, asking questions. But the silence went on.

How can this be? We have our whole lives to talk about. She knew nothing about Jewel, and Jewel knew nothing of her. There had to be something to talk about.

As Caroline opened her mouth to speak, Jewel asked, "Do you want to freshen up?"

The idea sounded wonderful.

"And put your things in your new room?"

Caroline nodded with a sigh. "Yes please!"

"I've picked a room with an ocean view for you. But if you don't like it, you can pick your own room."

She laughed. "Who would say no to a room with such a view?"

"That's what I thought. But I wanted to ask."

Together, they walked to Jewel's house without saying a word. As they walked, Caroline stayed close to Jewel. Her eyes scanned each house they passed. The architect was so different from Washington. The huge houses looked new, each painted either a light blue or a bright white. Not one house was missing a wraparound porch or a grand stairway to the front door.

The air had a happy feeling to it. In a few front yards, families' laughter echoed as they took their things into their houses.

"Those are rentals," Jewel explained. "They come, stay in those houses for a week, and leave. Then the next family comes in and so on. There are only four houses with permanent residents in this neighborhood, and I am one of them."

"How did you find this place?" Caroline asked.

"My late husband Lester." Jewel looked down at her. "Your grandpa. His grandmother owned the house, and she left it for him. We moved into the house and raised our girls here."

They followed the road as it bent, and the ocean came into view. The sound of waves crashing in rhythm filled their ears.

"How did he pass?" Caroline asked as her eyes danced over the ocean. The sun was almost set, making the sky half pink and half filled with stars.

"He died when your mom and aunt were still kids. Always had heart problems and never took it as seriously as he should have."

I hope that doesn't run in the family. "I didn't know you raised my mom alone."

Jewel pointed at a house. Her house.

It took Caroline's breath away. The large house had many windows. It seemed so peaceful. But it also seemed like a lonely place to live alone. She glanced back at her grandma as she went on.

"I didn't really raise them alone. My best friend Dutch— you'll meet him—helped me. He'd take them to school dances and help with homework. He even walked your mom down the aisle at her wedding."

As they got closer to the house, Caroline's mouth dropped. The house was so tall from where she stood. More than a dozen steps led to the front door and porch with a few rocking chairs.

"Don't trip. The steps are a bit steep," Jewel called over her shoulder as she went up to the front door.

Caroline loved the blue color of the house and the plants growing by the stairs.

"Come on!" Jewel called.

Caroline moved to go up the steps.

She opened the door to reveal a beautiful open space. "Come in quick!" she said as she practically shoved Caroline through the threshold.

"Jewel!" Caroline gasped as the door shut hard behind them.

"Sorry. When the sun goes down, these bugs called midges come out. They are very annoying, flying into houses because they like the light." She pointed up toward a few already sitting on the ceiling.

"Do they bite?" Caroline asked.

"Nah. They won't hurt you, but it's gross to have them in your house."

She looked toward the rest of the beach house. It seemed like its own world. A peaceful energy came from every corner. What was left of the sun shined through every window, filling the house with a warm light. As she walked in further, she took it all in.

An overwhelming feeling filled her as she continued to take the house in. It was *huge*.

"If you want, you can explore the house and see it for

yourself," Jewel said with a smile. "It's more fun to discover each room. Or I can give you a tour."

She looked over and smiled. "I kind of like the exploring idea."

"I'll put your bag in your room and meet you there."

As Jewel went up the stairs that sat next to the living room, Caroline slowly walked around the house. Pictures of the beach and birds were up on the walls. Her heart leaped when she saw old pictures of her mom and Aunt Tilly playing by the ocean on a table behind the sofa. She had only seen a few photos of her mother before.

One picture that caught her eye was of her mom when she was maybe fifteen or sixteen years old. She sat on a low tree branch with a large smile. Her long brown hair came down over her shoulders and seemed as though it had blown lightly in the breeze. Frozen in time.

Tears stunned Caroline's eyes as she touched the photo with her finger. Her mother had lived here. She had walked these rooms, laughed between these soft yellow walls.

Caroline felt closer with her mom now than she had in years. Living a little bit with each of her uncles had given her a lot of information about her dad. But joy grew within her at the idea of now learning about her mom.

She continued through the house, finding an open kitchen by the stairs. She took the two steps up to get into the room and looked out the windows at the end of the room. The windows reached all the way up to the ceiling from the floor. Through them, she could see into the house next door.

The neighbor, a man, was eating a donut inside his kitchen. He looked up, making a shudder run down her spine. He waved at her, but she turned out of the room with speed, away from the donut man. She stood on the two steps for the kitchen and looked to her right, where a small hallway led to a small bathroom. Next to the bathroom was a short hallway that led to a shut door.

She turned away, knowing that if it was closed, Jewel didn't want her in there.

As she went up the stairs, her heart beat excitedly to see what the next floor would hold. The space opened to four primary bedrooms and a porch on the front of the house. A glass door led to the porch, which faced the ocean.

"Oh wow." She gasped as she opened the porch door with a soft click.

The ocean winds danced across her face and lifted her hair off the back of her neck. The beach was so close. Only a road stood between them and the beach. The ocean itself looked like it lasted forever. A small ship off on the horizon caught her eye as the sun set over the horizon.

She closed her eyes, enjoying the salty smell that filled the air. She had never felt so relaxed. The thought of staying here maybe forever brought a smile to her lips. *What if she's like Uncle Edmund?*

Her eyes snapped open, and anxiety twisted her stomach. She had lived with him after Aunt Tilly—her mom's sister— had another baby and moved her out. Uncle Edmund had her for seven years, and she felt so safe with him. She had felt at home. *Till he kicked me out.*

"It's pretty, right?" Jewel asked, taking her out of her thoughts. She stood next to her, placing her hands on the railing.

"This place…" Caroline looked over at her grandmother as she swallowed her anxiety. "How do you not just stay up here all day?"

"It's hard not to. But I love the town and the people who live here."

"Even that neighbor? I made eye contact with him in his kitchen!"

Jewel laughed. "Ready to see your room?"

She nodded. "Oh yes! I need to get out of this outfit."

Jewel led her back into the house. The door to her room was on the left. She bounced as she realized she would have the same view from her room as the porch. When Jewel opened the door, she moved aside to let her walk in.

Caroline gasped. "Are you sure I can have this room?!" she asked, scanning everything around her.

The cozy room wasn't big, but it wasn't small either. The wallpaper was a soft off-white color with small rose details. Somehow, it made the space feel big. She looked out the window and was met with the same view as the porch. Her smile grew. The windows stretched from the floor to the ceiling like the kitchen.

"Yes, I'm sure," Jewel said.

"I've never had a room so elegant before." She ran her hand over the white bed frame. Her bag was waiting for her on the mattress.

"And feel free to change anything you don't like," Jewel said as she watched Caroline with joy in her eyes. "Like we can paint the walls if you like. The wallpaper is kind of old."

"No! It's gorgeous!"

"I went to the store last week and got you some new sheets and pillows."

"Thank you."

It was so wonderful to know that Jewel wanted her to have such a nice room. That she wanted her to feel at home. It had been a long time since someone went out of their way to give her something as nice as this.

She scanned the dresser, seeing nothing on its white surface. A blank canvas for her to do what she pleased.

"One more thing." Jewel pulled out a small book from one of the dresser drawers.

She couldn't help but notice clothing folded inside the drawer. "Did you…get me clothes?" she asked in a small voice.

"Oh, I did!" Jewel said, holding a light blue notebook. "I'm glad I did because I don't think you could have fit much in that bag." She pointed at the bag on the bed.

Caroline was at a loss for words.

"Anyhow, I had a diary when I was your age, and it helped me a lot. I thought you might enjoy writing down the things you do or anything else you can think of."

Caroline didn't like the idea of having her thoughts or feelings written for anyone to see them but took the small book anyway. "Thank you." She flipped through the pages. "And not just for this." She gestured to the book. "But for everything."

Jewel's eyes got a bit watery before she blinked any tears away. "Well, I will give you some time to get ready for dinner."

"Okay."

Her grandmother shut the door.

She turned and looked out the window again, knowing an ocean sat just outside her window, even in the darkness. She smiled as she flopped onto the soft bed. *I might never get up again!* After the train and the bus ride, the bed felt like a cloud. Her eyelids felt heavy. But she needed to wash the six days of travel off.

Jumping out of the bed, she took her dresses out of her bag she had forced them in and went to hang them up in the closet by the door. As she opened the closet, she noticed that dresses were already inside. It felt like Christmas. She put the dresses she held down on the bed and went back to the closet. A letter sat on top of some shoes at the bottom of the closet.

I didn't know how much you could bring on your train ride from Washington, so I got you some new dresses and shoes. A few new pajamas are in the dresser drawers as well. I hope you like them and that they suit you well!

Your grandmother, Jewel

Caroline smiled as she looked at her new dresses. Everything she owned was hand-me-downs from Norna, Edmund's only daughter and her favorite cousin. She had never minded, but the excitement of finally having outfits of her own brought a huge smile to her face.

Maybe this won't end like Uncle Edmund!

Hope bubbled in her chest at such a thought.

Chapter 4

The next morning, the sun shined in through the windows of Caroline's new room, waking her up earlier than she wanted. She rolled over to find the ocean outside the window. It was the most stunning view to wake up to.

Smiling, she sat up and got ready in one of her many new outfits. She settled on a one-piece jumper. It fit her like a glove, the belt around her waist helping just a tad. Looking in the mirror over the dresser, she smiled. The outfit was a lovely blue and white plaid that had a matching headscarf she tied into her hair. The outfit had no sleeves. Bows held the top up on her shoulders. Knee-length culottes stopped an inch or so below her shins. Blue flats made her feel like a doll.

After one last scan in the mirror, she went into the kitchen and found Jewel already there.

"Good morning, sweetie." Jewel smiled, still in her green nightgown. Her hair held soft curls as if she had just removed her curlers. She put a plate of pancakes on the table.

"Good morning," Caroline said. She sat where her grandmother had set her plate and poured syrup on top of her golden-brown pancakes before taking a bite.

Jewel sat next to her with her own plate of food. "You look very nice today."

She smiled. "Thank you. My stylist is a genius."

Laughter burst from Jewel. "I wouldn't go that far!"

They fell into silence, but Jewel was quick to stop it.

"Today, we should go into town and meet everyone!"

"The entire town?" Caroline asked.

"Just a few friends. Everyone is excited to meet you."

She took a bite. "That sounds like fun," she said.

Soon after they finished eating, Jewel got dressed so quickly it was odd. As fast as she went up the stairs, she came back down in a white blouse and a green skirt. Her hair was pinned back in a bun that she had put up unnaturally fast.

"How did you do that all so fast?" Caroline asked as they walked down the porch steps.

"I already had everything laid out."

With a shrug, she followed her back into town.

"So, I'm a little confused with your uncles," Jewel said.

"What do you mean?" Caroline asked.

"Who did you live with and who didn't you live with? There are two of them, right?"

She fell into step with her. "I have three uncles: George, Edmund, and Robert."

Jewel nodded. "I always forget about poor Robert. Such a quiet soul."

She went on. "I lived with Uncle Edmund for seven years—"

"He kept you in one place for that long?!" Jewel all but yelled.

Her eyebrows came together. "I don't understand what you mean."

Jewel scratched her head. "Keep going. Sorry I interrupted."

She brushed it off and continued. "Anyway, he was like my dad, and I don't know what I did wrong, but he made me leave." She hated that she felt tears building in her eyes. *Edmund is not worth crying over.*

Jewel's voice was soft. "You did nothing wrong."

Something in Jewel's voice made her almost believe it.

"I lived with Uncle Robert after that for about a week," she said.

As they made their way to the neighborhood's exit, Caroline spotted that same boy who almost got hit by the bus yesterday. He was playing with a small cocker spaniel in the yard of the first house on the street. Her eyes lingered on him once more.

Words George had said weeks ago came to mind. *You're too insignificant for anyone to notice you.* She looked away from him.

"Just a week?" Jewel asked.

"Yeah. We clicked and enjoyed our time together, but Aunt Elizabeth got in a terrible car crash when she was twenty-four weeks pregnant. She almost died and lost the baby."

"That's horrible."

Caroline nodded, recalling how just days before she had helped her aunt paint what would have been the baby's room. "They moved me to live with Uncle George because of how badly they were suffering. And I understood. She was really depressed."

As soon as they entered the town, a tall man walked right over to them with a big, warm smile. He had dark skin and not one hair out of place. His gray suit was wrinkle free, making him look almost like a president from a history book. He held his matching hat in his hands. "Well, hello there!"

"Hi, Scott. How have you been?" Jewel asked as she shook his hand.

"Good. And how are you, Mrs. Walker?"

"I'm doing really well. And please, Jewel is fine."

He looked over at Caroline. "Is this the granddaughter you told me about? The one coming to live with you?"

She smiled. "Yes! This is my granddaughter. Can you believe it? She's here!" She gave her a side hug.

Caroline smiled. "Nice to meet you."

"Same to you!" Scott said. "You both look almost the same! There is no denying you're family." His light green eyes shined with the sun. "Are you liking it here?"

She had not even been in this small town for twenty-four hours yet. But her heart had somehow fallen in love with the cute town around them. "It's so refreshing," she said as Jewel let go of her.

"I'm so glad. And you'll love the schools here. They have great teachers."

She hadn't even thought that far ahead. "Well, that's good to know. Do you have kids who go to school here?"

"No. I only know because I'm running for mayor. I have been working to get some great teachers for kids your age."

"The town is looking for a new mayor," Jewel explained, pointing toward Scott. "When the summer ends, there will be an election, and the town will pick a new one."

He fixed his tie and stood a little taller. "And it will be me!" A smile overtook his face. "Or at least I hope."

Caroline's mouth wavered as she tried to hide her smile. Everyone walking by smiled and waved his way, showing that he had a few supporters already.

"I have no doubt," Jewel said, making him glow with pride.

Another man came out of the shadows and walked over to them. "Sadly, you will lose," he said.

Scott's eyebrows furrowed as the other man joined their

small circle. This new man was tall and fit. His black suit fit as if tailored just for him. His dark hair was brushed back, a few strands moving with the breeze from the beach nearby. An old scar crossed his face in a strange way.

Scott whipped around to look him in the eyes. "Keep telling yourself that, *Remy*." He pointed his finger toward the other man.

"It's Remis," the man commented with a roll of his purple eyes.

"But I will win this election," Scott said, raising his voice.

The other man nodded, seeming unamused.

Jewel and Caroline shared a confused glance.

"Don't get too worked up, Mr. Dickerson." The man's voice stayed calm. "People might change their votes at the sight of you yelling in front of such fine company." He glanced toward Jewel and Caroline.

Scott let out a puff. Anger was written across his face, and a vein popped out of his neck. "Will you ladies excuse me?"

Jewel nodded.

Before walking away, he faced the other man, giving him an intense stare.

"Such a fool," the other man muttered before he turned his attention toward Jewel and Caroline. A thin smile appeared on his lips as if nothing had happened. "Sorry about that."

Jewel dismissed it with a wave.

"Good morning, Jewel. How are you doing today?" He shook her hand.

"Good, and you?" she asked as he let go of her hand.

"I'm doing well. Thank you." He turned to Caroline with curiosity. "Who is this?"

"This is my granddaughter, Carol," Jewel said.

Caroline tilted her head, confused by the nickname.

The man shook her hand. "Nice to meet you," he said as they made eye contact.

His scar caught her attention; she tried to meet his eyes and not look at it. She wondered what had happened to him to have that.

"The name is Achilles Remis," he said as he let go of her hand.

"I'm guessing you're running for mayor too. Or you like yelling at Mr. Dickerson."

He laughed. "I do enjoy making that vein of his pop. But yes, I am running for mayor, and I plan on winning."

Jewel spoke up. "Achilles just moved here a few years ago," she explained, looking back over at Caroline. "He's really helped the town in many ways."

"Nothing I didn't enjoy doing," he said with a small smile.

"Oh, come on. After the big storm hit a few months ago, you helped many people fix their homes. That was a lot of work." She looked at Caroline. "My house flooded a bit, and he helped me get all that water out."

"Jewel!" a woman with a strong Spanish accent called from across the streets.

The three of them looked her way. She had light brown skin, and her dark hair was pulled back into a long braid that ran down her back. She cleaned her hands that were covered with flour off on her apron. "I have made strawberry donuts! Come and try them!"

Jewel waved. "Be right over!" Her eyes went back to Caroline. "Do you like donuts?"

Achilles laughed. "I don't know who wouldn't."

"I do," Caroline answered as he pointed at her.

"See? Smart girl."

"Would you like to join us?" Jewel asked.

He shook his head. "No thank you. I have so much work to do."

She nodded and said her goodbyes before crossing the street to the small donut shop.

"Let me know if they are any good," he told Caroline as she moved to follow her grandma.

"Will do!" With that, she jogged off and caught up with Jewel. "Carol?"

Jewel laughed. "I was trying a nickname." She put her hand across Caroline's shoulders. "We'll stick with Caroline."

Chapter 5

Somehow, Caroline had been in Duck for a whole week. Time seemed to move differently by the beach. The days moved by quicker.

Though she did find the town lonely at times with no one her age to talk with. It seemed not many people her age lived in the town; the only other teenager she had seen was that boy. And nerves kept her from walking up to him.

Even alone, she still enjoyed sitting by the ocean and swimming in the backyard pool. The sun always made the pool sparkle and look so welcoming.

Now, as she lay in bed late into the night, her mind wandered off to her family back in Washington. Should she send word to George? Tell him she had made it safely? *Would he care?*

Her mind then wondered about Edmund like it did ever so often. Did he even know she had left?

A banging came from somewhere downstairs, snapping her from her thoughts. She rolled over, getting tangled in the blankets. She kicked her way free and looked toward the clock on the wall across from her bed.

It was midnight. Why was Jewel still up?

The noise continued downstairs.

Caroline pulled off the bedsheets, sliding her legs over the side of the bed. She put her feet into her slippers that were next to the window. Her pink nightgown fell into place around her legs as she stood. She opened her door and walked out into the dark house.

For some reason, she didn't know why Jewel kept the house dark at night. And she hated it. Her eyes glued to the stairs as a small amount of light floated up the steps from downstairs.

She glanced into her grandmother's room, which was next to hers. The door had been left wide open. She squinted, trying to see if Jewel was in bed. But Jewel's figure could be seen under the covers. A chill ran down her spine. *Who's downstairs?!*

Slowly, she turned away from her grandmother's room and headed down the stairs. Her heartbeat was like a drum. The noise downstairs had stopped, making her pause as she held onto the railing. It seemed like the person had stopped making noises because they had heard her loud heart.

She moved her foot to go down one more step but froze again. What was her plan? She couldn't just walk down the steps empty-handed. She needed something, but she had nothing. She lifted her right leg high enough to grab her slipper off her foot. It shook in her hold.

Now with something in her hand, a bit of courage grew within her. She continued down the stairs, making sure they didn't creak under her weight. Halfway down, she stopped as a different sound came to her ears: whooshing.

She played with the buttons that ran down her nightgown. She lowered to her knees as she tried to peek into the living room.

Through the railing, she saw a broom moving around the room on its own.

She blinked hard. *That's not right. I'm seeing things.*

When she opened her eyes once more, the broom was pushing some sand or dirt along with it. It made its way back toward the dustpan that hopped closer to it.

She pinched herself. Nothing she was seeing could be real!

The broom swept the floor as the dustpan hopped by the stairs and into the kitchen. Her eyes widened as they followed the little living dustpan. It dumped the dirt it held into the trash bin before heading back toward the living room. Each hop it took made a soft thud.

Which was what she had heard.

She noticed a mop moving on its own, leaving a wet trail behind it. A feather duster moved over the tables. Everything moved as if they were alive with work to be done.

She raised both of her hands to her face and rubbed her eyes, not believing what she saw. *I've lost my mind!* She slowly stood from the step and walked over to the living room, where most of the cleaning items were.

Jewel sat on the sofa with her feet up on the coffee table, reading a magazine. Her hair was in curlers, and her rope was tightly closed at her waist. As if this was a normal night in her house. As if this was no big deal.

"Jewel!"

She jumped at the sound of her granddaughter's voice, and the magazine she held dropped from her hands. She stood so fast her knees hit the coffee table, causing a teacup to spill over and leave a small puddle on the hardwood.

The magic mop pushed past Caroline, making her trip to the side, as it went to clean up the spill. She screamed.

Jewel looked at the mop by her side and then at Caroline.

She nervously laughed and snapped her fingers. Everything that had been cleaning the house dropped to the floor with loud bangs as if they had just lost their life.

Caroline looked down at the lifeless mop and then back up at her grandmother.

"What are you doing down here?!" her grandmother asked.

Jewel bent over to put the magazine on top of a book on the coffee table, but it was too late. Caroline had seen the cover of the book. *The Enchanted Spells* written in gold letters flashed in her mind.

Her grandmother had lost her mind! *That* was why she had never reached out to her and why no one in the family talked about her.

"What is happening?" Caroline asked.

"Um…" Jewel looked around. "H-housekeeping."

Caroline picked the mop up. As she did, it wiggled in her grasp. She cried out and dropped it to the floor. Her whole body shook.

"Why are *you* awake?" Jewel asked, taking a step closer. Something in her tone gave away that she was annoyed.

"No!" Caroline snapped, backing away. "I-I ask the questions! Why is everything moving?!"

Jewel didn't answer her. Instead, she looked over at the book and back at Caroline. She then pulled a sticklike object from the front pocket of her robe.

A wave of panic overcame Caroline.

They held eye contact as Jewel spoke. "Look. I know this looks…weird, but let me explain."

"You're a…a witch?" Her words were barely audible.

Growing up, she had read horror stories about witches with Norna around Halloween. The stories would keep them up all night. The same childlike fear came to life as her eyes fell on what was in her grandma's hand.

"Answer the question!" she snapped, taking another step back.

Jewel smiled. "This will all seem like a dream tomorrow!" She lifted her wand up and flicked her wrist at Caroline. "Forgetsy."

Caroline screamed and dropped to the floor.

The spell missed her.

She looked up at Jewel, her eyes watering. She then threw the slipper she had been holding up at Jewel. Her grandma gasped as it hit her face.

There was no way Caroline would stay there with her. Tripping over her feet, she raced to the front door.

Chapter 6

Caroline raced down the beach, her legs moving faster than she thought they ever could. They burned and felt like they would fall off. But she kept running.

Her slipper had fallen off ages ago. Her heart wildly beat in her chest. She wished with all her heart that she was back at home in Washington with any one of her uncles. At this point, she'd take George if it meant getting away from Jewel.

"Caroline!" Jewel called out from somewhere behind her.

But there was no way she would stop and let her grandmother near her again. Not after she tried to kill her back at the house.

"Wait! Stop!" she called. Desperation rang in her voice.

Caroline looked over her shoulder. Jewel was nowhere in sight. She looked back at where she was going and screamed. Jewel had somehow gotten in front of her and had her arms out to grab her. She turned the way she had come from and kept running.

Each time her foot dug into the sand, she fought to keep up the same pace. The sand pulled her in with each step. The steps were painful each time a seashell got in her path.

"Get away from me!" she yelled over her shoulder. A

wave broke where she was running, making her steps feel so much heavier.

Jewel appeared in front of her again. "Let me explain!"

Caroline screamed. As she turned to run, something caught her leg, and she fell onto the wet sand with a cry. Her mouth filled with sand. She coughed everything out. Another wave crashed into her, soaking her.

"Caroline!" Jewel pulled her to her feet.

As the wave pulled back, she saw what had tripped her. A piece of washed-up wood. "Don't touch me!" Pain shot up her leg, making her bend over with a gasp.

"Are you all right?" Jewel asked, guiding her away from the water.

She looked down at her leg and saw a big gash. Blood ran down her leg. "Please…don't hurt me."

Jewel helped her sit and glanced down at her leg. "Oh, my goodness! You're bleeding a lot!"

"Get away from me!" Caroline cried out, yanking her arm out of her hold.

"Can I help you?" Jewel asked, lowering herself next to her granddaughter.

"No! I want you to get away from me!"

"You're bleeding too much."

Blood stained the sand.

Caroline watched as Jewel put a hand to her cut. She hissed out in pain. Then as if she had never fallen, the pain disappeared.

Jewel lifted her hand off her leg. The cut was gone. As if it had never been there. The blood slowly vanished too.

With wide eyes, she looked at Jewel.

"Yes," Jewel said, tucking her legs under her. "I am a sorcerer. I have powers. But I would never want to hurt you or anyone else."

Tears rolled down Caroline's face.

"What I did back at the house was wrong. But it was not meant to hurt you. Only to take away your memory of the past hour."

She jerked back. "That's somehow even more scary! Have you done that to me before?"

Jewel shook her head desperately. "No. I promise I never have."

With the little light, Caroline could see the sadness in her grandma's eyes. She looked down at the sand, not wanting to meet them.

"Please believe me. I wanted to tell you, but I didn't know how or when."

"I'm so scared," Caroline whispered. "Will you hurt me?"

Jewel reached for her hand but stopped as if thinking better of it. "No, I won't hurt you. Or ever use magic on you."

So many questions ran within her mind, her stomach in knots.

"Let's go back home," Jewel said softly. "I will tell you everything. I promise."

Caroline noticed that she kept looking around as if someone would appear. Only the darkness and the waves breaking on the beach surrounded them. Fear of going back in the house brought her heart rate up.

"No!" Caroline pointed toward the house. "I am not going back there! Do my uncles even know what you are?"

"You come from a family of magic."

Her eyes went wide, and her body filled with chills.

"I started using magic when I was about your age. Your mother, Lucy, also gained powers at a young age."

She shook her head. "No… My mother was normal."

Jewel's face had a weak smile. "Compared to your father, she was."

"I don't understand."

"He also had magic. Dilandro was very powerful."

Caroline clutched her stomach; she was going to be sick. Nothing made sense.

"The magic in your father's family—the Smiths—goes back hundreds of years." Jewel looked around again.

She looked around too. "Who do you keep looking for?" she asked, her voice shaky.

Jewel's tone lowered to a whisper. "No one can know this."

Caroline looked back at her.

Her eyes were soft and pleading. "Let's go back home, and I can tell you more," she said, getting up and holding her hand out for Caroline.

Caroline held her hand close to her chest, her mind split in two.

"Trust me," Jewel said after a beat, her hand still out to take.

Caroline looked into her grandmother's eyes and saw only goodness in them. *If she wanted to hurt me, she would have already.* She inched her hand toward her grandmother's. "I trust you."

Chapter 7

Within the kitchen, Jewel made Caroline some tea.

The warm cup in Caroline's hand shook. She sat at the table as Jewel sat across from her. The light over them coated the room in a yellow glow.

"I know you're shaken up," Jewel said, "but I'm excited you know the truth."

Caroline looked down at her tea. She was numb. It was a lot to take in. Everyone had hidden this secret right under her nose for years. Her voice cracked. "Why did no o-one ever tell me?" She looked up at her grandmother, meeting her eyes.

"They wanted to keep you safe," Jewel said as she placed her mug down on the table.

Nothing made sense.

"From what?" Caroline asked.

"Remember when you told me how Edmund kicked you out of his house?"

She nodded.

"There is an evil man who wants to hurt *you* because of your family's power. Edmund moved you to keep you safe. He didn't want to. But it's not good to keep you in one place for too long. We fear *he'll* find you easier."

Caroline had never seen her grandmother so serious. Her eyebrows furrowed. She hadn't done anything wrong.

That thought melted away with fear.

The warmth of her mug was like a comfort in her hands. "That sounds scary. Who is *he?*"

"I don't know if they would want me to tell you."

"Please Jewel. I've been hurt. I deserve to know why."

Her grandma nodded. "There is a man who is after you because you are a Smith."

Chills went down her spine. She could see in Jewel's eyes that she was thinking over her wording carefully.

"Before your parents…drowned…um…they prevented *him* from hurting you. And since then, he's been searching for you. He's killed a lot of Smiths. Like your grandparents and many others. But for some reason, he really set his target on you."

She was speechless.

"That's why Tilly, your aunt, moved you out after a year. Edmund was only meant to keep you for two or three years."

"Then why did he change his mind after having me for seven years?" she heard herself ask.

"*He* was seen nearby, and Edmund grew worried."

Caroline leaned back in her chair, her mind spinning. *Do I have to leave after two years?* Her throat grew tight. Each breath was shallow. "Are you serious about that man? That someone wants me dead?"

Jewel nodded with sorrow in her eyes. "I am."

It seemed all the air was sucked from her lungs. "Who? Who is he?!"

"The masked man. We don't know who he is. His face is covered when he attacks your family."

Caroline let go of her mug. Her shaky hands covered her face as her breath grew frantic. "Why me?" she asked as Jewel stood and moved over to her. "Why my family?" She lowered her hands as her grandma reached her side.

"He's been after your family for as long as anyone can remember." Jewel's voice was gentle. "Something happened generations ago that none of your uncles understand."

Tears built in Caroline's eyes. She blinked them away, not wanting to cry in front of Jewel.

"You should go to sleep. It was wrong of me to tell you this after the shock of learning everything else."

She shook her head. It was late, she knew that, but adrenaline and fear kept any tiredness she should feel at bay. "I can't sleep. Not now," she mumbled as Jewel sat in the chair next to her.

Jewel took her hand. "Do you have any questions?"

With a nod, she spoke. "I do."

Lightly squeezing her hand, Jewel urged her on.

"Because of this masked man, Uncle Edmund moved me out. Right?"

Jewel nodded.

"So, why didn't he ever write me?" She hated how broken her voice sounded.

After she moved away, not once did she ever hear from Edmund. Not a phone call. Not a card wishing her well. She would send him and her cousin Norna cards weekly. But she had given up after six months of being ignored.

Jewel's eyes watered. "Aw, Caroline. We should have told you sooner to keep you from getting hurt."

An unwanted tear rolled down her face.

"We feared it would be too dangerous to send anything with your name and address on it. Too risky for it to be found by him."

Caroline nodded.

"If you like, you can give him a call tomorrow."

Her bottom lip wobbled. "I don't know…"

Jewel smiled softly. "Any other questions?"

"George… He was such a bully. And Mia was physically abusive. I hate them."

Her eyes moved to the faint bruises on Caroline's arm.

Her hand was still within her grandma's "But I have to know if they kicked me out because I had to leave or because—"

"They are awful people! Time-wise, you should still be there!"

Caroline sighed. Of course, George and Mia didn't care about her wellbeing.

"Anything more?"

An odd part of her brain whispered, *Do I have magic?* "You said everyone on my dad's side has magic, right?"

Jewel nodded.

"So, does that mean I can learn to be powerful like you or my dad?"

"Well, you're a Smith. So, it's within you."

"So, I can have powers?!"

"Yes."

Caroline flipped her shaky hands over, and her eyes landed on her palms.

"I don't think you're ready for it yet. It's not something to play with. Magic is very serious."

She put her hands back down on the table.

"You can get hurt if you do something wrong."

She took a deep breath and looked down. "Like what?"

Silence fell over them for a beat. The only sound throughout the house was the waves crashing on the beach. And Caroline's mind shouting that someone wanted her dead.

"When I was a little older than you," Jewel said, "I didn't take my magic seriously, and I hurt my sister one night."

Caroline nodded. A yawn escaped from her mouth, her mind tired.

"It's late. Tomorrow will hold more answers."

"You just said someone wants to kill me. I don't think I can fall asleep even if I wanted to."

Jewel sighed. "Maybe I should have told you that later," she mumbled.

"You think!"

She placed a hand on her shoulder. "I promise you are safe here. It's been years since we have seen him. He has no idea where you are."

Caroline nodded, trying to find a hint of comfort in her words. But there was none.

****

As the sun came up, Caroline could smell breakfast. She lay in her bed, her eyes scanning the ocean just outside.

Edmund still cares about me.

Tears built in the corners of her eyes. It seemed the world had been lifted off her shoulders. For the first time, she felt she was not the problem.

In her mind, she could still see herself much younger with him and his big family. He and his wife Mary had eight children. Only one girl. So much love filled his house. So much joy. And just the right amount of chaos.

She recalled the way a night would not pass without him coming into her room and tucking her in. Wishing her sweet dreams.

It had pained her that he left her with George. But now, there was a reason, and it made the cut in her heart heal just a bit. *Should I call him?*

She didn't even know what she would say if he picked up. It had been two years since she had last seen him. But the thought of hearing his voice again brought a weak smile to her face.

"Caroline, are you up?" Jewel's voice rang from downstairs.

"Be right down!"

Jewel flipped a pancake as Caroline walked into the kitchen. She was dressed this morning: a flowing red dress with white dots, her hair twisted up and out of her face. She looked much nicer than the jeans and pink blouse Caroline had thrown on. "Did you rest well?"

"Um…" She walked over and sat in the same chair as last night. "I slept okay."

Jewel turned around and placed a stack of hot pancakes in front of her. "Take as many as you want!" She turned back around to get two empty plates and sat next to her. "I was thinking we can go get more donuts." She used her fork to pull a few pancakes onto her plate. "Then we can go to the beach if you want. The weather is great—"

"Well," Caroline interrupted, "I would love to get more answers. I have about a hundred more questions. I couldn't sleep with everything you dropped on me." She took a pancake from the stack and dropped it onto her plate.

"Me too."

Caroline smiled as she poured syrup over her pancakes. "Let's go with an easy question. First question: the other day when you got dressed freakishly fast, was that magic?"

Jewel laughed. "Yes. I saw you looking at me all confused. I knew I messed up there."

Despite everything, she chuckled. "Do you use magic on any other things like that?"

Jewel picked up a pancake with her fork. "This is magic."

"What?!" She looked down at the perfect pancake on her plate.

"It's all magic. I can't cook." Jewel took a bite of her food. "Now eat my fake food before it gets cold."

Once they finished their meal, Jewel stood. "Come on, kiddo," she said, waving her arm for Caroline to follow her.

Caroline followed her grandmother to the closed door at the end of the hallway. Curiosity bubbled inside her as Jewel put her hand on the metal doorknob. The door opened with a loud creak.

She stood on her toes, trying to see over her grandmother's shoulder. But the room had no light. Jewel walked in, snapping her fingers. Light filled the room.

"Okay. That's cool," Caroline commented.

She scanned the new space. It was a medium-sized room with pastel floral wallpaper. Pine bookshelves filled each wall with an old ink and dusty smell. Each bookshelf held books of different sizes and colored spines.

"I have a feeling this is more than a library," she said.

Jewel clearly did not go into this room a lot. Cobwebs took up every corner, along with dust bunnies. The dust tickled Caroline's nose, but she ignored it. Unlike the rest of the house, this room had no windows to provide light. A dusty lamp stood in the corner with more cobwebs resting on its yellow shade. It lit up the space with a soft yellow glow. The room had a magical yet spooky feeling to it.

"I can share what this place holds now that you know," Jewel said as Caroline ran her hand down the books.

Caroline wondered what she meant, but she didn't give any further explanation.

She sat on some off-white pillows on the ground. As she sat, a cloud of dust lifted into the air around her, making her cough. She waved her hand, trying to get the dust away. "I need to clean this room."

Caroline coughed as the dust reached her. "No kidding." She pinched her nose a few times.

Jewel stood while dusting off her dress. She looked at the many books and put her hands on her hips. "Can you close the door please?" She reached out for a book.

Caroline raced over and shut the door with a loud creak before going back to her grandmother's side. "Now what?"

Jewel held a book with a velvet green cover, showing it to her.

She looked at the book with a blank expression. "You want me to read?" When Jewel didn't reply, she added, "Why can't you just tell me? You're being so cryptic. It's kind of spooky."

Jewel turned around to face the table in the middle of the room with a smile. She placed the book down on the table. "I'm going to use my wand. Don't get scared," she said as she reached into the pocket of her dress.

Caroline took a small step back.

She turned her attention to the book as Jewel opened it. No words were within the book, just one photo per page. Each looked like they had been painted with watercolors.

Jewel flipped through a few pages before looking up to meet Caroline's eyes. She held her wand out in front of the book with a large smile along her face. "Ready?"

"For what?" Caroline asked, unsteadily.

"Trust me. You'll love it!" She closed her eyes. "Pastgona."

The tip of her wand lit up, and Caroline's eyes widened. The air around them seemed to stand still, while the book pages glowed a bright yellow. Caroline looked over at Jewel as she held her arms out between her and the book. Her eyes closed. Gravity disappeared, and everything lifted off the ground.

"Whoa." Caroline gasped as her feet came off the floor. *Is the whole town floating? Or just us?*

Before another thought could come to her mind, everything shined bright, making it impossible for her to keep her eyes open.

Chapter 8

"Where are we?" Caroline asked, blinking a few times to readjust to the light. With each blink, her mind registered more around her.

She was not in Jewel's dusty library. In fact, she didn't know where she was. Bright green grass grew to her ankles, and a vibrant blue sky glistened overhead. Fluffy white clouds moved across the sky at a slow pace.

A small house sat in the middle of the beauty around her. The front door had a pair of muddy boots sitting next to it. Some of the windows on the top floor were open, making the curtains flow with the breeze. Trees surrounded the house. Some leaves were faintly changing from green to orange. A chilly wind blew a few leaves from the trees, making them dance through the sky. One yellow leaf landed by her foot.

"I don't understand what just happened!" she said.

Jewel smiled as she put her wand in her dress' large pocket. Only the end of the wand stuck out. "We are at your parents' home before you were born."

Caroline turned around to meet her eyes with her eyebrows raised. "Before I was born?!" Her voice was loud. "How?! We were just in your house in 1953!"

Jewel laughed. "Magic, my dear."

Her mouth dropped as she looked around once more.

"At this point, they were getting ready to move into the house you lived in."

"I still don't understand!"

"The books can take you back in time, to moments in our family history."

Caroline felt a knot in her throat. She looked at the house before her with a newfound love. Tears filled her eyes. "Is this really happening?"

Before another word could be shared, a voice filled the air. "Pancake!" Lucy called out.

A small brown dog raced out the front door and down the few porch steps. A pregnant Lucy opened the front door so strongly that it bounced off the wall and flung shut with a bang. She ran down the porch steps after the dog.

Caroline gasped at the sight of her mother. In that moment, she saw how much she looked like herself.

Her mother's brown hair was pulled out of her face in a loose bun. A pink dress hung over her stomach; her feet were bare as she moved across the grass.

"They had a dog?" Caroline asked as the dog looked back at Lucy and ran with a wagging tail.

Although Lucy could not catch up to her puppy, she seemed happy.

"They did," Jewel said. "That poor dog got loose a few days after they moved."

Lucy turned, facing where Caroline stood.

Caroline's heart all but soared. "Mama! It's me!" she cried as she walked over to her.

But Lucy's eyes looked through her.

"Mom?" she asked under her breath as Lucy turned and scooped up the dog that had walked up behind her.

"She can't see you," Jewel said sadly, walking up behind

her granddaughter. "That's one hard thing about these books. The people within it can't see or hear you."

Caroline bit the inside of her cheek to keep herself from crying. As Lucy kissed the puppy, she reached up toward her mother's face, getting as close to her as this world would let her.

"Did you find him?" Dilandro asked, letting the door close much softer than his wife had.

"It's my dad!" she yelled. Tears rolled down her face.

His brown trousers were slightly wrinkled. A casual dark yellow button-up shirt made his brown eyes pop. He looked happy. He looked alive.

Lucy smiled, turning to face him. "I did, but if he keeps running off, we are going to lose him."

"Did he get far this time?" he asked once he was face-to-face with her. He patted Pancake behind his ear.

"Not as far as last time."

They walked back toward the house together, leaving Caroline standing where they had been a few seconds ago.

"This was two months before you were born," Jewel said as she watched them walk.

Caroline wanted nothing more than to follow them. To hear all they had to say. To hug her father and never let him go. "We really are back in time!" She flipped back to face Jewel with a radiant smile.

Her heart felt like it was soaring. Never in her wildest dreams did she ever think she could see her family like this. To breathe the same air as them once more.

Lucy walked past her again. She had a basket of laundry sitting on her hip as she walked out to a tree with clothing lines tied to it.

"This is amazing!" Caroline laughed. Tears hung in her vision.

Jewel sat on a bench under a big shady tree, watching her with a smile.

Dilandro called out to his wife as he crossed the yard. "What are you doing?"

"I'm doing the laundry," his wife said, putting the basket down on the grass.

"Let me do it." He pulled a tan jacket with square shoulders out from the basket and hung it up.

"I'm pregnant, not sick, Landro." She rested her hands on her hips. "I can hang up the laundry."

He smiled, placed two hands on her baby bump, and kissed her forehead. "I have to look out for you two."

Caroline, who was standing right next to them, watched as both of them jumped back a bit. They looked at each other with joy on their faces.

"Did the baby just kick? That hard?" he asked, laughing as he placed his hands back on her belly.

"The baby has been kicking all day, but it kicks more when you're nearby. It's crazy about you already."

"This beautiful baby is my whole world. And I don't even know it yet."

Caroline reached out to him. There was something about her dad that she missed more than words could say.

Pain stabbed her as she remembered that they would only get to see the first four years of her life before they died. That this happiness would not last.

"You're my world too, and I don't even remember you well," she muttered as if he could hear her.

She looked over toward Jewel, who patted the spot next to her on the bench. She glanced at her parents once more before she walked over and sat next to her grandmother in the shade.

"It's incredible," Caroline said. "Just a moment ago, I was at your house, and now we're here with them."

Jewel smiled. "The most beautiful thing about having magic is to see this." She pointed back toward Lucy and Dilandro; Lucy was talking to him as he hung the rest of the clothes. "Any book you grab from my library will take you to that time and place that is shown within the pages."

"Thank you for sharing this with me."

She pinched her cheek. "I wanted to share this with you the second I heard you were coming this way."

Caroline smiled and looked back at her parents.

After a beat, Jewel sighed. "Let's go back."

"Why?" she asked. She just got her parents back. Saying goodbye so soon would hurt.

Jewel smiled at her, her cheeks a shade of pink. "Time does not stop back home, and I have a friend coming over for lunch. He's dying to meet you."

She sighed.

"We will be back," Jewel said, patting her knee before standing.

She took one more look at her parents.

Her father, who was playing with Pancake, called out to Lucy. "I think if the baby is a boy, we should call him Dilandro Junior!"

Lucy laughed under her breath.

"And if it's a girl, we should call her Caroline."

"I love the girl's name," she said, watching her husband. "The boy's name needs some work…"

****

The spell to come back felt the same as it had heading into the book. Gravity returned when they came through the pages. And as if they had never left, they were back in the library.

Once Caroline opened her eyes, readjusting to the light, she saw the familiar books and table. "I can't believe I saw my dad. And my mom! She was beautiful."

Jewel put her wand back in the drawer and shut the book with a peaceful smile. "It's been so long since I have done that. I have a feeling that I'll be doing it more now." She glanced at Caroline, joy showing in her green eyes.

"That was amazing!" Caroline said. "I just wanted to run up and hug them both!"

"I felt the same way," Jewel said as she put the book back among the others.

Caroline looked around at all the other books, wondering what each one held. Whose lives were waiting to be explored? "We need to do that every day!"

"I'm so glad you liked it." Jewel's eyes fell on a book by the door, and the smile on her face fell.

"What?" Caroline asked as she moved to open the door.

Jewel moved across the room and grabbed one book off the shelf. "We just can't go into this one."

She furrowed her brow. And curiosity built within her. "Why?"

Jewel tucked the book under her arm and met her eyes. "There are just things I don't want you to see."

That surprised her. "After the news you dropped on me last night, I don't think much else is going to shake me up."

Jewel softly smiled, but the book stayed tucked away from her.

"Trust me," her grandmother said. "No daughter needs to see the day their parents died."

She swallowed as her eyes fell on the book. She hadn't even thought about that fact. That it would be drawn within the pages of the books around her. "You're right. Thank you."

A knock came from the front door.

"Can you get that, dear? I want to put this away upstairs," Jewel said as she opened the door.

"Yeah," Caroline answered. She stepped out of the room, closing the door behind her, as Jewel went up the steps.

Chapter 9

When Caroline opened the front door, she stood face-to-face with a man in his early fifties with a handsome face. He had blue eyes like the ocean. He stood tall with a welcoming smile on his sun-kissed face. His dark hair rested neatly on his head, even with the ocean breeze coming from behind him. A short white sleeve shirt and jeans somehow looked more casual on him than most.

"Hello," Caroline said. *Is this the man who helped raise my mom?*

"You're her granddaughter!" he said in a heavy but sweet voice. "No doubting that fact. You look just like Jewel."

She wondered just how many people Jewel had told she was coming because everyone seemed to know who she was. "I'll take that as a compliment."

He held his hand out to her. "I'm Dutch Thomas. It's so nice to meet you at last."

She took his hand. "It's nice to meet you too, Mr. Thomas. I'm Caro—"

"Mr. Thomas was my father." He laughed as he shook her hand and let it go. "Dutch will do just fine, youngin."

"Okay, Dutch. I'm Caroline."

He smiled.

"Come on in."

He walked inside as she shut the door. "Boy, it is hot out there."

Before she could say anything, he left and headed for the kitchen.

She followed. "Do you want something to drink?"

"Don't worry. I know where she keeps the lemonade." He opened the refrigerator, showing more comfort than she did in Jewel's house.

As he pulled out a pitcher, she stood off by the table, unsure what to say. *What is taking Jewel so long?*

"Would you like some?" he asked, and she couldn't help but laugh. After all, he was their guest, offering her something to drink.

"Sure." She opened the cabinets by the refrigerator to find bowls and plates.

"They're over here," Dutch said kindly as he opened the cabinet by the stove. After filling two glasses, he passed one to her with a kind smile.

"I guess since you knew where the glasses were, you are a regular here."

He laughed, the sound as refreshing as the ocean. "Pretty much."

Jewel came into the room—lipstick now on her lips— and smiled at the sight of him. "At last! I've missed you!" She crossed the room and wrapped her arms around him.

****

"It's only been a week!" Dutch laughed as Jewel let go of him.

Boy, she had missed him. It felt perfect to have him over once more. They both had thought it best for him to give her a week with Caroline alone before he came over. To let her get adjusted first. And if she was being honest, she missed him more than she thought she would.

"I know," she said, "but I have never gone that long without talking to you."

He put his glass down and poured her a glass, which she took with a smile.

"Caroline, this is the friend I was telling you about." Jewel looked over at her granddaughter, who seemed a little out of place.

"I have to say, Jewel," he said as he moved to the table, pulled out a chair, and sat. "She could be your clone."

Jewel gesture for Caroline to sit as well. Caroline sat in the same chair as before. She then grabbed her wand from her pocket and flicked it at the table. A cherry pie appeared.

"I love cherry pie," Caroline said.

She waved her wand again, cutting eight even slices. Plates floated down from the counter and in front of each of them as a slice of pie landed on them. The pie smell filled the room as she sat.

"She does look like me, but I can also see Dilandro in her," she said, glancing at Caroline.

Caroline gave her a soft smile.

"Though I'll give it to you. You seem much calmer than your mother was."

Dutch laughed as she put her hand to her face. "She was one wild child." He looked at Caroline, seeming excited to share a story. "She would climb the fence to my house almost every day. Just to take the strawberries I grew in my backyard."

Jewel smiled at the sound of Caroline's laugh.

"I will never forget the first time I saw her taking them. I was in my living room, reading the newspaper, when I noticed this small child jumping over my fence with a bucket."

She rested her hand on top of Caroline's, making her

look her way. "It was the middle of the day, might I add. She didn't even wait till it was dark out to commit this crime."

"Your grandmother was so embarrassed when I brought Lucy back to her house."

Caroline smiled.

"Don't remind me," Jewel said, shaking her head.

"She was nothing like her sister," he said as he took another bite. "Your mother would jump my fence or dig holes in the sand big enough to break an ankle. And your aunt would read all day."

"That's how we met," she added with a smile. "I was looking for Lucy, but then there was a knock at my door. I opened it to find her and Dutch. He started telling me how she was in his backyard, and then we started talking and have never stopped since."

"Yup!"

Caroline giggled. "I had no idea about any of that."

"Well, there are a lot more stories like that." Dutch smiled as he picked up the last piece of pie with his fork.

Jewel watched as Caroline cleared her own plate with a soft smile on her lips. She hoped she could do enough to keep Caroline happy. To always keep a smile on her face. "Caroline."

Caroline looked up to meet her eyes.

"I have your uncle's number if you want to call him today."

She sucked in a slow breath. "A-all right."

Jewel stood and opened the junk drawer that the cabinet by the sink held. A small spiral address book sat on top of everything else. She pulled it out and flipped to Edmund's page.

"What if we go to town and get some donuts?" Dutch said as she passed Caroline the book.

She gave him a weird look. "We just ate pie!"

"So? Your point is?" He stood with a serious face before he smiled.

Her heart fluttered at the beauty of it.

"Then after we get donuts, what do you say we have a beach day? Give youngin here the full vacation experience."

"That sounds like fun," Caroline said, looking down at the book in her hands.

Jewel couldn't help but notice it shaking in her hold. "We'll meet you outside," she said, resting a hand on her shoulder.

Caroline nodded.

****

Caroline watched as Jewel and Dutch walked out of the room. As the front door clicked shut, she released a breath. Looking back at the address book in her hands, her eyes scanned over Edmund's name. His address was still the same, still the house she had grown up in. And his number was still the same.

Standing, she made her way to the living room, where the black rotary telephone sat. There was a table by the front door, and a mirror hung behind it. Putting the address book down, she picked up the phone, stuck a finger in the rotary dial, and spun it. After speaking with an operator, the phone rang.

Her mouth was dry, and her throat was tight. It had been two years since she had heard his voice. Would he be excited to hear from her? Or would he…

"Hello! This is Edmund Smith. May I ask who is calling?"

Tears built in her eyes. He sounded so happy. His voice was just as joyful and comforting as she had remembered. She closed her eyes. Words failed her.

"Hello?" he asked.

She couldn't bring herself to speak. Fear overtook her. *What if he still wants nothing to do with me?*

"Hello?" he asked one last time before she placed the phone down, hanging up.

Tears rolled down her face, and her eyes locked onto the phone.

The front door cracked open. She wiped her face quickly as she turned to see Jewel peeking her head inside.

Jewel's smile fell as she scanned her. "Are you all right?" she asked, coming in and closing the door behind her.

Caroline forced a smile on her face. "Yeah. Let's go."

"Did he say something to you?" she asked, walking up to her.

Caroline just wanted the moment to pass. To dry her tears and go on with her day. "No. I'm a coward. He picked up, and I didn't say anything."

She wrapped her arms around Caroline, and Caroline melted to her touch. "You're not a coward. He hurt you, and healing takes time."

"It was a long-distance call. I wasted—"

"Stop, love." She pulled back enough to lock eyes with Caroline. "You can call back when you're ready." She wiped Caroline's face free of any tears. "Ready to go have fun?"

Caroline softly smiled with a nod.

****

As the three of them walked toward the town, Dutch asked, "Have you had the donuts here yet?"

Caroline hadn't stopped dreaming about them. "I had them on my first day here."

He put a hand to his flat stomach. "I wish I could teleport at night to get a donut when the cravings hit, but can I? *Nooooo!*" He looked over at Jewel, who slapped his arm.

"We already talked about that!" she snapped. "That's wrong, and you know it!"

Caroline's head snapped up at him. "You have magic too?"

He nodded and pulled a wand out of the pocket of his jeans. "Of course."

Does everyone here have magic?

"Here." He smiled, passing her the wand.

Before she could take it, Jewel ripped it away.

"Dutch, put that thing away before someone sees!" Jewel snapped as she passed it back to him. She looked around like she had on the beach, but no one was near them.

He slid it out of sight.

"How many times have we talked about this?! You can't talk about magic in the street."

He rolled his eyes. "I'm not ashamed of my powers. Unlike *you*!"

Jewel's eyebrows came together in thought. "I'm not ashamed."

He laughed as they made their way out of the neighborhood and into the town. "Yes, you are!"

"I just know how much people can hate people like us." Her voice was low; Caroline had to strain to hear her.

His tone was soft. "That was one person."

Jewel shook her head. "Listen, I don't want to talk about my father. We need a code word for magic while we're out here."

"Fine. You want a code word? Merlin the Wizard—"

"He's not real!" she snapped, slapping his arm.

Caroline looked back and forth between the two of them and laughed.

Chapter 10

"So, you both have powers?" Caroline asked in a whisper to put Jewel at ease.

"Oh, she knows," Dutch said, smiling at Jewel like a child.

"Well, if she didn't know, she would know now because of you," Jewel said, looking down at her feet.

"How did that happen? She's only been here for a week!" His deep laugh sounded from his belly.

Caroline couldn't help but giggle with him. "I walked in on her cleaning the house with magic."

"Doing it the easy way came back and bit you, Jewel."

Jewel crossed her arms. "I know. But it worked out. I can be myself now."

Dutch smiled and turned back to Caroline. "Yes. To answer your question from before, we both have powers."

Amazement filled her eyes, and questions stormed her mind. *Did they learn together? Could they both teach me?*

As they neared the donut shop, a loud booming voice took her out of her thoughts.

"Vote for Scott!" Scott drove down the street in an old-looking convertible Ford. He sat behind the wheel with a megaphone in hand. Off the car's back and sides, banners hung with "Vote for Scott" written in big lettering.

Dutch moved faster toward the donut shop. "Each time I see him, he is so pushy about me voting for him."

At the same moment, Scott took notice of their presence and called out. "Jewel! Wait!"

Jewel stopped, gaining a sigh from Dutch. Caroline laughed under her breath as he shifted his face into a smile. Scott pulled the car over and jumped out. The banners shined in the sun.

"Nice ride you got today," Jewel said kindly.

Scott blushed. "Thank you! I was hoping to get some attention." He pointed at Dutch with a wide smile. "I got your vote, Mr. Thomas?!"

Dutch laughed, pointing two finger guns at the man. "You sure do!"

Though Caroline didn't know Dutch, she could hear the lie in his voice.

Scott reached into the breast pocket of his tan suit. "I know Achilles is passing these around as well." He pulled out three flyers. "But I wanted to be the one to invite you all."

Each were handed one.

Caroline looked down at the small yellow paper.

Come one, come all!

Next week, the town is holding a carnival! It will have many fun games to enjoy with many prizes to win. Along with lots of carnival food!

You can also get to know the candidates for mayor better when they give their speeches on their plans for the town and its future at eight p.m.

This will be held on Courthouse Street at seven p.m. on Saturday night!

The road will be closed from six p.m. to ten p.m.
We hope to see you there!

Jewel looked back up at Scott. "This sounds like fun!"

"I'm not going to lie," he said. "I am a bit nervous about the speech. I have half of it written and don't think it's any good."

She waved off his worry. "Oh please. You'll be fine."

He smiled. "Well, I better get moving again." He jumped back in his car as she waved bye. "Vote for Scott!" he called through his megaphone as he drove off.

"I thought you said you were not voting for him?" she asked as she turned to Dutch.

"I can't lie to his face, Jewel!"

Caroline laughed. "You kind of did."

He chuckled as he wrapped his arm around her shoulders and guided her to the donut shop.

****

From across the street, Achilles watched as Dutch held the donut shop's door open for Jewel and her granddaughter. The smell from the treats inside reached him from where he stood. His stomach growled, reminding him it had been hours since he had eaten.

He waited for Scott to drive past in his obnoxious car before crossing the street. Families walking by jumped each time Scott yelled into his megaphone. Rolling his eyes, he walked toward the shop.

The whole morning, he had been walking down the beach, talking to people who lived in the town and handing out flyers for a carnival he hoped would give him more votes. He needed to win.

As he reached the door, he looked down at his brown

saddle shoes. Sand lined their rims. He kicked the door frame a few soft times, the sand fell off, and he went inside.

The scent of fresh donuts welcomed him. His mouth watered. He scanned the shop, quickly spotting where Carol sat with her back to the door.

The shop was narrow and long. A counter stretched down most of the space with red bar stools in front. Jewel and Dutch were ordering with the owner. The family who worked there made more donuts for the workday ahead behind the counter. A large jukebox by the front door played a song he didn't recognize. A few booths lined the walls across the counter. Where the girl sat.

In that moment, he felt she looked lonely.

He made his way to her. "Are you liking the town?"

She jumped and gasped, turning to face him. "You scared me!" She put a hand to her chest.

"Sorry," he said, putting the flyers he was holding away in the pocket inside his brown suit jacket.

"I'm sorry. What did you ask me?"

As she looked up at him, he noticed how she looked so much like his mother. From her hair color to the shape and size of her eyes. It brought a small joy to his heart.

"If you liked the town so far," he repeated with a smile.

"Oh. Yes, I really like how peaceful it is here." She gestured for him to sit in the empty booth across from her.

He lowered himself into the plastic booth. "I hope you are also enjoying living with Jewel."

She nodded. "I am. I didn't think we would click as soon as we did."

He was glad for her. "She was excited to meet you. She hosted me over for dinner a few nights before you came, and she could not stop talking about everything she wanted to do once you came."

Her cheeks blushed a bit. "I'm excited too. It was a big move, but I've adjusted nicely."

In that moment, he realized he didn't know much about the town's newest member. "Where did you come from?"

"I lived in Moose Lake, Washington."

His interest piqued at the mention of Washington. "Really? I am quite familiar with the state and have never heard of that town."

"A lot of people don't know about it. It's small."

He made a mental note to look for the town on his maps. "Still, it is such a big move. What brought you this way if you don't mind me asking?"

"My parents died. Jewel was the only one willing to take me in."

He could hear the pain in her voice. One he understood all too well himself.

"I am so sorry," he said.

She smiled sadly. "It's been a few years…"

"That doesn't make it easier. I lost my mother when I was maybe a year older than you."

Her eyebrows rose. "We have something in common."

He sucked in a breath. "What happened to your parents?"

"They drowned when I was four. I still miss them. And your mother?"

"She got sick."

They fell into a comfortable silence.

"Losing one's mother is a pain that lingers forever," he said.

Her eyes showed understanding. "I bet she is proud of you, running for mayor."

Her comment took him by surprise.

Jewel and Dutch walked up to the booth. "Look who it is!" she called out as he sat a box of donuts down on the table.

Achilles cleared his throat. "I was just getting to know our newest member."

She sat next to him, trapping him in the booth.

"Would you like one?" Dutch asked as he opened the box. The smell of glaze and sugar was strong.

"I can't say no to a donut." He picked a glaze donut and took a large bite.

Jewel pushed the box to her granddaughter. "Caroline, do you want—"

"Caroline?!" He choked on his bite as he snapped his head toward her, looking puzzled. "I thought your name was Carol."

She let out a laugh. "No. When I introduced the two of you, I was trying out a nickname."

He stayed quiet for a moment.

If lost, please return to Caroline Smith.

His eyes fell on the girl. *Caroline.* Was she the Smith girl? No! He was being foolish. There were so many girls named Caroline; he was jumping to conclusions. The girl in front of him could not be the young girl from ten years ago.

Could she?

"Are you all right?" Caroline asked, snapping him from his thoughts.

"Yes," he said. "I was just thinking of everything I have to do." He finished his donut and reached for the flyers inside his jacket.

"You must be busy with the elections coming up," Jewel said, cleaning her hands on a napkin.

"That I am." He passed them each a flyer. "I'm handing these out. It would please me if all three of you could come. Maybe get your support." He glanced from Jewel and Dutch.

She rested her hand on his arm. "You know you already have my vote."

He smiled.

"And it sounds like fun. It's been so long since I've been to a carnival."

"It will be great to see familiar faces," Achilles said as she stood for him to get up.

"Thank you for joining us," she said once he stood.

"And thank you for having me. If you excuse me." He left the shop, feeling uneasy.

If lost, please return to Caroline Smith.

Pushing that thought aside, he went to secure more votes. Because at the moment, nothing was more important than getting into the mayor's office.

Nothing.

Chapter 11

hours later, Caroline sat at the beach, the warm air traveling through her hair. The beach was filled with families enjoying the weather. Some were playing with their dogs, others were laughing while they ate, and a few were running with a kite. But most were in the ocean, talking and swimming. With all the joy around her, she hated how overstimulated her mind was.

She watched Jewel and Dutch float in the waves and talk. She didn't know how they could be so carefree after what she knew. Someone wanted to kill her. Someone she didn't even know or hurt wanted to see her suffer. Chills went down her back, even with the sun beating down on her.

She closed her eyes, listening to the waves. Jewel had promised she was safe here. That she would protect her. Taking a slow breath in, she tried to make herself trust those words.

Looking up at the blue sky with its fluffy clouds, she took another breath in. A seagull flew by, gliding through the air. Four large pelicans flew low, almost touching the waves before flying higher.

Digging her fingers into the sand, she made herself take a few more breaths. *I am safe. Nothing's going to happen.*

In front of her, someone fell hard into the sand with a grunt, missing her by inches. She screamed as he cursed.

"Darn tourists making holes!" He lay face-first in the sand before pushing himself up. Sand covered his lips covered.

She stood, facing him. "Are you okay?"

Her heart seemed to flip in her chest. This was the same boy who she had seen around town. The one her eyes couldn't help but linger on.

His eyes closed as he brushed off the sand covering his face. Sand also covered his dirty blond hair and his eyelashes, and it stuck to his bare chest. His cheeks turned a light shade of red, matching his swimwear. "I'm fine. Just a damaged ego." His blond hair moved with the wind as his blue eyes met hers.

"Why were you running?" she asked.

"I was running to the ocean, and my stupid foot got caught in a hole and… Well, you know the rest."

"You…you fell really h-hard." Her mouth went dry. She had never stuttered like that before. It made the tips of her ears burn.

"I didn't hurt you?" he asked, rubbing the back of his neck.

"Oh no. You didn't. Y-you just scared me."

He smiled as he put a hand through his hair, shaking the sand away. She pulled up her swim shorts, very aware of the small amount of skin she was showing. Her two-piece pink swimsuit felt small.

He reached his hand out to her. "I'm Sal."

She shook it. "Caroline."

A smile grew on his face. "You're Jewel's granddaughter!"

She smiled at the fact *another* person knew she was coming. "Yeah. I moved h-here almost two weeks ago. You know Jewel?"

"Of course! She has dinner with my grandparents sometimes. I've known her since I was maybe two."

Butterflies flew in her stomach as she let go of his hand. George's words echoed in the back of her mind, but if she was so insignificant, why was this boy still talking with her?

"You live here?" she asked.

"Yeah," he said with a smile that could light up the world. "I live in the blue house by the entrance." He pointed down the road off the beach.

"I know which one that is. It's a lovely house."

"I'll have to tell my grandpa you said so. He's done a lot of work on it. He's very proud."

She put her hands behind her back, unsure what to do with them. "Do you g-go to school around here?"

Sal put a hand to his forehead, blocking the sun. "I do. I'll show you around the place once summer is over."

She blushed, tucking a loose hair behind her ear. "I would like that."

"It is hard to study when you know all this is out here waiting." He gestured to the ocean.

She glanced at her grandma, seeing that she was still enjoying her time with Dutch. *Good. I want to keep talking to Sal alone.*

"I can imagine you come here a lot with your sweetheart." Sal laughed under his breath. "I don't have anyone special enough to bring here. Not yet at least. Unless you count my dogs, but that just sounds sad."

She tried to hide her smile. For the first time since arriving, she was glad there was really no one her age around. "That's too bad."

He smiled at her. "Not really. Because if I was here with someone, I wouldn't have noticed you."

She glanced at the sand with a soft smile.

"D-do you maybe want to bike around town tomorrow?"

Her heart seemed to simply burst.

Quickly, he added, "To help you get more familiar with Duck."

Her cheeks were pink, but she hardly cared. "I would really like that." *Take that, George.*

Bashfully, he smiled. "I'll pick you up at your house around five."

****

Once the sun disappeared from the sky, everyone headed back home. Dutch lived right next door to Jewel. Standing on his front porch, he watched Jewel unlock her front door.

"Good night, Dutch," she and Caroline both called as they went into the house for the night.

"Sleep well," he called.

After the door shut behind them, Jewel spoke. "I saw you talking with Sal. He's a good kid."

Caroline smiled, her face pink once more. "He is."

"Do you want to jump into a book before bed?"

She gasped. "Yes!"

Jewel laughed. "Let's take a shower and eat something. Then we have a date!"

****

Once Caroline and Jewel showered, got in their nightgowns, and ate a quick dinner, they headed into the library.

"Where are you going to take us?" Caroline asked as she closed the door behind them.

Jewel smiled. "I don't know. I'm a little tired. Why don't you take us inside the books."

Excitement grew within her as Jewel took out her wand. "I'm going to do magic?!" she asked and held her breath.

Her grandmother laughed. "Go ahead and pick one!"

She looked around at each book with a watchful eye. For her first book, she wanted it to be perfect and fun. "This is so exciting!"

Standing on her toes, she spotted a book that seemed as if it had fallen behind other books on the shelf. With some effort, she pulled it out. The brown velvet cover was dusty and seemed old, which only made her more curious as to what was inside it. She ran her hand over it before turning and placing it down on the table.

"This one," she declared.

"I don't remember this one," Jewel said, looking down at it. She flipped through its pages.

Dust lifted from it, filling the air and tickling her nose. "Is it a good one?" she asked.

Jewel stayed silent. Her eyebrows pushed together. "I don't know what is in it. What if it's something bad?"

She took Jewel's wand into her hands, and something odd shot through them. "Then we'll just have to find out."

Jewel snatched the wand out her hands and placed it back down on the table.

Caroline stilled as her grandma's face hardened.

"Okay," she said with a bit of an edge in her voice. "Rule number one: never take a wand into your hand when you are not ready."

Caroline tilted her head to the side. "How come?"

"When you're new to magic, and you hold a wand, you can hurt someone because you don't know what you're doing," Jewel said in a low voice. Her eyes turned red. She then blinked a few times as if trying to keep a memory at bay.

"You all right?" Caroline muttered, not wanting to upset her further.

"I just want you to be safe. So, you're not going to touch anything until I tell you that you can."

She nodded.

"All right. You ready?"

Her eyes lit up.

Together, they worked on the spell for about an hour: how to say the spell, how tightly to hold the wand, and how much force to flick the wand with.

"All right. One last thing," Jewel said, resting a hand on her shoulder. "You might get tired after doing the spell because it's your first time."

Caroline nodded. She moved from foot to foot, her body restless. She couldn't wait any longer. "Okay. Can we try it now?"

Jewel picked up her wand and held it out to her. "All right. Take the wand, say the spell, and focus."

Caroline's heart pounded as she took the wand into her hands. Power flowed through her. Her arm shook a little bit as she held it up in front of her.

Jewel held her breath.

She closed her eyes. "Pastgona!"

Chapter 12

Caroline held the wand, pointing it at the open book. The room glowed like it should and they both lifted off the floor. She smiled. She was doing *magic*, and it felt amazing.

"I'm doing it!" she called out as she opened her eyes.

Abruptly, the room stopped glowing, and they hit the floor hard, along with everything else that had been lifted into the air. A loud bang filled the space.

"What happened?" she asked as Jewel stood up straight and took the wand out of her hand.

"You can't get distracted!"

"Sorry!" Her eyelids felt heavy. She bit back a yawn to hide the fact she was already drained.

"We'll try again tomorrow," Jewel said as if she could hear what she was thinking. "I don't want you to drain yourself."

Caroline stood up taller. She knew Jewel might change her mind tomorrow, and she was too excited to let this pass. "I'm fine! Let me try again."

Jewel paused. "Don't lie to me."

"I'm not. I promise."

She handed her back the wand.

It was heavy in her hands as she closed her eyes and held it over the open book in front of her. "Pastgona." She put all the energy she had left into the spell.

The small room glowed as they lifted off the floor once more. But this time, she stayed focused.

When Caroline opened her eyes, they no longer stood in her library but in a living room that oddly felt familiar. There was a fireplace with a mantle filled with pictures, green sofas, and a desk off by some windows that revealed a yard.

She smiled. She had done her first spell.

"You did it, sweetie!" Jewel cheered, but she sounded so far away.

Spots came into Caroline's vision as her smile faded. The wand dropped out of her hand. She swayed on her feet, feeling like the room was spinning. Fear crept into her.

"Caroline?!" Jewel walked closer to her.

Her eyes rolled to the back of her head. And before Jewel could reach her, she dropped to the floor.

"Caroline!"

****

With her heart in her throat, Jewel dropped to Caroline's limp side. Regret for not stopping after the first spell overtook her.

"Are you okay?!" she asked as panic grew within her. She took hold of Caroline's shoulders, shaking her. She knew Caroline would get tired, but she didn't know it would be this bad. "Caroline!"

Caroline's eyebrows moved together.

"Can you hear me?" she asked as Caroline's eyes fluttered open.

"Everything is spinning," Caroline whispered.

With a sigh, she put a hand to her chest.

"I did it…" Caroline called out weakly as she smiled up at her grandmother.

"You scared me!" Jewel took her hand. "Can you stand?"

She nodded. "The room stopped spinning."

Her grandmother pulled her to her feet.

"You were right. We should have tried again tomorrow." She laughed, still seeming a bit pale. As she scanned the room, Jewel's eyes lingered on her. "Where are we? I feel like I've been here before." She turned back to Jewel.

For the first time since arriving, Jewel took the room in. This had been Lucy and Dilandro's living room in the house they had lived in when the masked man had found them. The afternoon sun brightly shined in through the windows, and the house was still.

"This was your home," Jewel said.

Caroline's jaw opened slightly as she moved around the space. "Yes!" She looked back at her with bright eyes. "I remember! We did puzzles on this table." She pointed at the round coffee table.

Jewel smiled.

She looked up at the windows. "I used to run through the yard! Dad would help me catch fireflies in a jar!"

Blinking back a few tears, Jewel listened. Her heart hurt for the girl before her, the one who didn't know what had happened to her parents. That they had never drowned. That they had fought till their last breaths to keep her safe. *I'll tell her the truth when she's ready.*

"My room was up the steps! And to the left, I think." Caroline looked up at the stairs behind the sofa.

Before Jewel could say anything, a door slammed shut, and they both jumped.

A man with a cape and a broken mask over half of his face walked into the room.

"Who's that?" Caroline asked, stepping back.

It seemed as if all the air rushed out of Jewel's lungs. Chills crawled up her back. *The masked man.* With a shaky breath, she took a few steps back.

His fists were down by his sides, and blood covered his face.

"Who is that?!" Caroline asked, moving as he grabbed a picture off the wall and threw it.

"We need to go!" Jewel choked out as she reached for her wand in her pocket. But she found nothing. *Caroline has it!*

Caroline moved to her side as he threw a vase at the front door. "Why was he in my house?"

"Where is the wand?"

"I don't have it!"

He held his face, groaning in great pain. He then removed what was left of his mask.

Everything seemed to freeze around Jewel. Her eyes widened.

"Is that?!" Caroline asked as she looked at her grandmother.

Words could not be formed as Jewel looked at the face of Achilles.

"No…" she muttered, backing up. Her whole body shook. "This can't be right!"

"Why is Achilles here?" Caroline asked, sounding far away.

Her bottom lip quivered. How was it that she had become so friendly with the man who killed her daughter?

"We need to g-get out of here," Jewel said, holding back her tears.

"I will find your child, Dilandro," Achilles said. His tone had an angry undertone.

Caroline's eyes froze on the man before them.

"I hope you know that your Caroline won't get away," he said to the house as if Dilandro was trapped in its walls. "I hope you both rot!"

Jewel lifted her hand, not taking her eyes off Achilles. "Wand, come to my hand!"

Caroline jumped back as her wand rolled from under the sofa and flew into Jewel's waiting hand. With a flick of her wand, they were gone.

****

"What happened in there?" Caroline asked, out of breath. So many questions racked her mind that she felt ill. Her heart beat uncomfortably fast.

They were back in Jewel's magical room, but the panic from the book lingered within her.

Jewel lowered herself to her knees as she put her fist to her head. "I think I'm going to be sick," she mumbled as her body shook.

Caroline put a shaky hand to her back, moving it in soft circles.

Her shoulders shook as a sob came from her. The sound held so much pain that Caroline lowered herself next to her as she sat.

After a few minutes passed, and Jewel calmed down enough to speak, Caroline asked, "Why was Achilles in my house?"

Jewel lifted her head, looking over at her. "I haven't been honest with you."

Her mouth grew dry.

"That was the day your…parents…" Pity filled Jewel's eyes as they locked with hers. "They never drowned, Caroline."

A sharp pain stabbed her chest.

"The masked man murdered them."

Caroline jerked back as if Jewel had hit her.

Tears filled her grandma's eyes once more. "I never wanted to tell you. None of us did."

Caroline's whole world broke into pieces. Someone had *stolen* her parents' lives. Everything everyone had ever said was a lie.

Words failed her.

"They were murdered by a strong sorcerer," Jewel said. "The masked man I told you about."

She shook her head. Nothing she was hearing was true.

"He's in our town…" Jewel whispered.

She wanted to scream. How was this true?

Jewel put her hands to her head.

"Why did no one tell me about this?" she asked as a tear rolled down her cheek.

Jewel wiped it away with the back of her hand. "Oh, love. We didn't know how to tell you." She cupped her cheek. "You were so young."

Caroline shook her head. "Are you sure that was Achilles?" she asked in a weak voice. She knew it was him, but her denial was strong.

Jewel nodded. "His scar—"

"It was the same as the cut we just saw." She watched as panic twisted on Jewel's face.

"The man who wants you dead knows where you live."

Chapter 13

The next day, Caroline sat in a large rocking chair on the porch by her room. Her eyes were swollen and red. She closed them, listening to the waves breaking on the beach. She could hear people talking. Opening her eyes, she saw a family walking down the beach, laughing together. A family much like the one she once had. The parents each held their daughter's hand, swinging her between them.

Life is not fair.

A strong urge to sob filled her heart once more. She pulled her eyes away from what she once had. What had been taken from her by an evil man. *And for what?* Her parents were good people, and they should have never been killed.

She pulled her knees close to her chest, burying her head in them. Since last night, her stomach had been weak. Growing queasier at the thought that she talked to Achilles in the donut shop. That she had shared that she missed her parents with the man who had killed them.

Clearly, he didn't know who she was, and that was why he had spoken to her. But how long did she have until he found out?

Someone riding their bike in the street caught her eye. *Sal.* She had completely forgotten his offer to take her into town. She sucked in a breath and darted back inside.

A knock came from the front door.

Caroline moved to the top of the steps and saw Jewel walk toward the door. "Jewel!" she called down.

Jewel turned and locked eyes with her.

"I can't go out. Not like this." Her eyes burned from how much she had cried, and she was still in her nightgown.

Jewel smiled before answering the door.

"Hi, Jewel!" Sal said as Caroline moved out of sight.

"Hello. You're here for Caroline, right?"

Caroline held her breath.

"I am." Sal's voice sounded worried. "Is something wrong?" "Well, she's feeling a bit under the weather," Jewel said.

Caroline listened as he disappointedly said his goodbyes. Moving slowly to the porch, she watched as he biked away.

****

A few hours later, Jewel invited Dutch over. She knew he could help her figure out what to do next.

He sat on the sofa next to her, his arm over her shoulders as she leaned into him. Her heart felt so heavy—from the pain of what she had learned and the pain of seeing Caroline suffer the loss of her parents as if for the first time.

"Are you doing all right?" he asked after she told him everything.

She didn't even know how to answer him. "I don't know. I'm in shock."

"What do we do now?"

"I don't know."

"Are you sure it was him?"

"I *saw* him."

Dutch's hand rubbed her shoulder as she closed her eyes. She couldn't help but enjoy how he smelled of cotton.

"He's in our town, Jewel." His voice was low. "He wants to kill Caroline. Is it safe to keep her here?"

When Achilles had met Caroline, nothing showed that he had any idea who she was. But he could've been acting for all she knew. Everything seemed so complicated.

"It's only a matter of time before he finds out." Her panic grew. "Just like we did."

"I agree," Dutch said. "So, what do we do?"

"I'll s-send her back to live with her uncles. She'll be safer there, away from Achilles."

Tears formed at the thought of living alone again. The short amount of time she had with her granddaughter had been like heaven, but this was what was best for her granddaughter. She was not safe here anymore.

She saw Caroline in her mind, suffering because Edmund had moved her out. What would happen to her if she did the same?

"No!" She pulled away from Dutch to meet his eyes. "I can't do that to her."

"If you are keeping her here, you need to have her ready, so she can keep herself safe."

"I don't know if I can teach her."

"Why not? She has powers that can keep her safe from him. You just have to show her how to use them."

"What if I do something wrong? What if I hurt her?"

Dutch took her hand. "You won't. You are amazing."

Her eyes locked onto his, and her face grew pink.

"With your magic!" he quickly added. When she said nothing, he went on. "Your father was a fool for treating you as less because of your powers."

Tears built in her eyes. She could still see herself, young and scared the day her father had disowned her.

"You have what it takes to help Caroline."

She sighed.

"Jewel, she needs to know how to defend herself if you are keeping her here."

"You're right," she whispered. "I just can't train her…"

He stayed quiet for a beat. "You can't hold onto what happened to you forever. You've come so far."

Her eyes filled with unwanted tears. She turned her face away, not wanting him to see her cry.

"If you won't train her, I will."

She said nothing as she closed her eyes. She was exhausted. For a second, she wanted to forget about her childhood, about befriending the man who had killed her daughter, and about the stress of everything else.

Dutch spoke low once more. "Rest. You both are safe here with me. I promise."

She let her body relax into him and dozed off.

Chapter 14

Achilles walked out of the courthouse, fixing the cuffs of his brown suit, and stopped two steps from the street. He took a deep breath. The meeting he had just attended was a bit stressful in ways it didn't need to be. *I just have to win.*

He watched as the townspeople walked around the town, talking and going from shop to shop. Making his way down the street, he waved at whoever looked his way.

With the carnival looming closer, the stress to win was growing. He needed to get the votes. He needed to get into the mayor's office.

As he continued his walk through the town, he noticed Dutch holding the door open for Jewel as she walked out of the donut shop with a small box in her hands.

Achilles hadn't seen Caroline with Jewel for the past two days. It was odd. In her short amount of time in the town, he had gotten so used to seeing them together. He wondered if she was sick or had headed back home.

He decided to ask about the young girl. "Jewel!" he called out, walking over to her with his fakest smile.

She looked up. He waved, making her eyes meet his. He

couldn't help but notice her eyes widening and Dutch putting a hand to her back. A smile that didn't reach her eyes overtook her face.

"Good morning, Achilles!" Her voice was stiff.

"How are you this fine morning?" he asked once he was in front of the pair.

"I'm d-doing good. What about you?" She fidgeted with the box in her hands.

"I'm doing well." He nodded and glanced over at Dutch, who stared at him. "Where is your granddaughter?" he asked, clearing his throat.

"Why?" she asked a little too fast. She cleared her throat too. "Why do you ask?" Her voice was a bit calmer.

"I just haven't seen her in a few days, and I wondered if she was all right," he explained. In all the time he had known her, she never was one to be so uneasy. She always spoke with a confidence he envied. "Jewel? Are you all right?"

"Caroline is just fine," Dutch said. "She just came down with something."

Achilles kept his eyes on Jewel as she nodded. The tension in the air grew heavier.

"I hope she'll be all right," Achilles said.

Jewel smiled.

"Maybe it was something she caught on the train."

"That's what I was thinking," she said, sounding a bit more like herself.

He took in a slow breath, never had he felt so uncomfortable in Jewel's presence. "I hope to see you all at the carnival!" he said, waving his goodbyes as they made their way past him.

****

Achilles opened the front door to his house and took a deep

breath. He walked into the small foyer, letting the door shut as hard as it pleased. As he stood in front of a small mirror he had by the door, his eyes caught his scar running across his face.

"1943," he whispered as he ran the tip of his finger over the long scar. "April sixteen."

So many people had asked him how he had gotten it. Which was to be expected. He told people that he had gotten it from fighting in War World II. Everyone believed him without question. Who would think a war hero would lie?

The scar on his face was a sharp reminder he had failed. That even after what had happened with Dilandro and his wife, he didn't kill their child. He had failed.

He slammed his fist onto the table that sat under the mirror with frustration. A vase with old flowers fell off it and onto the floor, shattering. He looked over at it and cursed under his breath.

He picked the flowers from the glass shards, held up one of the lilies, and smashed it in his hand. "I will find her."

He left the glass and the mess on the floor.

He faced the bookcase beside the mirror and pulled a large red book back. The bookcase moved to the side, revealing a room hidden behind it.

Candles around the walls lit up the space well enough. Not one window took up space on the walls, making the room seem even smaller than it was. A large desk sat near the back of the room with a large map of the world behind it. A few bookcases filled the wall to the right, while the wall on the left held a large golden mirror. The room itself smelled stale and dusty. Snapping his fingers, the bookcase behind him slid shut.

He moved past the large mirror while dragging his fingers over the cold glass. Glancing at the map behind his desk, his eyes followed the *X*'s that covered most of the East and West Coast, along with some throughout the country.

"You're out there," he whispered as he moved to the map. And he would find her.

He had a list of the remaining Smiths pinned next to the map: George, Edmund, and Robert. Dilandro's name had been scratched out years ago. His daughter's name, which was under his, had been waiting to be scratched out as well.

Wherever the Smiths were hiding, he would find them.

His eyes moved to the far top left corner of the country. Caroline had said something about a city in Washington. Maybe they were there.

There was something odd about that girl. Something that didn't sit right with him. He didn't know how old she was, but he imagined Dilandro's daughter would be about the same age, if not older. Could fate be so kind as to put the Smith girl right under his nose? And could he be dim enough to not know it was her?

Sighing, he turned away from the map, not wanting to stress over anything. Not yet. He had to focus on winning. But he would keep his eye on her.

Stepping away from his secret room, he decided to go down to the beach and take a walk. The stress of acting like someone he was not weighed heavy. But since moving to the seaside town, he had found peace in grabbing seashells on the beach.

He grabbed the bag he used to collect seashells before taking one last look at the map as the bookcase slid closed.

Chapter 15

Still in her nightgown, Caroline sat on the sofa. The television was on; Lucy and Ricky were talking within their own living room. But she didn't pay them any attention. Her mind was wrapped in everything and nothing at all. With each beat of her heart, her mind echoed. *You have magic. Achilles wants to kill you. They were murdered.*

She hated the idea that the man who had destroyed her life lived in the same town as her. She didn't want to ever see Achilles again or to even go back to town and risk seeing him. *I hate him.*

All her life, she had read stories with villains who did unspeakable evils. Never in her life did she think her life would be ruined by someone like that. That people like that actually existed.

She glanced out the windows, the ocean seeming so close. The sun was high in the bright blue sky, and the even brighter ocean reflected the daylight in a playful manner.

The front door opened, and the house filled with Dutch's and Jewel's voices. A sweet smell came in with them.

"Hey, youngin," he called with a smile as she turned off the television and walked over to them.

"Hi, sweetie," Jewel said, sounding happy as well.

He passed her the box of donuts he held. "Have you eaten today?"

Caroline shook her head.

"I'll warm up dinner from last night," Jewel declared as she walked past her and into the kitchen.

"I'll just eat one of these," she said as she followed her into the other room.

Jewel waved her wand over an empty plate, and with a flick, it filled with green beans, mashed potatoes, and chicken. "That's not food. You can have that after you eat something."

Setting the box down on the table, she sat where she always did. She said nothing as Dutch walked into the room and took a donut for himself.

"Here you go!" Jewel placed the plate in front of her.

She looked at the plate with no appetite. Slowly, she picked up her fork and poked a green bean.

Jewel turned her back to them, put a cobbler apron over her green dress, and started cleaning something on the counter.

Dutch sat next to her. He lightly grabbed her arm, pulling her chair closer to him. The chair's legs squeaked on the tile. She looked at him, confused.

"I'm going to start training you," he whispered.

Caroline smiled at the thought.

"There she is!" he cheered.

She put her hand to her face as she realized she had not smiled in what felt like days.

Dutch looked over his shoulder at Jewel before opening the box of donuts and handing one to her. He slid her dinner in front of himself.

"Really? You mean it?" she asked, gladly taking the donut.

"I do. With everything happening, you should learn."

Jewel turned back toward them. "You're going to do that today?"

Caroline couldn't help but notice the fear in her voice.

"Why not?" he said. "She's a Smith. Might even be easy!"

She took a bite of the donut with a smile. Learning magic seemed like the best way to get her mind off everything else.

"Not tonight," Jewel said. "What if—"

"Nothing is going to happen," he said.

Jewel put a hand to her forehead as she sucked in a deep breath.

"Caroline, let's go and try some spells."

They both stood, leaving Caroline's meal and the donut box on the table, and went into the living room.

"Wait!" Jewel called, following them. Her heels clicked with every panicked step. "You must give her a training wand!"

"We'll skip that step," he whispered to Caroline.

She smiled as he gestured for her to sit on the sofa.

"Dutch!" Jewel yelled.

"I'm only joking!" he called out.

"Dutch! Stop it!"

"What?" He stood in front of Caroline, looking over toward where Jewel stood behind the sofa.

"I agree she needs to learn her powers. But not like this! You must walk her through everything! You must be careful!"

Caroline turned on the sofa to see her grandma.

"She needs a training wand! If not…"

"Jewel…" Dutch's voice was soft. "She's going to be fine."

Caroline could see the anxiety on her grandma's face. Her grandma's eyebrows were close together, and her green eyes held fear. "Jewel, are you all right?"

As their eyes locked, Jewel took in a slow breath.

"Because I was not old enough or trained with enough caution, I almost killed her."

"Who?"

She took a shaky breath. "My sister. I hurt her so bad. From such a simple spell too!" Her eyes moved to Dutch. "If you're going to train Caroline. Do. It. Right." Her voice was hard. "Give her a training wand! Walk her through everything. And overexplain everything."

"I understand," he said.

Caroline bit the inside of her cheek.

"Dutch, I'm trusting you with this."

After a few seconds of silence, he said, "She'll be fine. I know you had a horrible experience, but I promise we will be safe. She will be safe."

Jewel nodded. "Thank you, Dutch."

He smiled. "She's not alone like you were. She'll have us to keep her on the right path and keep her powers under control."

The way they both spoke about her with so much love and care overwhelmed her. She blinked back the sting in her eyes and looked back over at her grandmother. "I want both of you to train me."

Both looked at each other, seeming surprised by her answer.

She glanced between both of them. Something in her heart told her that having them both would be wise.

"I never thought about that before," Jewel said, still looking at Dutch.

"What?" he asked.

"Working together."

Caroline laughed. "You both already work well together." She noticed Jewel's face heat. "I think having you both train me would be a good mix."

Jewel smiled. "I agree."

He laughed as he patted Caroline's back. "This is going to be fun."

Chapter 16

A loud whistle woke Caroline up before the sun had risen. Sitting up, she screamed as the door to her room flung open.

Jewel walked into the room with a smile. Far too happy for the sun to not even be up. "Can we come in?" she asked.

Caroline hid under her pillow. "Yeah. In like four hours!"

"Dutch, come on in!"

The whistle rang in her ears again, only louder.

"Get up! Get up!" they both chanted.

Caroline sat up, her hair a nest. She watched as Dutch sucked in a breath and brought the whistle to his lips. "Dutch, I swear to God!"

He laughed as he lowered it.

Jewel chuckled as well. "My granddaughter is not a morning person. Noted."

Caroline rubbed her face with her hands. "I'm a morning person when the sun is up! What time is it?"

"Almost six. We wanted to get an early start."

She scanned over them both. Dutch had sweatbands on his wrists, white shorts, and a red shirt, ready for the day ahead of them. Jewel also had on her own sweatbands that matched his. She looked beautiful in her white short-sleeved shirt with a collar that buttoned in the front and matching shorts. Her hair had been pulled back into a ponytail.

How they looked so put together so early, she would never know.

"Anyway! Come down once you feel awake." Jewel smiled before they both walked out of her room.

Caroline lay back down with her face in her pillow and sighed.

****

A little while later, Caroline got dressed in the first dress she found—the yellow color seemed too cheerful—and ate some breakfast. She then made her way into the living room where Jewel and Dutch waited.

A large chalkboard filled with many words that looked like a whole other language stood by the sofa.

"Okay…" she said. "And why did we have to do this before the break of dawn?"

"Two reasons," Jewel said, moving next to the board. "We were excited, and we have less chances of anyone seeing us during odd hours."

She nodded, rubbing the sleep from her eyes.

Sitting on the sofa, Dutch joyfully called, "Let's begin!"

"A very important thing to know is that magic does not come from this world," Jewel explained.

"Where does it come from?" Caroline asked.

"No one really knows. But legend has it that there is another world. A place said to be filled with magic and powerful people."

Dutch nodded.

"The legend goes that magic comes from there, and it

flows into a few lucky people on this Earth and gives us our power."

Caroline laughed. "That sounds made-up."

Jewel softly smiled. "I agree. I don't really believe any of it, but that is what people believe. They believe that some great wizard king watches over what gives us magic."

"That sounds even more made-up."

Dutch rolled his eyes with a smile. "Well, say what you want, but I believe it. Merlin the Wizard is real and—"

"Dutch, we're getting off track," Jewel said as Caroline chuckled under her breath.

"Today, you begin a new chapter in your life," Dutch said, locking eyes with Caroline.

"After today," Jewel added with a smile, "you will be able to do magic! And as the days pass, you will find it easier. You'll never grow tired like the first time."

Caroline grinned. Today was the day she had been waiting for.

"Your father's family—the Smiths—has natural, strong magical abilities. That means it will come way easier to you than it did to me and Dutch. Each Smith also has a birthmark on their right wrist."

She turned her right wrist over, and her eyes fell on the familiar mark. "Norna and I always wondered why we both had this!"

"Your family is so powerful that it's marked on their bodies."

Amazing.

"Now, let's look at this spell."

Caroline held her breath. The stress that had formed since moving in disappeared. She looked over at the chalkboard, which had odd words: lifterit, stone-soul, float itera, fire itera, and opena. Excitement bubbled in her.

"I wanted to add flying to the list," Dutch mumbled, gaining a look from Jewel.

"Dutch, that's outdated!" Jewel snapped. "No one uses that spell anymore."

Caroline smiled. "You guys can fly?"

"I can!" he called out happily. "She can't, and she's jealous."

Jewel sucked in a breath. "I am not jealous, Dutch."

He playfully rolled his eyes. "You're jealous. I can see it in your face."

Caroline looked over at her grandmother. Her cheeks were, in fact, a light shade of pink.

"Enough about the flying!" Jewel said.

Dutch turned back to Caroline. "Today, we will start with the easy ones." He pointed at the odd words before her.

She mumbled the written words under her breath. Her tongue was in knots, the words strange in her mouth.

"Some of the pronunciations are tricky, but we'll walk you through it."

Jewel picked up a shoebox off the coffee table and moved closer to her. "We want you to have this."

She took the box and pulled it open. A wand sat securely in tissue paper inside. Her throat grew dry, and she looked up at Jewel. "I thought you said I couldn't hold one until I was ready."

"This is a training wand."

Carefully, she removed it from the shoebox.

"It was Dutch's when he was your age."

Her eyes fell on him, his smile full of pride. "Thank you so much, Dutch."

"No problem, youngin."

Her eyes scanned over the wand. It was made with simple

oak wood and had a slight bend. The wood formed something like a grip where she could hold it.

"It won't hurt anyone like real ones can," Jewel said. "It's not strong enough. You'll use this one till you're ready for a real one."

"To break this new wand in, start with this spell." Dutch pointed at one of the odd words on the board next to him: float itera.

"We'll start on things like books, pots, pans, shoes, and anything else that is small and lightweight," Jewel said as she took the empty shoebox from Caroline and sat it down.

"How will this help me stop Achilles?" Caroline asked with a raised eyebrow.

"We all start somewhere. You have to crawl before you can walk."

"And we'll be right here with you!" Dutch said.

****

One hour later, ten items had lit up in flames during Caroline's training. Ashes suffocated the air as Dutch sat on the sofa with a tired expression. He held onto a fire extinguisher.

Caroline was frustrated. They had lied to her, making her believe nothing could go wrong because she was a Smith. That she could do magic well.

George's harsh voice creeped into her mind. *You can never do things right!*

"Why is everything catching on fire?" she asked after the book she sent the spell to lit up in flames.

"I didn't like that book anyway," Jewel said, never taking her eyes off the book.

Dutch sprayed it with a blank expression. He was much calmer now than the first fire she had made. Their yells and panic still echoed in her mind. Jewel had used her wand to make the fire disappear from the book, and he had raced to get the fire extinguisher from the kitchen.

As fast as he had left, he had come back, but the fire had already been gone. "Come on!" he had cried. "I've always wanted to use one of these things!"

He, in fact, had a few more chances to use the fire extinguisher afterward.

"You have to clearly say the *itera* part of the spell," Jewel said with a calm voice, bringing Caroline back to the moment.

"And I keep telling you," Dutch added as he looked up at her, "you have to hold the wand right."

"I am!" Caroline said.

"It's not a pen. You don't need to hold it like one."

Looking down at her hand, she saw that once again she was holding it like a pen, ready to write. "Okay… Noted," she mumbled as she adjusted her grip.

"And try not to flick it as hard," Jewel said as she lowered herself into one of the chairs by the windows. The sun was coming up behind her.

"Try it again," Dutch ordered.

Caroline sighed.

"Lift this pillow." He pointed at the yellow one next to him.

"No!" Jewel called. "I like that one."

He laughed. "Okay. Try what's left of the book."

Taking a slow breath, Caroline turned to face the burned book. "Float iteraaa!"

Oddly, the spell jumped off the book and went to the floor. Dutch's shoes lit up in flames. He screamed as he stood, dropping the fire extinguisher with a bang.

Caroline backed away.

Jewel gasped and pulled her wand out from her pocket.

She waved her wand, and the fire was gone. Caroline put a hand to her chest as she saw that the fire hadn't burned the shoes enough to hurt him.

He looked at Caroline with fear written on his face. "You tried to kill me!"

Jewel laughed, covering her mouth with her hand.

He turned to her. "Don't laugh! Your granddaughter just tried to kill me!"

Her laughter grew. "Come on, Dutch. We all saw that spell jump."

He put a hand to his chest, his breath shaky.

Caroline looked down at the wand in her hands. Disappointment filled her. It had seemed so easy! As smoke filled her lungs, she knew it was going to be a lot harder to keep herself safe from Achilles. Tears stung her eyes.

Jewel's hand went to her shoulder. "It's all right. The way it jumped was impressive. You'll get it."

"I thought you said this was going to be easy because I was born with it!" she said, raising her voice. "I don't get it. Why am I not good at this?"

"That's a good question!" Dutch said as he looked down at his burned blue suedes. "Nothing we won't figure out in time."

"You're just overthinking it," Jewel said. "That's all."

He walked off toward the kitchen. "I need a beer!"

"It's not even eight yet."

"It's five o'clock somewhere!"

Jewel laughed under her breath before looking at Caroline. "You did great."

"Are we done for the day?" Caroline asked.

She nodded. "Sometimes, taking a break when something is hard just makes it so much easier later."

She placed her arm over her granddaughter's shoulders,

and together, they walked into the kitchen. Dutch sat at the table with a beer in his hand, drinking it with a straw.

"Dutch!" Jewel gasped as she walked up to him and removed the drink from his hand.

"I need the alcohol to work faster," he said.

"It's her first day. She'll get better!"

Caroline inched into the room, making her way to the table. "I'm sorry I lit everything on fire," she said, sitting and folding her hands in front of her.

Jewel threw his straw away and passed the drink back to him.

"I just don't understand why it kept happening," Dutch said after a small sip. "You gave me a heart attack with the first fire and the last. I have never seen a training wand do anything that strong before."

"Is it something I did wrong?" Caroline asked, trying to hide her disappointment.

"No," Jewel said as she leaned on the back of the chair next to Dutch. "I mean, you held the wand funny, and you overpronounced the spell—"

"Only because you both kept saying how important it is to say it clearly!" she remarked.

He set his beer down. "The point is we have to work on it. We are not going to give up on you."

She swallowed, her throat tight.

He was not family. In fact, she hardly knew him. But he didn't want to give up on her. For once, she felt she had someone in her corner. He wanted to be there for her because he wanted to.

"Really?" Her voice was small.

He smiled at her. "Really what?"

"You're not going to give up on me?"

He shook his head. "No way. You're stuck with me, youngin."

She blinked away forming tears. Only one rolled down her face.

"Together, we can do this," Jewel added as she put a hand on her back.

"So," Dutch mumbled, "who's going to clean the mess in the other room?"

Chapter 17

As night fell, the carnival came to life. The live band—playing the latest hits—could be heard from Caroline's bedroom. As she hooked her earrings on, she looked out her bedroom window, seeing high beams dance in the sky as the sun worked its way down for the night. If she closed her eyes and took a deep breath in, it seemed she could smell the funnel cakes from where she stood.

Caroline could hardly wait to join. As she lingered at the window, she saw families, dressed in their finest, heading toward downtown. Turning to her mirror over her dresser, she scanned herself. The color of her plaid dress reminded her of Dorothy from *The Wizard of OZ*. It fit tightly enough around her waist that the skirt seemed bigger. The skirt reached her knees, ending in white lace. The same lace was wrapped around her chest and shoulders. Her short bubble sleeves made her feel as if her hair should be up, but each time she worked to get it out of her face, it held bumps. Her arms were sore after her third attempt.

She hadn't left the house in what felt like forever. She didn't want to see Achilles, but she hoped to see Sal. And she wanted to look her best. She had stood him up once, and she wanted to make up for it.

Running her hands through the knots in her hair, she sighed.

A knock came at her door.

"Come in," she called.

Jewel opened the door, popping her head in with a smile before she walked into her room. She was all dressed up for the carnival. Her brown curls were pulled in a low bun, out of her face. She had on a lovely dress that was the softest color of yellow with a thick black belt around her waist. Her matching earrings sparkled in the setting sun. "You're not ready!"

Caroline sheepishly smiled. "I don't know what to do with my hair."

"Give me the brush."

She handed her a brush and stood in front of the mirror. "It doesn't want to cooperate with me."

Jewel stood behind her, meeting her eyes in the mirror. "Let me work my magic." She ran her hand through her brown hair, guiding the brush through.

As she watched from the mirror's reflection, she scanned Jewel's eyes. Something about the way her eyes fell on her felt so motherly, so caring.

Jewel pulled her hair up into a high ponytail, making it seem so easy. Not one bump in sight. She grabbed a ribbon that matched Caroline's dress and wrapped it around her hair. "I cannot cook," she said as she tightened the ribbon into a bow. "But I can do hair."

Once the bow was set, she used her hand to curl Caroline's ponytail. She then rested both hands on Caroline's shoulders. Their eyes locked in the mirror.

"You look just like your mother," she said.

"Thank you," she said as her vision blurred.

"What's wrong?" she asked in a soft tone.

"It's silly. Are you ready to—"

"Nothing you feel is silly. Your feelings are validated."

She sucked in a soft breath and turned to face Jewel. "It's just been a really long time since I have felt loved the way I do here."

Jewel smiled as she put a hand to her chest. "You're happy here?"

She nodded. "I haven't felt anything close to the love of a mother in so long. It's overwhelming. But it makes me happy."

They both stayed quiet for a moment before Jewel spoke.

"I am sorry that I was not there for you."

Caroline swallowed.

"That I didn't reach out to you."

"Because of Achilles?"

"We were all so scared that a letter might get into the wrong hands, or a phone call would be heard, and he would find you." She took a deep breath in. "But that's not an excuse. I could have teleported to you. I should have been there."

"But we're together now," Caroline said with a soft smile.

She laughed under her breath. "That we are. I love you with all my heart."

Caroline wrapped her arms around her. "I love you too."

She melted to the touch, resting her head on top of hers.

A knock came from the front door.

Jewel pulled away. "That must be Dutch."

Caroline couldn't help but notice her grandmother's cheeks growing pink once more as her grandmother checked her hair in the mirror. "Do you like Dutch?"

Jewel's wide eyes locked with hers. "What?!" Her cheeks darken.

"You blush around him."

Her hands went to her face. "He is my best friend. It would be wrong!"

Caroline smiled. "That didn't answer my question."

Another knock came from the front door.

She slid her white Penaljo Candy Twist heels on. After buckling them at her ankle, she stood.

Jewel spun to leave, her dress raveling around her legs before falling back into place. She made her way to the front door.

Caroline bit her lip to keep from laughing.

"Let's go have fun!" she called.

Chapter 18

As Caroline, Jewel, and Dutch walked into town, the carnival sounds filled Caroline's ears. The band played a bouncing song, and the smells of treats being served became even more present.

Jewel sighed as she closed her eyes. "Wow! That smells amazing!"

Caroline spotted a stand with a tall skinny man behind it. He was handing out burgers as if they were free. It seemed everyone wanted to try one.

Dutch gasped. "I want one of those burgers."

So many people walked within the street. Some talked, some danced to the music, and others ate off to the side with their friends. Everyone looked so happy. Banners with bright colors hung over the street, and some carnival games decorated the area. The lights around Caroline glowed in a comforting manor, making her want to join in faster.

"Why don't we get in line for one?" Jewel asked Dutch as she pointed at the burger stand.

"Whatever you want!" He held his arm out for her to take.

She blushed again.

"Caroline!" someone called, making Caroline turn to see who.

Sal pushed through the crowd as kindly as he could.

"Go have fun," Jewel told her as she looked at the pair. "Just stay safe, and we'll meet back up later."

"Are you sure?" Caroline asked.

Fear of Achilles resurfaced. He was here. Somewhere.

"There are too many people for anything bad to happen." Dutch gave her a comforting smile. "Have fun," he added as he and Jewel joined the line for the burgers.

As Caroline turned around, Sal pushed past one last person.

"Hey! I haven't seen you in a while!" he said over the noise around them. He wore black pants that made his light green button-up pop in a pleasing way. The joy of seeing her again was clear on his face.

"I was sick," she lied, not wanting to share the truth of why she had stood him up. "Listen, I'm really sorry about the other day."

He waved his hand dismissively. "You got sick. Nobody's fault. I'm just glad you're here."

The band finished playing a song, and applause sounded around them as the next song started. She didn't know which song it was, but the beat sent people around her running to dance.

"Have you played any of the games?" Sal asked.

"Not yet. I just got here. Would you like to play them with me?"

Even in the setting sun, she saw his cheeks blush. He held his arm out, much like Dutch had to Jewel, and she placed her hand in the crook of his elbow, letting him guide her.

"You look really nice tonight," he commented, bringing a smile to her face.

"Thank you."

"You might get some dog hair on that dress if you stand too close to me." Laughter rang in his voice.

She looked down at his arm seeing a few small blond dog hairs. "I don't mind. What type of dog do you have?"

"Four cocker spaniels."

Caroline looked up at his face. "You have four?!"

His head tilted back as he laughed; she loved the sound. "Yep! They're all pretty young, so they're a handful."

The game lights came into sight. Though there were still too many people in her path to see what they were.

She strained to see, everyone towering over her. "What type of games do they have?"

Sal, who stood a foot or so taller than her, looked ahead. "They have a ring toss with some spooky dolls you can win. Oh! I see one of those booths where you throw a dart at balloons."

"My aim is terrible."

"Me too. I see one where you have to knock down some clown dolls with a ball. And a dunk tank."

She jumped a little. "I've always wanted to try one of those!"

He looked back at her with a smile. "Dunk tank it is!"

They made their way to the tank. String lights hung over it, casting a warm yellow glow over them. Hector—one of the owners of the donut shop—happily sat over the dunk tank. He kicked his legs over the water, as dry as can be. A young boy threw a ball at the target that would send him into the tank but missed by feet.

Hector laughed. "Better luck next time!"

Caroline looked at Sal. "Well, Sal."

He turned his face to meet hers. His face was so close.

"I-I think it's time he took a splash. What do you think?"

Once more, he laughed. "Caroline Smith, that is the best thing I've heard all day!" He turned to Elena—Hector's wife—who was working the booth. "How much for four balls?"

Hector spit out another chuckle. "You'll never get me in!"

She moved closer to Sal. "Twenty-five cents."

He reached into his pocket and pulled out a quarter. "Here you go."

As she got the balls, Caroline whispered, "I'll pay you back."

"Don't worry about it."

She smiled as Elena returned.

"You're going to need more than that!" Hector called.

Caroline grabbed two balls as did Sal. She watched as he closed one eye and aimed. He missed the target by a few inches, making Hector's laughter grow.

"You try." Sal moved aside for her to stand in front of the target.

She held her breath and threw the ball. It bounced off the tank and came back to them. They both yelled, stepping out of the way before bursting with laughter. He picked up the ball and threw it, missing the target. His last ball missed as well.

"Suckers!" Hector laughed.

Sal ignored him. "I believe in you," he whispered to her as she moved in place with their last ball.

"No pressure," she mumbled with a laugh.

Caroline felt her determination grow. After throwing the ball hard, she watched as it hit the target. They both yelled out as Hector dropped into the water below with a satisfying splash.

"You did it!" Sal cheered as he wrapped his arms around her. He lifted her off the ground and spun her, resulting in a joyful squeal. After setting her back down, he put a hand behind his neck. "Sorry. I got excited."

She smiled. "Don't be sorry. That was exciting!"

"You're the first couple of the night to win!" Elena said. She handed them both donuts from the bakery.

Sal laughed. "We get a donut!"

"Enjoy!"

"Thank you!" they both called in unison.

As they turned around, Caroline froze as she saw Achilles. Watching them.

"Great job," he said.

Chills spread throughout her body. Fear like no other took over.

"It was about time someone hit the target." In the string lights' yellow glow, his scar stood out as if confirming his identity.

"It's a lot harder than it looks." Sal took a bite of his donut. "Caroline made it look easy."

He smiled at her. "How much did you two spend to get him in?" He dug into the pocket of his brown pants, his suit jacket matching perfectly.

Caroline's eyes widened. All the air seemed to leave her body. *Does he have a knife? A wand…?*

"Just twenty-five cents," Sal answered with a shrug.

"Here you two go!" Achilles pulled his hand out of his pocket, handing Sal a dollar with his thin smile. "I don't have change on me, so just take the dollar."

"Thank you, sir!"

His eyes fell on her, and her heart drummed. "And how are you feeling? Jewel said you were sick."

Clearing her throat, she found her voice. "I feel much better. Thank you." She was proud that her voice stayed even.

"Well, I am glad," Sal said. "I would have been disappointed if you had to miss tonight."

"Well, I have to go and get ready," Achilles said, making both their eyes fall on him. "My speech starts soon. I want to ensure that my cards are in order." He tapped his breast pocket.

"Good luck, Achilles!" Sal called out as he left, blending in with the crowd.

Caroline watched him, wondering how someone so deadly could just blend in. To become one with a crowd as if he was good. As if he didn't destroy her whole world.

"My grandparents hate him," Sal said as he took the last bite of his donut.

Caroline hadn't touched hers yet. Her eyes lingered where Achilles had gone.

"I feel like I have to be extra nice to him to make up for the rude comments my grandpa an—" His hand went to her shoulder, snapping her back to the moment. As their eyes locked, he kindly asked, "Are you all right?"

"W-Why?" she asked, her throat dry.

"You look pale." He removed the donut from her hand and put his free hand to her back. "Let's find a place to sit, and I'll get you some water."

She moved where he guided her, her heart rate high and hands shaky. An empty bench came into sight, and they made their way to it. His hand never left her back.

"Sit."

She sat and took in a slow, shaky breath.

"Let me get you some water. You're pasty white."

A hush filled the street. Everyone around gave them their backs and faced the courthouse steps. From where she sat, there was a clear path through the crowd, allowing her to see an older man walk up and stand in front of a microphone.

"I'll be right back," Sal whispered, leaving to get the water.

George's voice echoed in her mind. *You ruin everything! Just keep your mouth shut.*

She glanced at where Sal had gone. Did he think she had ruined the night? *In and out. In and out.*

The old man spoke into the microphone. "Well, I'm happy to see everyone is having a good time! Really brings a smile to my face." He shook, his boney hands tightly holding a dirty cane. He was short and thin. A few white hairs on his head moved in the light breeze. "As most of you know, I am going into a late retirement." He pushed his large glasses up on his nose. "It has been an honor to serve this lovely town and to have seen it grow."

Standing off to the side were Scott and Achilles. Both stood tall with their eyes on the mayor. Scott fiddled with his green tie while Achilles stood with his hands behind his back. His gaze was hard. *Why would he want to be mayor? Here of all places.*

"Today," the older man continued, "I want to bring the two men running for mayor out here with me. Gentlemen, if you may."

Achilles and Scott made their way next to him, both towering over him. A few cheers came from the crowd.

Sal appeared with a cup of water. "You look better," he whispered as she took the cup. He sat next to her.

She took a sip. "I'm sorry I was a bother."

The older man kept talking as Sal leaned in closer. "You are not a bother, Caroline."

She smiled.

Maybe George had been wrong.

"I hate to leave the office, but at eighty-three years old, I thought it was best to leave the town to someone younger," the mayor continued.

"This guy is older than air," Caroline whispered.

Sal bit his lip, trying not to laugh. He looked at her with delight in his eyes.

"I now introduce to you, Scott Dickerson and Achilles Remis," the mayor called out. "Give them a big round of applause."

****

After both men finished their speeches, the carnival continued. The band played an upbeat jazz song that Caroline didn't know, but the beat was inviting to dance to. The saxophone was loud and bright.

"May I have this dance?" Sal asked, smiling at her. He stood and held his hand out for her.

"I have no idea how to dance," she said shyly.

"The music is jazzy. We're not waltzing. Let's just have fun."

She took his hand. It felt comforting in a way that she had never known.

He pulled her to her feet, and together, they joined the other dancing couples. She was glad the sun was down. If not, she knew he might see her blushing cheeks. As everyone around them did the boogie-woogie and the bunny hop, they laughed and jumped along with the music.

"See! You're a natural!" Sal laughed as he spun her a few times.

Her skirt opened around her legs before falling back into place. He then pulled her close and dipped her.

"You're just saying that because I have not crushed your toes yet!" she called out over the music.

When the band stopped playing, everyone cheered for them. Sal and Caroline turned to the band and clapped.

"Thank you for that." She laughed as she fixed her hair.

"You dance amazingly. You sold yourself short."

The band started to play a song by Bing Crosby called "I Don't Want to Walk Without You." His smoothing voice filled the night.

Everyone around them moved closer to slow dance.

Sal and Caroline looked at each other. Before her nerves could get the best of her, she slowly reached for his hands. His hands filled hers as he pulled her toward him. One of his hands went to the small of her back, and the other held her hand near his chest. They moved softly in beat.

"I have never felt this comfortable with anyone so quickly before," he said in a hush tone.

A smile came to her lips. "Me either."

His face grew closer to hers, making her stomach flip in the best way it could. "Is it all right if I kiss you?" he asked.

Their eyes locked.

She nodded and slowly closed her eyes. His lips softly touched hers, and a jolt of joy washed through her. She melted to his touch as his hand on her back pulled her a bit closer.

The band finished their song, and everyone around them clapped. Sal and Caroline pulled apart. A smile held both of their lips, and a soft pink stained their cheeks.

"You're groovy, Caroline Smith," he whispered as she laughed under her breath.

"I'm groovy?"

"Yeah. You are amazing."

"You're wonderful too."

He smiled.

One of the band members took the microphone. "We'll be back in ten minutes. You all have been fantastic!"

With that, the band left their spot on the sidewalk, and the street filled with conversation.

"I'm going to go check on Jewel," Caroline said.

Sal nodded as he scanned the crowd. "Okay. I'll be waiting by the donut shop."

Her face hurt from smiling. "All right. Be back soon."

As she walked away from him, she gently touched her fingers to her lips. Her stomach still fluttered. *I can't believe that happened.*

She scanned the crowd for Jewel or Dutch, but with everyone in the street, it felt impossible to spot them. Stopping, she stood on her toes as much as her heels would allow. Even with a few inches more, she had a hard time finding them.

Someone backed into her, taking her off-balance. She gasped as gravity pulled her down to the asphalt. But before she reached the road, a strong hand grabbed her arm and pulled her back to her feet.

"Thank you so—"

The words died on her tongue as her eyes locked with Achilles.

"Good thing I was near by," he said with a smile.

She stayed still for a moment as he let go of her arm.

"That fall would have led to a doctor visit."

Swallowing her fear, she pushed aside everything she knew of him.

"Probably would have broken something." He put his hands in the pockets of his pants, his suit jacket pushing back, and she tensed. "Are you enjoying the carnival?"

"I am. It's been a perfect evening."

"You started it off well. Hector is still upset you got him."

She laughed through her nerves. Scanning his face, she wondered if his smile was forced or genuine. Either way, he was an amazing actor, fooling everyone around them.

"If you excuse me, I'm looking for Jewel," she said, smiling kindly. "I want to take her to the carnival games."

A good two feet taller than her, he scanned over the crowd. "I last saw them talking with Mr. and Mrs. Clark by the courthouse."

Running her hand through her hair, she looked toward the courthouse. As she met his intense eyes once more, her blood went cold.

Achilles, with his sharp eyes, reached out, grabbed her right arm, and pulled it toward him.

"Hey!"

He turned her wrist over to the Smith mark just on the inside. It stood out like a sore thumb.

Air rushed out of her lungs. *Why didn't I cover it?*

His eyes hardened, and his face twisted. "Well, hello, little Smith," he whispered in a low hiss.

She yanked her arm free.

The band played music once more, the song nothing but noise. Someone called out to Achilles, pulling his eyes away from her. Slipping away, she forced air into her lungs.

****

Achilles looked back at where Caroline *Smith* had been. She was gone.

But it didn't matter. She was here. In Duck.

He had let her go for now, but he knew where she lived. He knew everything. There was no hiding.

"Achilles!" someone called out once more.

Before he could turn to look for the source, Scott jumped out in front of him.

"Hey!" he said energetically as he fixed his tie.

Achilles yelped as he jumped back, surprised.

"The mayor wants us to come back to the courthouse. The press is ready with the camera."

Together, they made their way back to the courthouse,

but his mind was far from the carnival around him. *Tonight, I will go to her home.* A thin smile came to his lips. *Tonight, she will die.*

"It has been fun going up against you," Scott said, removing him from his plans. "I'll be a little sad when we go our separate ways at the end of summer."

"It has been an honor going against you," Achilles said, lying through his teeth.

As they reached the building, they climbed the few steps to where the mayor stood. He smiled up at them. Both men stood on either side of him, facing the man with the camera.

The cameraman had on a gray suit with a matching hat that was slightly leaning off his head. With both hands, he held his black and silver press camera and brought it up to his face. Off the side of the camera was a bowl-like item with a small light bulb inside.

As he gestured for the three to move closer together, Achilles spotted Caroline with Jewel and Dutch. They stood off to the right of the cameraman, and her eyes fell on him. Fear was clear on her face.

Enjoy the night. Your hours are numbered.

"Mr. Remis, please look into the lens," the cameraman said.

Achilles turned his eyes back to the camera. And with a flash, the picture was taken.

Chapter 19

"**A**re you having fun?" Jewel asked Caroline with a loving smile as Mr. and Mrs. Clark sat on the bench beside her and Dutch.

"Yeah," Caroline said. "Sal and I were at the games—"

"Sal is our grandson!" the older woman on the bench called out. "Are you Caroline?"

She nodded.

"He was so excited that he might run into you tonight." A shy smile grew on her face.

"We have had a wonderful night, Mrs. Clark."

"Please call me Patti. And this is Bob." She pointed at the older man next to her. "Any friend of Sal is a friend of ours."

She looked over at Jewel and Dutch. She wanted to tell them about what had happened with Achilles, but guilt for possibly ruining the night held her mind.

"You all right?" Dutch asked.

She forced a smile. "Oh yes. I just feel a bit off."

Jewel grabbed her arm gently. "Have you had any water tonight?"

How she wished it was something as simple as hydration.

She knew she had to tell them. Eventually. *Now or later?*

She couldn't wait until later. With him knowing who she was, she might not *have* later.

Fear overtook common sense. *What if Jewel sends me away now?* Still, she knew she owed it to her grandma to tell her.

As Patti and Bob talked, Caroline lowered her voice. "Well, Ach—"

"This is yours!" Sal called out, walking up to her. He held a donut in his hand. "Hector's mad at me."

Despite everything, she laughed and took the treat from him.

"Where did you get that?" Dutch asked as she took a bite, her stomach in knots.

"The dunk tank," Sal said. "Get Hector in the tank, and Elena gives you a donut." He pointed in the direction of the tank and the other games.

Dutch laughed. "I want one."

"Me too," Jewel said. Her smile was odd as she scanned over Caroline. Did she know the fear inside of her?

He held his arm out to Jewel, and she took it. "Let's go."

They walked off toward the games.

****

As the three of them walked home, Jewel held a bear that Dutch had won for her after they had gotten their donuts. The stars over their heads seemed dim with all the lights from the town.

"What a great carnival!" he said as they turned into their neighborhood.

"It really was," Jewel said. "Thank you for the bear."

He laughed and threw his arm over her shoulders. "Anything for you."

"What did you do, Caroline?" Jewel asked, reaching over to eat some of the cotton candy that he held.

"You're going to eat it all!" he complained as he held it out for her to take it easier.

"Sal and I had a really good night," Caroline said.

She settled on keeping her run-in with Achilles to herself. For now. As she watched them laugh, the last thing she wanted was to ruin their fun night.

Tomorrow, she would tell them.

****

As the clock reached four o'clock in the morning, Achilles stood in Jewel and Caroline's living room.

All the lights were out. The only sounds came from the crashing waves.

He held his wand tight as he made his way up the steps. A spell kept each step silent. The first door he peeked in, he saw Jewel sleeping, her breathing deep. Moving past her room, he looked for his target.

The next room's door was slightly open. He pushed it open more and saw Caroline sleeping in her bed. She lay on her side, her face peaceful.

His knuckles grew white the tighter he held his wand. After her, all that would be left was the Smith brothers. She had said she moved from Moose Lake, Washington. Perhaps that was where he would find them.

He lifted his wand to her sleeping figure. *Plaguonyx.* The poison spell sat at the tip of his tongue. With one flick of his wand, she would be dead.

But something hissed in his mind. He wanted to see her suffer before she died.

He would kill her uncles first. Once her heart was heavy with loss, he would take her life, slowly and painfully.

With a flick of his wand, he teleported back to his house. Once he was inside his hidden room, his eyes fell on the map behind the desk. Moose Lake. A smile twisted his lips at the idea that she had given away such information about her uncles. That her words were what led him to them.

Yes, they all would die for the pain their family had put him in years ago.

Shaking his head, he tried to clear his mind; he would not think of who he had been. But no matter how hard he tried, his past held onto him.

****

"I sold the last of the milk jars," a young Achilles said, giving his mother the coins he was given.

She took them from him with a smile. She stood tall and thin. Her dark hair that matched his own had been pulled out of her face and into a bun. Her skin was a little tanner compared to the pale complexion he had gotten from his father.

His father—who had sat at their small dinner table—laughed under his breath. "Only five coins? We're starving, and that's all you could make?"

Achilles looked down. If his father saw the tears forming in his eyes, he would never hear the end of it.

"Why can't you be more like your brothers?"

Achilles swallowed hard at his father's words and closed his eyes.

His older brothers were his dad's favorites. His father didn't hide that fact. He always took them out with him, teaching them many useful skills.

They were twins, sharing the same face and the same long black hair and the same awful personality. Being almost ten years older than Achilles, they helped the most around the house. They also overshadowed Achilles, no matter what he did.

"He did his best," his mother said.

He looked up at his mother like she was an angel. And for him, she was. She had been the only one who treated him with love, the only person he knew to treat him well.

"Well, his best is never good enough," his father snapped.

"Albert, stop!" she yelled.

He gave Achilles a dirty look. "I don't have time for this. Someone needs to feed this family."

As the door shut behind his father, he cried, and his mother picked him up.

Years later, Achilles learned it was him and his mother against the world. Against his father.

It seemed like the family had broken into two parts. Albert and his sons versus Achilles and his mother. This became clearer when she grew ill, and only Achilles held her hand and worked to bring her strength back.

After weeks of her illness taking hold of her, he kneeled by his mother's side as she lay in bed. "Mother..." He grabbed her cold hand in his.

Her eyes stayed closed, but her eyebrows moved, letting him know she could hear him. She wheezed with each breath.

"Mother, I will get you help. You won't die. I promise."

He could not lose her. He would not.

Achilles had learned of a powerful family—the Smiths. Rumors had spread that they could heal the sick. Years ago, he might not have believed such a thing existed, but he was now desperate.

He kissed her hand and looked at her still form before heading out to find the only hope he had left: *magic*.

The trip was long, but he finally reached the Smith's house.

"Please!" Achilles begged Willison Smith. "My mother is dying. You're the last hope I have!"

Willison looked down toward him with mournful eyes. "Young boy, I wish with all my heart that I can help you, but I cannot."

Anger filled him. "What? Why?!" He could not lose his mother. Without her, he didn't even know what would happen to him. "You have the magic to help her!"

Someone walked into the room, went straight to Willison, and whispered into his ear. "Don't waste your powers on this filth."

Willison looked back at Achilles. "I'm so sorry, but my powers are needed elsewhere."

Achilles' heart froze. He opened his mouth to protest, but Willison raised his hand to stop him.

"I hope your mother gets well," he said flatly before he walked away.

Achilles felt like he had no air left in his lungs.

He came home to a dark house, meaning his brothers and father had not come home from work. Lighting a candle, he walked over to where his mother lay. He placed the candle down on the floor next to her bed and kneeled.

"Mother, the Smiths failed me. They won't help you."

Saying the words out loud hurt just as much as they did to hear them. How could someone with the ability to help just choose not to? If she died, it would be their fault, and he would let them know. He'd make them pay.

Achilles raised his head, looking at her face. "Mother," he muttered, barely above a whisper. He shook her arm, but she didn't move. Dread corrupted him.

She was gone.

He kissed his mother's hand as his shoulders shook with his sobs. Blowing out the candle, he walked out of the room and into the night.

He had never felt more helpless and alone in all his life.

He could not stay home; he knew he was unwanted. He curled his hands into fists. He never wanted to feel that way again.

Years later, Achilles headed back to Willison. He was now taller, and his eyes no longer looked like they belonged to a young, sad boy. They instead belonged to a wicked man with no heart or soul.

"You may remember me," he said as he walked up to Willison.

Willison had not changed one bit. He stood high as if he was better than anyone else. "I'm sorry, but I don't seem to recall who you are."

Achilles gave him a thin smile, not surprised. His tight fists hid behind the cloak draped over his shoulders. "I was the young boy you turned away years ago. The one whose dying mother you didn't want to save. The filth you refused to help."

Willison stayed quiet.

"I remember that day like it was yesterday." He took a few steps closer. "You did nothing to save my beautiful mother. *You* walked away."

The man's face paled.

"I have learned the craft you are so arrogant about. Though unlike you, people will fear what I can do with it."

"Wait!" Willison held his hands out in front of him. "My family needed me that day!"

"Now you remember me?" he hissed. "The boy too below you to help."

Willison said nothing.

"My mother needed you, and you let her die." He pulled out his wand and pointed it at Willison. "Every Smith to walk this Earth will pay for what you've done!"

With a flick of his wand, the first Smith was killed.

Chapter 20

Jewel watched as Caroline rode off with Sal on their bikes. A picnic basket sat awkwardly on Caroline's bike's rear rack. It wiggled with every pedal. The bike was hers, making it a bit too tall for Caroline. Stopping would be a task. Mentally, she added to the growing list of things Caroline would need.

Laughter rang from Caroline as the pair turned down the street and out of sight.

Smiling, she made her way down the porch. She was glad how happy Caroline seemed and how quickly she was adjusting to everything.

A car passed by as she made her way next door to Dutch's house. She knocked on his front door.

He opened it after a few seconds. "Hey. What's up?"

She glanced at the old-looking jeans he wore and his white T-shirt that was tightly wrapped around his biceps. *What would it be like to be held in his strong arms?*

She snapped her eyes back to his, and her cheeks grew warm. "I w-wanted to see if there was a book you could think of that could help us train Caroline."

"Good idea." He closed the door behind him. "Has she been working on the list we gave her?"

They had given Caroline a list of all the easy spells they wanted to start with. In between her lessons, she would practice the pronunciation for each.

"Every day at breakfast, she recites them to me," Jewel said. "She's speaking much clearer."

Once inside Jewel's house, they made their way to the library. Dutch opened the door for her, and her skirt brushed his legs as she passed.

"I was thinking we show her how to teleport next," Jewel said. "Every sorcerer knows how, and I think it will be something that can help with Achilles."

She moved to the table and opened her spell book that sat there. The last book she and Caroline had traveled into sat on the other side of the table. She glared at it.

"Is that the book you told me about?" Dutch asked as he stood across from her.

"It is."

He opened it, flipping through the pages.

"You know what has stayed with me after seeing what's in there?"

He locked eyes with her.

"How Achilles looked exactly as he does now." She could see that Dutch didn't understand by the way his eyebrows moved together. "This was ten years ago." She rested a hand on the book's dusty cover. "How can someone not age in ten years?"

Dutch tilted his head. "I don't get what you're saying."

"Ten years ago, you and I didn't have wrinkles or much gray hair. So how—"

"Whoa! Easy!" He put a hand to his chest. "Honey, we've aged like fine wine. No white hair or wrinkles here."

She sighed with a roll of her eyes. "I'm serious, Dutch.

Something is not sitting right with me. How can he look the same as he did ten years ago?"

"What are you saying?"

"Is there a way to stay young with magic?"

He let out a puff of air. "You really think Achilles has some aging spell on him? Jewel, maybe he just ages really well. Like us."

Pushing away from the table, she pointed at the book she had seen Achilles in. "Dutch, go in and see if you don't believe me!"

His hands went up in surrender. "I believe you!" He took a breath and spoke gently. "Let me look for something like that in here." He grabbed the spell book she had opened.

She watched him flip through the pages.

"You might be on to something," he mumbled as he held the book open on a page with a clock drawn near the text.

Jewel leaned in, following the words with her eyes as he read.

"'Who wants to grow old? Who wants to feel as if each click of the clock is one click closer to death…'" He glanced up at her. "Well, that's enlightening."

"Keep going."

"'But with this simple potion, stay your age forever. Only need a fistful of grass, the eye of a hog, two hairs from your chin, tears of pain, and blood from your left index finger. Drink this for a year, and you will remain the same age for the rest of time. Only death will come from a violent act of another.'"

They locked eyes.

"Okay," Dutch said. "That's nasty, Jewel."

"How do we know if he has this?"

He looked down at the page once more. "'Beware: this spell can be discovered. If someone with magic blows dry magnolia leaves in your face, the spell will be revealed to those around. The spell also may be removed by a potion made of tree bark, blood, and the hair of the person with the spell on them.'"

"How do we get his hair?" Jewel asked.

Dutch stood tall. "We don't even know if he has this!" he all but yelled.

"And we don't know if he doesn't!" She knew she sounded as if she had lost her mind, but something in her believed it anyway. "Dutch, what if this is true? He can—"

"How would you even get him to drink that?"

She shook her head. "I don't know."

He sat on the floor pillows and sucked in a deep breath. "If you're right, how old do you think this guy is? Maybe he met Merlin the Wizard!"

Jewel's mind spun, thinking of an idea. "Merlin the Wizard is not even real."

Dutch looked at her deeply. "Jewel, we can't act on this."

"I made a promise to keep Caroline safe. If this is something I have to do, I'll do it for her."

He shook his head. "You getting killed will not help Caroline!" The worry in his voice made her lock her eyes with him.

"I'm going to keep those dry leaves on me in the meantime."

"In the meantime of what?!"

"He doesn't know who we are. Not yet. I'll make that potion and invite him over for dinner."

Dutch stood. "Jewel, do you not hear yourself?!"

She nodded. "I do. We need to get some of his hair."

"And how do you want to do that?"

"We go to his house."

****

Caroline enjoyed the freeing sensation of the wind hitting her face. As she and Sal made their way past the donut shop, she waved at Elena. Behind the window, Elena waved back.

The sidewalk flowed into a curve, taking them past the town. As the sidewalk ended, she rode in the street, following Sal. The road then turned into a tight two-lane road with sand and trees lining it.

"Watch this!" he called out.

She watched as he did a wheelie. The front of his bike moved with every small movement. A car passed them in the other lane, making her tense.

"Be careful!" she said.

He brought the front of his bike back down with a bang. The whole bike wobbled before he regained control. Nervous laughter bubbled from him. At first, Caroline thought he slowed down out of fear, but he pointed to the left, where a break in the trees created a path.

"Let's turn here, and we can eat."

She followed him to the sandy path. Once off the road, he jumped off his bike, and she did the same. Together, they pushed their bikes into a small park.

Sand and rocks made up the small beach. The water calmly broke on the sand, and a pier stretched out in front of her, going out a few feet over the water.

It seemed like years ago when she had been on that bus that had taken her over the water. She looked at the bridge now, happy to be one of those dots she had seen.

"How did you know this place was here?" she asked as she leaned her bike against a tree.

"I've lived here all my life," he said, helping her remove the basket Jewel had packed from her bike.

"You said you lived with your grandparents?" she asked as she followed him to the pier.

"I do!" He smiled back at her as they made their way down the pier. The wooden planks thumped with each step. "I was born in Richmond, Virginia."

They reached the end of the pier, and he put the basket down. They sat with the basket between them. As she sat, she was grateful she had worn her jeans. Sitting over the water was a bit breezy.

"What brought you here?" Caroline asked, hoping she was not overstepping.

"A month after I was born, my parents wanted to go on a date. My grandma was watching me. On the way home, it started raining, and I guess they were distracted and didn't notice a truck stopped in the road."

Her hand went to her chest.

"Their car slid underneath the trailer and…"

"That is terrible!"

He took a slow breath in and nodded. "My grandma says I look just like my mom."

She smiled gently. "She lives on in you."

He beamed before opening the basket. "After they died, my grandparents moved here. Too painful to stay in Richmond."

He reached in and pulled out their lunch. The sandwiches Jewel had "made" were wrapped in a napkin.

As he passed her a sandwich, he asked, "Your parents died as well, right?"

"In 1943. I was four." A part of her wanted to share what she knew now. That the very man who took them from her was in this town. "They were murdered."

Well, it was half the truth.

His eyes widened. "By who?!"

She unwrapped her lunch. "I don't know," she lied as he took a bite of his sandwich.

It felt so wrong to lie to him after he had been so open with her. Before she could change the subject, he spoke.

"That was ten years ago. What took you so long to move in with Jewel?"

She looked toward the water, not wanting to meet his eyes. *How can I answer that without lying?* "I lived with my Uncle Edmund for a while, but I…um…"

As words failed her, a seagull cried out above them. They both looked up as it lowered toward them.

"Get out of here!" Sal yelled, waving his hand over his head.

The bird cried out again as another showed up. Both flew far too close. The sound of their wings flapping filled the air. Caroline bent over her sandwich as she screamed.

"Leave us alone!" he yelled.

She looked up as one stole his sandwich from his hand. He stood with a gasp as the birds both flew off, fighting for the ham sandwich. He looked back at her with his mouth slightly ajar. She bit her lip, trying to withhold her laughter.

"What the hell…" he said.

Laughter broke free from her. It was loud and unladylike, but she could not stop it. He looked back at her with delight in his eyes.

"I'm sorry!" Her stomach protested her laughs. "How did that happen?!"

Sal joined in, chuckling as he sat back down. "I hope they get food poisoning!" he called toward the water, making her laugh more.

Her eyes watered. "You must still be hungry." Her laughter under control, she sat straight. "You only had a bite." She ripped her sandwich in two uneven halves and gave him a piece.

"That was not groovy," he mumbled as he took the half.

"Will they come back?" she asked after taking a bite.

He scanned the blue sky. "I hope not." His eyes found hers. "Eat quickly."

She giggled as she took another bite.

"Are you enjoying living here?" he asked as she finished her sandwich and cleaned her hands on her jeans.

She nodded. "I didn't think I would or that I would get along with Jewel as easy as I do."

Yet her life before had been easier, which was a wild thought. George and Mia seemed like a walk in the park next to the danger she knew she was in now.

Her mind wandered off to Achilles. He knew who she was. Why had he not attacked? She would have to tell Jewel and Dutch what had happened the other night soon.

"Why didn't you think you would like it here?" Sal asked, removing her from her thoughts.

"I was never close with Jewel before." She thought over her words and how much she could tell him. "So much kept her away."

"I guess it was now that she was meant to be in your life," he said, making her lock eyes with him.

With everything happening now, she was so happy it was Jewel who was holding her hand through it all. Maybe he was right. Now was when she needed her the most.

"Everything has a reason," she agreed.

"Like those seagulls taking my lunch." He laughed. "I'm still hungry."

He looked into the basket and gasped. "Sweet lord! She packed pie!" He took out a Tupperware bowl with two pieces of pie. "It's cherry." He handed her a fork and held the bowl where they both could reach.

She smiled, thinking of how thoughtful her grandmother

was for remembering the little things. "Cherry's my favorite."

Cries from seagulls came from above. She scanned the sky, seeing a few flying nearby.

Sal laughed with his mouth full. "Eat faster!"

Four seagulls loudly cried out as they lowered themselves. They flapped over their heads loudly.

"I'll handle it!" she declared as she stood.

Sal covered the pie as best he could with his hands. "You guys already had a sandwich!"

A few more swooped down toward him as she swung her arms at them. A large and dirty-looking one flew close to her, making her take a step back. Right off the pier.

She screamed and flailed her arms before the chilly water welcomed her.

As she broke the surface, Sal gasped out, "Caroline!"

Coughing, she cleared the water that had gone up her nose. The seagulls still flew around him in a mess of white and gray.

"I'm all right!" she called.

He stood, laughing. "Help is on the way!"

He jumped off the pier, tucking his legs to his chest. He splashed in next to her, and she chuckled. His arms then wrapped around her waist as he came out from under the water. She squealed with delight.

"You're safe now." His arms stayed around her waist, keeping her close.

She rested her arms around his neck, their faces inches apart. The sounds of the seagulls fighting over their pie were loud.

"What about our pie?" she asked, never taking her eyes off his.

He shrugged. "I don't feel like dying for a pie."

The giggle in his voice brought a smile to her face. She laughed. "I'm willing! I didn't even get a bite!"

He pressed his lips to hers as they bobbed in the water.

Chapter 21

The sun started to set once Sal and Caroline made their way home. Soaked from their swim, they rode back. Her striped, green skirt clung to her like a second skin, while his white shirt had become quite translucent. She enjoyed the view the whole way home.

As they rode up to Jewel's house, they both jumped off their bikes, put hers back where they had found it, and went up to the front door. Their shoes squeaked.

"Next time we eat together, let's pick a spot where the seagulls can't reach us," he said.

She laughed as she held the empty basket in her hand. "I think that's a really good idea."

He smiled as he waited for her to open the door.

"I don't have a key."

He nodded and knocked.

Jewel opened the door a few beats later.

"Just dropping her off," he declared as he wiped away the water that dripped from his hair and down his face.

She took a good look at the two of them. "Where did you both go biking? The bottom of the ocean?"

Sal laughed while looking down at himself and the small

puddle he made under his feet. The puddle stained the wood a darker color for the time being.

Caroline walked into the house, passing her the basket. "We fell off the pier." She looked back at Sal.

The memories of him holding her close were still fresh in her mind. Along with the way his mouth had played with her earlobe. A blush crept up her neck.

Jewel smiled. "Sounds like fun!"

As he still stood outside the door, Sal's stomach growled.

She looked back at him. "Did you not eat?"

"Not really. I picked a bad spot. Seagulls took my sandwich and came back for dessert."

Caroline covered her mouth with her hands to muffle a laugh.

"Apparently, the seagulls were viciously hungry today."

"You're more than welcome to eat dinner with us if you like," Jewel said as she stepped aside, so he could come in.

"Thank you, but I want to get out of these wet clothes," he said, pushing his hair back out of his face. "Besides, my grandma made my favorite today."

"Okay. I understand. Maybe some other time then." Jewel walked away, leaving them alone to say their goodbyes.

"I had fun," Sal said, taking Caroline's hands in his.

"Me too."

He leaned in and locked his lips to hers. She pulled away after a beat.

She watched as he got on his bike and disappeared. As she shut the front door, Jewel's voice filled the room.

"Go and shower. I want to train with you tonight."

Caroline turned toward her.

"Have you been reviewing the list we gave you?"

"I have been." She pushed a soaked lock of hair back from her face and pictured the list in her mind. "Fire itera, to make fire. Stone-soul, to paralyze someone where they stand. Sundfulle, to remove the paralyze spell."

Jewel nodded.

"Float itera, to make things float. And teleportsheam, to transport from one place to another."

Her face broke into a smile. "Perfect! Now, go and shower. We'll eat, and then we can start."

****

Caroline ate her second serving of dinner. The potpie was aggressively filling, but she kept eating. It was possibly better than the one Aunt Mary was famous for. Possibly.

Dutch sat next to her, unusually quiet, and Jewel seemed tense, making her wonder what had happened while she had been away.

"What did you guys do today?" she asked with a shrug, her tone nonchalant.

"Nothing much," Dutch said, never looking up from his plate. "Your grandma came up with the worst idea to ever be said out loud."

Jewel sighed as she rolled her eyes so hard that Caroline feared it hurt. "Dutch! Come on!"

He shrugged as he filled his fork. Caroline looked over at her as she went on.

"This is not how I want to tell her this…"

"Tell me what?" Caroline asked.

She sighed once more before looking at Caroline. "I think I found—"

"*Think* is the key word here," he interrupted, gaining a dirty look from Jewel.

"Go on," Caroline said, locking eyes with her.

"I think I found a way to get rid of Achilles without him ever knowing who we are."

Everything she had eaten twisted in her stomach. Jewel already seemed annoyed with Dutch. Would Jewel yell like George if she told her what she had hidden from them? Or would the danger of Achilles knowing who she was make Jewel send her away? She was happy here; she didn't want to leave.

She sucked in a slow breath. She then blinked, and her mind was back in the kitchen. Jewel was explaining something she had not heard.

"That's why I think it's best to go into his house."

Her body jerked. That one sentence was enough to make chills race up her spine. "Jewel!"

Jewel put a hand to her temple. "I know it sounds so out of pocket, but I am willing to take a risk to learn."

"Let me get this straight," Caroline said, not believing what she had just told her. "You want to go to Achilles' house? The man who wants us dead's house?"

She nodded.

"I told you it was the worst idea," Dutch said.

"I know it sounds wild," she said, "but if he has this spell on him, it could be a safe way to get rid of him."

"How?!" Caroline asked, throwing her hands up in the air.

"Like I told you, we make that potion and invite him over for dinner. He drinks it, and then he'll die. This way, it'll keep us out of danger."

But they were already in danger.

She swallowed. "Guys, I have—"

Jewel reached across the table and took her hand. "I know this sounds wild. I'm willing to go to his house alone and—"

"No way," Dutch said, cutting her off. He crossed his arms over his chest. "I don't agree, but I won't let you do this alone."

She smiled softly. "Thank you."

"I want to help too!" Caroline added. It was the least she could do at the moment.

"Let's work on your magic more, so you can feel safer."

But it didn't make Caroline feel any better. Instead, she wanted to hide from the whole idea.

****

"If you find yourself in front of Achilles," Dutch said in the living room, "what spell would you use to get out of the situation?"

Caroline sat on the sofa, her training wand in one hand and the list of spells they had given her in her other hand. Her eyes scanned over the odd names she had grown familiar with. "I would use stone-soul and then teleport away from him."

Jewel, who was sitting in the chair by the sofa, nodded.

"Have you been practicing both of those?" he asked.

"I've been practicing stone-soul on bugs."

He smiled. "Good, but doing it on a person is harder."

Caroline put the list down on the coffee table. Her mouth was dry. She didn't want to leave! For the first time in a while, she was truly happy where she was. But the fact Achilles knew shouted in her mind. *I need to tell them.*

"Can I tell you guys something?" she asked.

"You haven't practiced the teleport spell?" Jewel said with a small smile. "That's fine."

If only it was that simple.

"Stone-soul requires your concentration," Dutch said. "And it's hard to do when you are afraid. With time, you will grow more used to using magic in stressful moments."

I hope not.

"No matter how stressful the situation is, focus on the target."

Jewel looked at her. "It's hard at first, but like anything, the more you work on it, the better you will become."

Standing, Caroline held the wand the way they had told her.

"Aim at me," he said, making her look at Jewel with wide eyes.

"What if I do it wrong?!" Her eyes landed back on him. "What if I hurt you?"

He smiled. "You're going to do fine. I trust you."

She took a deep breath and pointed the wand at him. "Stone-soul," she said.

It hit him, making him freeze like a statue.

Jewel gasped as she slowly stood from her chair. "I think you did it on the first try."

Caroline smiled. "How do I unfreeze him?"

She laughed. "Maybe we should have shown you that before you froze him." She pulled her wand out of the pocket of her dress. "I'll do it, but watch and learn."

Chapter 22

The next morning, Dutch walked into town. Jewel had wanted to get everything for Achilles' potion first thing in the morning. The plan was that when Achilles came out of his morning meeting at the courthouse, Dutch would talk with him and keep him away long enough that Jewel and Caroline could go into his house and get what they needed.

His stomach was in knots at the whole idea though. And his legs and hands were shaky. But still, he pushed on.

There was something about Jewel that made it impossible for him to say no to.

Dutch saw Bob and Patti eating donuts with some coffee outside the donut shop. Some clouds that promised rain covered the sun, and the air was humid. Looking down at his watch, he saw he had a few minutes till nine, a few minutes till the meeting would end.

"Good morning!" Patti called out with a kind smile.

"Those smell great!" Dutch said as he made his way to the pair. He hoped talking with them for a while would help calm his nerves. "How is your morning going?"

She handed him a glazed donut from the box. It stuck to his fingers the second he took it. With his anxiety so high, he didn't even know if he could eat the sugary treat.

"Good so far," Bob said. "Sit with us, Dutch."

His wife patted a spot for him to join them.

Dutch forced himself to take a bite from the donut. "I'm sorry, but I'm tight on time."

"What are your plans for today?" Patti asked as he looked over at the courthouse doors.

Scott walked out with a big smile plastered on his face.

"I don't want to be rude," Dutch said, "but I have to speak with Achilles."

Bob rolled his eyes. Patti nodded her farewell as Dutch threw away what was left of his donut.

Achilles then walked out of the courthouse, seeming a bit annoyed.

"Hey, Achilles!" Dutch called out.

Their eyes locked, and Achilles' face shifted into something close to a smile. "Hello, Dutch. How odd it is to see you in town this early." He made his way down the steps and faced Dutch.

Nausea turned Dutch's stomach; he regretted eating that donut. "Well, I had somethings I wanted to get done before noon."

He smiled thinly. "It seems a storm is coming, so that might have been a good idea." He put his hands into the pockets of his dark pants. His jacket opened, making his brown vest show.

"So, I think I know who I want to vote for!"

Achilles raised an eyebrow.

****

In the safety of their house, Jewel and Caroline teleported to Achilles' house.

In a second, Caroline stood within the house of the man who had killed her parents. Her mouth grew even dryer. She looked around, seeing that they stood in a dimly lit living room. The only light came from the small windows on the wall by a sofa. Two sofas sat facing each other, and there was no television. On the small coffee table between the sofas was a sculpture made from seashells.

Just by standing in one room, she got a sense that the house was much smaller than Jewel's.

"All right," Jewel said. "Remember to move fast and get as much hair as you can find."

Gross. Caroline nodded as she moved down a little hallway that she thought might lead to a bathroom. At the end of the hallway was what looked like the front door and a bookcase to her left. Where the bookcase met the wall, she saw light coming from behind it. Pushing on the case, she gasped as it moved, revealing a room.

"Wow…" she whispered under her breath.

Bookshelves surrounded the new room, and a large desk sat in the middle with an even bigger map behind it. As she walked into the space, she saw a large gold frame mirror on the wall to her left. She met her eyes in the reflection, but something seemed odd about it. The longer she looked, the harder it seemed to look away. As if something within the glass was pulling her to it.

Chills slid down her back as she forced herself to look away.

She moved around the desk, scanning everything on its surface. A book was open on a page about something she didn't understand. Something about an amulet. The rest of the book was covered by a piece of paper with names written on it.

Willison Smith—Dead
Ally Smith—Dead

Evelyn Smith—Dead
Daivd Smith—Dead
Robert Smith—Alive
George Smith—Alive
Edmund Smith—Alive

Seeing her uncle's names before her made her ill. As she picked up the paper, her eyes fell over her cousin's names.

Peter Smith—Alive
Micheal Smith—Alive
Linus Smith—Alive
Arthur Smith—Alive
Charles Smith—Alive
Jasper Smith—Alive
Thomas Smith—Alive
Norna Smith—Alive

They were living happily, not knowing their names were written down by the person who wanted them dead. The list unfolded in her hold.

~~Dilandro Smith—Alive~~
Caroline Smith—Alive

Her whole body shook.

"Caroline, I got a hair brush. Let's go!"

Jewel's voice sounded far away. Caroline looked up, seeing her standing in the doorway with a confused look on her face. Tears rolled down Caroline's face as she made her way to her. Caroline passed her the paper in her hands.

Jewel was quiet for a beat till her eyes landed on Caroline's name. Her eyes widened. "Oh my! He knows who you are!" The fear in Jewel's voice was clear. "How did he find out?"

Caroline looked away. "I d-didn't want to worry you…"

Jewel's voice now hardened. "Excuse me?"

"Jewel, he's known for a few days."

****

"Wow! You're right!" Dutch said with a smile.

Achilles nodded. "I know! Another fire station would be vital to the town, especially with all the new homes being built far from the current one."

He glanced at his watch, seeing that ten minutes had passed. That was all Jewel had asked for. *They should be safely at home now.* He smiled. "It was wonderful talking with you, Achilles."

Achilles shook his hand and wished him well before walking down the street and by the donut shop, where he lived.

Dutch walked as fast as he could toward the donut shop without being suspicious. He needed to see the girls' faces and know that they were all right. Once away from everyone's eyes, he would teleport to Jewel's house and start making Achilles' potion.

He opened the shop's door, and the bell rang over his head. Scott, Elena, and the few customers turned to look at him.

Bluntly, he asked, "Can I use your bathroom?!"

"Sure, Dutch. It's in the back." Elena pointed down the hall with a look on her face that was hard to read.

He smiled, fast-walked to the bathroom, and shut the door behind him. He pulled his wand out from his jeans' large front pocket. "Teleportsheam!"

In a snap, he stood right outside Jewel's house. He made

his way up the steps and knocked. No one answered. A horrible wave of panic took over him, and he flicked his wand at the door. "Opena."

The door opened, revealing an empty house.

"Jewel!" he called out as he stepped inside. He waited, but no one answered.

He wanted to hear Caroline ask more questions about magic. He wanted Jewel's laughter to fill his ears. Anything to let him know they were home. Safe.

"Caroline!" Dread overcame him. "They're still at his house!"

Chapter 23

Jewel turned red as her voice raised. "He knows, and you didn't tell me?!"

"He might have seen something that let him know who I was…" Caroline said. "But I didn't mean it!"

She put her hands on her hips, the brush in her hand held tight. "What did he see, Caroline?!"

"I made a mistake. I should've put something on to cover it, but he saw my birthmark that you talked about—" Caroline raised her arm, showing the mark.

"I can't believe you didn't tell me this! How dare you break my trust and—"

"I didn't want to stress you out the night of the carnival!"

Jewel jerked back as if Caroline had hit her. Her voice was no louder than a whisper. "It's been *days* since the carnival."

"I tried to tell you! I promise! But I-I was scared!"

"You put us all in danger, Caroline!" Her voice was sharp.

"Look, I didn't want to worry you."

"You had no right to keep this from me!" she yelled.

"I tried to tell you last night! I even tried to tell you that night he found out!"

"You should have tried harder! You should have not stopped till I knew!"

"I didn't think you would want to go into his house!"

Jewel gasped. "God, you knew, and you still let me go through with this!" She held the brush out. "You knew he would never come to dinner like before. You made us risk our lives when you knew this was for nothing!" She slammed the brush down on the desk.

Caroline swallowed. "I'm sorry."

"I don't want to even look at you right now." Jewel turned away from her.

Tears built in her eyes.

Jewel pulled out her wand with her free hand. "Come close so we can teleport."

As she made her way around the desk, the sound of a door opening made them both freeze. A light came in from the doorway by the bookcase. Her heart stopped.

Holding her breath, she watched as Achilles' body filled the doorway. Their eyes locked as a smile twisted his lips.

"Well..." he said. "This will be fun."

Jewel moved in front of Caroline and pointed her wand at him. "I won't allow you to lay a hand on her!"

He laughed, the sound wicked.

Caroline looked around the room. No windows. The only way out was through the doorway Achilles stood in. Her eyes burned with tears, but she blinked them away. She would not cry in front of this monster.

"Jewel, I am sad to see you here." He reached into the pocket inside his jacket.

Jewel tensed as Caroline grabbed onto the fabric of her skirt and shook.

"I really valued your friendship. You were my only confidant."

"You murdered my daughter!" she spat.

Achilles' eyes glanced at the mirror before they fell back on Jewel. "Step aside. You are not a Smith, and my fight is not with you." His eyes fell on Caroline.

Jewel flicked her wand at him. "Gunfoly!"

Light moved toward him, but he pulled his wand out and waved the spell away. "I see you choose to die for someone who is not worth it." He shook his head before smiling and flicking his wand at Caroline. "Gepsic!"

She pushed Caroline out of the path of his magic. The spell hit her instead, making her gasp in pain.

Pulling out her training wand, Caroline flicked it at him. "Fire itera!"

Fire shot at him, seeming to take him by surprise. It brushed his shoulder.

"Cute," he said. "A training wand."

Jewel waved her wand at him. "Float itera!"

She sent him up to the ceiling hard before he dropped down to the floor with a bang. As he stood, she moved close and reached into the pocket of her dress. She pulled out dry leaves, crushed them in her hands, and blew them into his face.

His face shifted as the leaves met his skin. His skin disappeared, and his skull showed. The only thing that remained were his purple eyes that locked onto Jewel with hate. Caroline screamed, backing away from him. His skull was dirty and ancient looking.

"I knew it!" Jewel said.

His face returned to normal, and he smacked her across the face. She dropped to the floor, and blood rushed down her nose.

"Jewel!" Caroline yelled.

Achilles held his hand out to her. Her body smashed

against the bookcase behind her and stayed there. Jewel looked up at him as he aimed his wand at her face.

"Goodbye, Jewel."

Dutch teleported into the space and tackled Achilles to the floor.

Caroline was released from the wall, and she rushed to Jewel. "Are you all right?" Her voice shook as she helped her grandma to her feet.

Blood dripped down Jewel's chin.

Caroline glanced at Dutch as he punched Achilles repeatedly in the face. Achilles grabbed a fistful of his hair, causing him to move away.

As Dutch stumbled back, Jewel flicked her wand, teleporting the three of them away from Achilles.

Chapter 24

After making it back to Jewel's house, Caroline felt so lucky to be back home. Then it hit her: this was her *home*. She hadn't felt that way in such a long time. Her eyes watered.

"I'm so sorry!" Dutch blurted as he moved to Jewel. "I had one job, and I failed. You guys could have been…" He didn't have to finish the sentence.

They all knew what almost happened.

Guiding Jewel by her elbow, he took her into the bathroom behind the stairs. Seeing the blood on her face reminded Caroline that this was her fault. Guilt built in her as she lingered in the doorway.

"I can use a healing spell," Jewel told Dutch, who grabbed a towel with a shaky hand.

"Let me at least get the blood off your face." He turned the sink on, and she leaned down into the water. Gently, he worked the blood off.

"I could kill him right now." His eyes were hard. "I can't believe he dared to touch you."

Once her face was clean, she put her hand to her face and healed the bruise that had been forming on her cheek.

"I'm so sorry," Caroline mumbled as Jewel looked at her with an expression that was hard to understand. She lowered her head.

"Why are you sorry?" Dutch asked with a kind smile.

"Because she lied to us," Jewel snapped as she passed her and went toward the magic room.

His eyes landed on hers. "What does she mean you lied to us?" he asked, hurt laced in his voice.

"Achilles knew who I was," Caroline said. "H-he found out the night of the carnival."

Dutch stayed quiet, his eyes never leaving her. "What?" he asked, no louder than a whisper.

Jewel walked back into the hallway with a spell book under her arm.

"I have done so much for you these past few weeks." Hurt and anger twisted her voice. "I never thought you would do this."

Caroline closed her eyes.

"I feel so betrayed by you."

She heard Jewel move past her and into the living room.

A warm hand touched her shoulder. She met Dutch's eyes, her own eyes watering.

"Let her cool off," he said with a weak smile.

"You're not mad at me?" she asked, no louder than a whisper.

"I am disappointed that you let us go into danger. But I'm not mad."

She released a sigh.

They walked into the living room, where Jewel was flipping through a spell book.

"What are you doing?" Dutch asked, staying by Caroline behind the sofa.

"Looking for a spell to keep our house safe," Jewel snapped, her back to them.

Caroline took a slow breath. "Jewel, I am so sorry." Her voice was small. "I can't give any more excuses. I—"

"Would you have done this to Edmund?"

She felt as if the air had been sucked from her lungs. "Jewel, I'm sorry!"

"Would you have done this to Edmund?" Jewel stood, turning to face her.

Taken aback, she stuttered. "N-no. I wouldn't. I-I was scared to tell you."

"That's not a reason!" she snapped as she rested her hands on her hips.

"I was scared that you would make me leave!"

Her eyebrows moved together. "I already told you I wouldn't move you." Her voice still held some anger.

Caroline nodded as she blinked back tears. She would not cry. She wanted to speak clearly. To let Jewel know how sorry she was.

Anxiety that Jewel would become like George and scream till she cried grew in her . Or get angry enough to hit her like Mia.

"I know," she said. "It's just…I haven't been this happy and comfortable in a long time." A tear escaped her eye, and she wiped it away. "I didn't want to risk me having to leave."

"You let me go into his house," Jewel snapped. "Caroline, I could have *died*. Dutch could have died. You could have been killed when you had the power to keep all of us safe!"

Tears rolled down her face. "I know. I'm sorry. I understand if you want me to leave."

George's voice rang in her head. *You'll mess things up with your grandma. No one likes a pebble in their shoe.*

When Jewel said nothing, Dutch spoke up. "Listen, what both of you are saying is valid."

Their eyes moved to him.

"From what your grandma has told me, you had a hard life before you came here. A lot of rejection that clearly has left its mark on you." His blue eyes fell on Caroline. "You thought keeping this was the best way to keep yourself from getting hurt again."

A part of her knew she had let herself get too close to Jewel and Dutch. That one day, they would make her leave like everyone else. She didn't know if she could handle the heartbreak of losing someone else.

How she wished she knew what was wrong with herself.

"And Jewel," he continued, "you have every right to feel betrayed. But she's so young, and this is so much for her."

Jewel's eyes closed as she took a breath in. A tear rolled down her cheek. "I'm just hurt."

"Me too. But I understand her, and I won't hold it against her."

When no one spoke for a while, Caroline looked down at the floor. "I'm scared…"

He put a hand to her shoulder.

"I am so afraid that you will do what Edmund did to me."

She could see herself at George's house, lying in her bed and wondering what she had done wrong for someone she saw as a father to leave her. Wondering how someone she loved with all her heart could never talk to her again. Wondering how he never came to take her away from Mia and her fist.

Jewel moved around the sofa and to her. "Caroline…" She wiped away a tear from her face.

"George…" Her lips quivered. "He would tell me horrible things about myself. I believed they were true."

Dutch's eyebrows moved together. "Like what?"

She closed her eyes. She didn't know if she was ready to say George's words out loud. To give them that power. But she had already given them power. They controlled her daily.

"He constantly told me I'm a fool," she said. "Or that I was better when I kept my mouth shut. That I was insignificant. That I am a pebble in everyone's lives. That that's why no one keeps me." Her throat grew tight.

"And you believe all those nasty things?"

She nodded.

Anger shifted on Dutch's face.

"Did he ever hit you?" Jewel asked.

"Never. But he knew Mia did."

She sucked in a deep breath. "Caroline, you left his house."

Caroline's eyebrows moved together in thought.

"You escaped that horrible environment. But every time you believe what he told you, you give him power."

Dutch looked at her with sad eyes. "You are as far away from him as you can get. Don't give him power over your life."

"I believed them so much," Caroline admitted. "I thought you would send me away like Edmund."

"I can't change what happened to you," Jewel said. "And I can't take away your suffering. But I can tell you that I am never sending you off. No matter what, you're stuck with me."

A tearful smile formed on her face.

"Each day that I am on this Earth, you will have a roof over your head and love all around you."

"I'm sorry."

"I love you."

"I love you too."

It had been so long since she had someone to say that to. She wrapped her arms around Jewel, and Jewel's arms fell around her shoulders.

"I love you too!" Dutch called, his arms draping around them both.

Jewel pulled out of the hug and took Caroline's hands into her own. "Caroline, I know Edmund hurt you by leaving you with George. But he didn't want you to leave; he was devastated to see you go."

Caroline bit her lip to hold back a sob.

"He loves you so much. I really think you should try and call him. Talk to him and heal what he broke within you."

Nerves bubbled in her stomach at the idea of talking to him again. But she still nodded.

Dutch gasped, putting a hand to his forehead. "Oh crap!"

They both looked at him.

"Elena still thinks I'm in her bathroom!"

Jewel glanced at Caroline, who shrugged. "What are you talking about?"

"I went into her shop's bathroom to teleport like thirty minutes ago! She must think I'm dying or something!"

Jewel burst out laughing as he pulled out his wand with panic.

****

"Do not go in there!" Dutch declared as he came out of the donut shop's bathroom.

Scott, of course, was gone, but Elena still stood behind the counter with a hint of embarrassment written on her face.

He waved his hand in front of his face with nervous laughter. "The wallpaper is peeling!"

She put a hand to her mouth as Hector came out from the back with a tray of donuts.

Dutch smiled awkwardly as he made his way to the exit.

"Are you okay?" Hector asked with the tray resting on his shoulder. "You've been in there forever."

Dutch gave them an awkward chuckle. "I just ate something bad." He headed to leave the shop, not wanting this moment to last any longer.

Elena's and Hector's disgusted faces made him wish he could melt into the floor.

"Are you sure you're all right?" she asked. "Do you want some water?"

"I'm all right!" *God, just take me now.*

Hector took a big sniff, and his eyes locked on Dutch. "I don't smell anything."

Elena turned to her husband and smacked his arm. "Hay, por el amor de dios, Hector!"

"Have a great day!" Dutch called as he walked out of the shop. His face was burning red as he walked as fast as he could away from the town.

Chapter 25

Dutch tossed and turned all night, and the few hours he had managed to sleep for, nightmares woke him up. His dreams fed on his fear. The anxiety he had experienced at the thought of losing Jewel forever. As he lay in bed, staring up at the ceiling in his dark room, he sucked in a breath.

He could not bear the thought that he had come so close to losing his best friend. To lose someone so important to him. If she would have died, what would he have done?

A part of him knew he would not have forgiven Caroline. But he would have taken her in and moved away with her. Somewhere where Achilles would not find her. Somewhere far away from the memories he had with Jewel. But those memories would always follow him; a part of him knew this.

Dutch had moved into his house with his wife Cecilia back in 1922. His work had brought them to Duck. Back then, it had been a very small and simple town. They had planned to fill their large home with children.

The thought of the life they had planned still ached in his heart.

No matter how much they had tried, Cecilia could not

get pregnant. Even all these years later, Dutch kept all the doors to the spare bedrooms shut, finding it too painful to see them empty when he had envisioned them full for so many months.

A year after they had moved in, Cecilia had grown ill. She had been infected with tuberculosis years before, but by the time they had discovered it, her lungs had been destroyed. The reason they could not have a baby had grown clear. Dutch had felt so foolish for not catching on sooner.

Jewel and Lester had moved in next door during the final week of Cecilia's life. Dutch recalled what a dark place he had been in the day he had spotted Lucy in his backyard. It was a welcome distraction to get to know Jewel and Lester.

Dutch had lost his family, but they had welcomed him into theirs.

Lester had become his good friend. Twice a week, they would go fishing in the ocean together. Jewel and Lester had helped him overcome the loss of his wife, and he had helped Jewel the same way years later after she had lost Lester.

Jewel had always been there for him, and he had always been there for her, but today, he had failed to keep her safe. He had almost lost another woman who meant the world to him. And that thought scared him.

He rolled over in his bed and looked at the clock on the wall. It read three a.m. Sitting up, he looked out the window by his bed. A light shined through Jewel's kitchen windows. She never left the lights on at night; she must be awake.

He grabbed his robe and slid it over his pajamas before making his way downstairs. He needed to talk with her. To see that she was all right with his own eyes.

Once in his dining room, he looked into her kitchen. She sat at the table with her hair down. Her brown curls rested on her shoulders as she looked down at the teacup in her hands.

Her robe was resting on the chair next to her, allowing him to see her white nightgown.

He swallowed as he moved to flick his lights and gain her attention.

After a few flicks of his light switch, her eyes moved toward his window. He waved as she reached for her robe and slid it on.

Can I come over? he mouthed.

She nodded with a soft smile, and in a second, he teleported into her kitchen.

"Can't sleep?" she asked as he lowered himself into the chair next to her.

"No," he said. "I have too many thoughts going through my head."

"Me too." She removed the tea bag from her cup. Tea dripped off it and onto the table as she placed it on a waiting napkin.

"I feel like I could've lost you," he said. "And Caroline. And it would've been my fault." He looked away from her, not wanting to meet her eyes.

"Dutch, what happened was not your fault! And we're okay." She reached her hand across the table, putting her hand on his.

"How are you feeling?" he asked.

She smiled sadly. "I'm still hurt from Caroline. But I am also mad at George. He treated her so poorly."

"Did she call Edmund?"

Jewel shook her head. "She's really hurt by things she doesn't fully understand. I think most of it might also have to do with the fact he left her with George."

"That man is nasty." He was surprised by the rage he felt toward someone he didn't even know.

Jewel took a sip of her tea. He scanned her face. Without makeup, her face still held beauty.

"Before she went to bed, she was telling me more about him and his wife," Jewel said.

"What happened?"

"Mia was physically abusive. Gave her a black eye once."

Dutch's blood went cold. Caroline was a good kid; she didn't deserve anything terrible. She was too young to have such a hard life already.

"She arrived here with bruises, and I didn't put anything together."

"It always amazes me that some people treat children so bad. Some people would do anything to have their own."

Her eyes saddened as they met his. "You would have been a wonderful father, Dutch." Her hand found his once more.

He swallowed the knot in his throat. "Today was really hard. I really thought I was going to lose you." Hoping his next words were not a mistake, he took a deep breath. "And I think I love you."

A blissful surprised look overtook her face. "What?" A soft smile formed.

His mouth was as dry as paper, but he pushed on. "I never thought I would love anyone like this ever again. But God, I look at you, and my heart skips a beat. And I feel so blessed to know you. I'm in love with you."

"You love me?" she asked. Her cheeks grew a shade darker.

"You are my home."

She leaned closer to him, and his heart banged in his chest as her eyes lowered to his lips. "Can I tell you something?" she whispered.

Having her face this close to his was doing things to his brain. "What?"

"I've cared about you for a while. I just didn't know if I should tell you."

Gently, he met his lips with hers. They were soft and welcoming. He tugged at her bottom lip before pulling away.

"I love you," she whispered as she rested her forehead on his. "It feels so good to finally say that out loud."

He smiled as he kissed her forehead. "I love you too."

Chapter 26

Achilles was done.

He had been humiliated. He should have won that fight! Living in Duck without using his magic in such violent ways had softened him.

The sun in Washington was surprisingly hot as Achilles stood in a full parking lot. His eyebrows came together. An old-looking general store stood nearby, and a few families walked out with paper bags in their hands.

Edmund walked out with a young girl. Both held a handful of bags.

Achilles moved in between the cars, the sun bouncing off the windshields and into his eyes. He held his wand tight in his hand.

As they got closer, the young girl asked, "What time does everyone get in?"

As they passed where he stood, he scanned over the girl. He quickly identified her as Norna Smith. There was no doubt that she was Edmund's daughter. Her face was identical, holding the same brown eyes and round face. Though her hair was dirty blonde unlike her father's brown hair.

I'll kill them both now.

"The party starts at noon," Edmund answered as the pair reached a green Ford Coupe. "Knowing your Uncle Robert, he'll be twenty minutes late." His laughter filled the parking lot as he opened the back door and placed the bags inside the car.

"And George?" Norna asked.

"He'll be late too!"

Achilles put his wand away. If they were having a party, it meant all his targets would be in one place. He could get rid of all the brothers and Edmund's family in one blow.

"All right. Get in, sunshine." Edmund put a hand to her back and guided her to the passenger door. He opened it and then made his way to the driver's seat.

Before he entered the car, Edmund scanned the parking lot, and Achilles lowered himself further. His eyes lingered where Achilles hid.

"Dad! Would Uncle Dilandro have been late or early?" Norna called from the car.

Edmund blinked and got into the driver's seat. "Early. Very early."

****

Achilles hid outside the house Edmund had gone into an hour ago. The white two-story house was built on a cul-de-sac, allowing him to stay hidden within the woods across the house. Each window had shutters that matched the dark green roof, and bright flowers grew in flower beds under each window. A bike lay on the grass, seeming as though it had been forgotten for some time.

More than a few cars were parked on the side of the road, and a few wrapped around the cul-de-sac. Edmund had been right. It seemed everyone had arrived, and yet the other two Smith brothers had yet to be seen.

Achilles grew anxious with each minute that passed. He took a breath, and his eyes fell back to the house. Birthday balloons—tied to a rocking chair—floated outside the front door. *Let them have their joy for now.* The rumbling of an approaching car took his attention away from the house.

A car pulled into the driveway.

He hid deeper into the bushes and waited. His time was coming.

George got out of the driver's seat and slammed the door shut. He was dressed well, tan khakis and a brown vest. He held a matching hat in his hand. *A good outfit to die in.* His brown hair was cut a bit long, allowing soft curls to form at the nabe of his neck.

The passenger door opened, and his wife—Mia—came out. She was dressed in a gold dress, and pearls hung from her neck. "Don't you dare slam a door at me again!" she hissed as she slammed her own door. The sound was loud from where Achilles stood.

George looked at the bright blue sky with a sigh. "Would having a baby really be that bad?" he asked, sounding annoyed.

"I already told you! I will not have a child! Ever!"

He slammed his fist on the roof of the car. "Mia, please try not to embarrass me today. Act like you're having a good time. And keep your mouth shut."

Achilles laughed under his breath. *Such problems will seem small in minutes.*

Another car pulled up to the house, notably slow. It stopped at the end of the driveway. The *happy* couple both watched as Robert climbed out of the driver's seat.

A wide smile overtook his face as he made his way to the other side of the car and let his wife—Elizabeth—out. Achilles noticed that they didn't have a kid with them. Meaning the car crash he had caused worked. One less Smith to worry about.

"It's been a while!" George called as he made his way to his brother.

Mia's mouth formed a fake smile.

"Too long!" Robert embraced him quickly. He held the same brown hair as his brother, along with his brown eyes.

Elizabeth's heels tapped the pavement as she made her way to everyone.

The house's front door flung open to reveal Edmund.

They were all here! And their families. Achilles smiled thinly. *This will work perfectly.* "Ah, look," Achilles whispered. "The three Smith brothers together for the last time." Reaching into the pocket of his vest, he pulled out his mask. As he looked down at it, his eyes scanned the line from where it had broken from the other half. The shape matched his scar.

"Family!" Edmund called, making Achilles look back. He gave each of them a hug.

"I missed you, Eddy," George said as he released the hug.

"Here you go." Elizabeth handed him a gift bag.

Edmund took it and peeked inside. "It means a lot that you came. I know this must be hard."

Robert put his hand on her back. "We could not miss Peter's birthday and the baby shower."

He took her hand, giving it a light squeeze. "Still, it warms my heart to see you here."

"Do you think you'll have another boy?" George asked.

He nervously chuckled. "Is it wrong if I hope it's a girl? Norna was just so much easier to raise. Though Mary's belly looks big enough for twins." He paused for a second, pointing at his brothers. "Don't tell her I said that."

Robert laughed.

Mia sighed. "I can't believe you're having another baby."

Achilles could feel the tension rise from where he stood.

"They are more work than they are worth."

Elizabeth's face fell. Robert put his hand on her shoulder, pain written on his face.

"Mia," George warned in a low voice.

Edmund turned to her. "Once you have your own, your thoughts will change."

She shook her head. "Trust me. There will be no child in my future."

Elizabeth bit her lip.

"Taking care of Caroline was the worst thing. The house has been so peaceful with her gone."

Edmund jerked as if she had hit him.

Robert's eyebrows moved together. "What do you mean?" he asked.

Achilles smiled at the unfolding scene in front of him. The fact their last conversation was not enjoyable only made his smile grow.

"Where is Caroline?" Edmund asked.

Before Mia or George could answer, Mary opened the front door. "There you guys are! I need help opening a jar in the kitchen."

In silence, they walked into the house.

Achilles readied himself.

****

Edmund put Robert and Elizabeth's gift down with the rest on the table in the living room. The house was full of friends and family talking and laughing, while his blood boiled.

George walked out of the kitchen after helping Mary and locked eyes with him.

"We need to talk," he hissed in a low voice. He didn't want to change the atmosphere, so he gestured for his older brother to follow him.

They moved out of the small living room and into the foyer that no one occupied.

George ran a finger over the round table in the middle of the space, and he glanced at the small amount of dust he had picked up. "This is about Caroline?" His tone didn't make his question feel like one.

"Where. Is. She."

He took a deep breath in. Robert walked up with his arms crossed.

"You said she was at a friend's house today!" Edmund snapped. "But your wife made it sound as if she had left."

George's eyes glanced around the space. "I had her for two horrible years and—"

"You agreed to three years."

"She should be safe where I sent her."

Edmund raised his voice. "Damn it, George. Where is my girl?"

George bit his lip. "She's in North Carolina."

"What?!" both brothers said.

The idea that Caroline was so far away from Edmund made panic grow within him. With everything happening with the masked man, it was always a comfort to have her nearby.

George glanced back at the room full of guests. "Lower your voice."

"George, how could you do this?!" Robert asked.

"How dare you send Caroline away!" Edmund hissed. "You didn't even ask or tell me!"

George rolled his eyes. "I don't have to ask you anything."

His heart sped up. Before he could snap back, Norna walked down the steps on his right.

"Oh. Hi, Uncle George. Hi, Uncle Robert!" She smiled kindly as she hopped down the last step. Her green skirt bounced with the movement.

"Hello, Norna," George answered.

Robert smiled. "Hi, sweetie."

Edmund took a slow breath. "Why don't you go see if your mom needs anything?"

She nodded and walked toward the rest of the house.

Edmund and Robert met George's eyes once more. "What is she doing so far away?" he asked in a low voice.

George slid his hands into the pockets of his pants. "She's with Julia."

"Since when?"

He threw his hands up. "I didn't want her. Besides, you got rid of her before I did. You are hardly one to judge." His eyes fell on Robert. "And you didn't want her—"

"You know the reasons!" Robert snapped. "It's insensitive of you to use that to make yourself look better."

Anger made Edmund's vision go red. "You know how much I suffered to leave her. She was a part of my family. Don't you dare say that to me again."

George scanned the room with a bored eye. "That's where you and I differ. She's a fool who acts like the world spins for her."

He grabbed his wrist tightly, and his eyes darkened. "Stop talking."

George looked at him with rage before pulling his arm free. "You can feel about me as you want. You're only mad because you know I'm right."

Robert shook his head, his brown eyes hard. "You are such a horrible person. We are all Caroline has. The fact that you would dare to say such things out loud is beyond me. Dilandro would not have stood for any of this."

"She's a good kid. And she deserves better than you," Edmund snapped. Everything that had happened to Caroline was unfair, and it pained him to think of his niece living with the man before him. "You've wanted kids all your life! Why do this to Caroline?"

George stayed quiet, not meeting his eyes. Instead, he smiled at someone behind Edmund.

Edmund turned to see Mia watching them from the other room.

"She is corrupting you," he hissed, looking back at his brother who kept his eyes on his wife. "You never spoke as harshly as you do now."

Robert nodded, his eyes locked on Edmund's. "I told you she was bad news."

"Let's not make a scene, guys." George rolled his eyes before locking them on Edmund.

"I know it's not safe to call," Edmund said, "but did you at least ensure she got in? That she's safe."

George put a hand to the back of his neck and looked away. The body language made him fear what he already knew.

"We don't know. We don't know if she even made it or not." He thought of all the worst things that could have happened to her.

Robert gasped. "What?!"

His eyes stung with unfallen tears. "What the hell? Why would you not call Jewel's house to make sure she's all right?!"

"To be honest, I don't really care," George said.

He took a step back; he was going to be sick.

"Do you not hear yourself?!" Robert asked, his face pale. "George, how can you—"

"We're done here," George said.

No words could be formed as he went to where Mia was still watching.

"I don't recognize my own brother," Robert said as he looked the way he had gone.

The noise of everyone talking and the light music faded into nothing. It seemed like an ice dagger went through Edmund's heart.

He walked through the party, not reacting to anything happening around him. Once he made it to the kitchen, he moved to the table with the gray rotary phone. Robert was close on his heels.

"It's almost time to sing happy birthday to Peter!" Mary said as she put a few candles on the cake she had made.

"I need to make a phone call." He lifted the phone up and spun the dial. Its clicks filled the room.

She turned back to him. Her dirty blonde hair was pulled back in a bun, though a few strains had fallen into her face. The apron she had on over her dress was stained with frosting. Her baby bump made the apron fit oddly on her. "Is everything all right?"

He shook his head as he brought the phone up to his ear.

Robert turned to her. "George and Mia moved Caroline to North Carolina."

She gasped, nearly dropping a candle. "What?!"

"They don't even know if she got to Jewel's."

Mary paled. She looked at Edmund. "Are y-you calling her?"

He nodded as the operator came on the line.

"Operator. How can I help you?" Her voice was light and airy.

"Hi. This is Edmund Smith."

"Hello, Mr. Smith!"

"Hi. I need to get in contact with Julia Marie Walker. She is in Duck, North Carolina."

There was a beat of silence as Mary walked closer to him.

She rested a clean hand on his arm as she waited alongside him.

"Connecting you now," the operator said.

"Thank you." He took a few deep breaths to slow his heart and calm his mind. He didn't even know what he would do if Caroline had never made it to Jewel's house.

"Your call is connected," the operator said. "Go ahead."

Jewel's voice followed. "Hello. Julia speaking. May I ask who this is?"

He put a hand over his other ear to hear her better. "Jewel, it's Edmund." His voice shook.

"Oh, hi! It's so wonderful to hear your voice! It's been so long since I—"

"I don't mean to be rude," he interrupted, "but I just learned that Caroline moved in with you. There's been no word on her arrival. I need to know she is all right."

His eyes fell on Mary and Robert as he waited for an answer. His fear and anxieties reflected in their faces.

"Yes," Jewel said. "She's here with me."

He sighed with relief as a tear rolled down his face. He lowered the phone. "She's all right."

Mary put a hand to her chest with a smile. Robert let out a shaky breath as his face also broke into a smile.

He put a hand on her shoulder. "She's all right!" he whispered as she nodded with tearful eyes. He brought the phone back to his ear. "Is she all right? Adjusting well?"

"Caroline is fantastic," Jewel said. "She misses you a great deal."

He blinked away the tears he could feel building in his eyes. "I miss her too."

Caroline's laughter echoed in the background of the call.

"Is that her?" he asked.

"Yes. She's been training all day and—"

"Training?" he interrupted once more.

"Yes. She knows about everything now. Took the news much better than I would have at her age."

A smile overtook his face. "I am so happy to hear that! So, she knows why I had to let her go?" His heart beat hard in his chest. Did she finally understand why he had to lose her?

"She does—"

The doorbell rang, pulling him away from the conversation. He turned to look at Mary, who held the cake in her hands. Robert held a high stack of plates.

"I'll get it!" one of her friends called from the other room. "Don't worry, Mary."

Edmund turned back to the phone. "I'm sorry, Jewel. I missed that. What did you say?"

"I think you need to talk with her," Jewel said. "She's still really emotionally damaged from everything that has happened, even knowing their reasons. She loves you so much."

His heart hurt for his niece. His daughter. "I love her so much. Breaks my heart to think I hurt her."

Whatever Jewel said next, he didn't hear it. The sound of a body hitting the floor echoed through the house. Followed by a scream.

Chapter 27

Caroline quietly shut the front door behind her. Each crash of the waves was loud in the night. The moon was full and bright overhead, and it seemed like thousands of stars shined down on her as she made her way down the porch steps. *They have to show me how to teleport.* She slowly made her way down the last steps, worried about making a sound.

"She's sleeping?" Dutch asked once she reached the driveway.

She was surprised he was still dressed. His jeans and white T-shirt made her glance down at her cherry pink pajama set. *Should I have gotten dressed?*

"Jewel's sleeping," she said. "Fell asleep about an hour and a half ago."

"Perfect! Come on."

She followed him across the street and to the beach. She was surprised by how bright the night was. The stars gathered in a way that almost looked like someone had cut a jewel in half and threw it into the sky.

"That's the Milky Way," he said. He pointed up toward the shining sky.

"Is that what that is?!" she asked with a laugh as her feet

dug into the sand with each step they took. She wondered how such a beautiful place could have someone so *deadly* hiding within it.

"Yep! The Milky Way!" Dutch said, bring her mind back.

The Milky Way was visible on most nights, though Caroline had not understood that was what she was seeing. "It's lovely."

The ocean seemed to glow with the stars above it. The waves crashed louder, making him have to speak up a little.

"Here on this barrier island, the Milky Way shows more clearly than anywhere else in the world."

Before she could answer him, a shooting star raced across the sky.

"Look!" he called out. He rested one hand on her shoulder and pointed the other toward the star.

She gasped.

"Make a wish!"

I wish to live here forever. Happy.

"Okay," he said. "Time to learn magic without Jewel."

Caroline smiled, feeling the cold sand under her bare feet as she dug her toes in. "Will she mind?" she asked as he pulled out his wand.

The wind from the ocean made both their hairs move freely around their heads. They turned away from the ocean.

"Remember, what she doesn't know won't anger her," he said as she pulled out her training wand. "Flying, it's kind of easy. You need to hold your wand like this."

She copied the way he held it with both hands in front of his body.

Her excitement grew by the second. "Now what?"

"You have to see yourself lifting into the sky in your mind." He closed his eyes. "The clearer you see it, the easier the spell will work."

Scanning the beautiful sky, she took a deep breath and then closed her eyes. Her mind blanked.

"Now, you say the spell," he said. "You can open your eyes for a second."

She smiled shyly as she met his eyes.

"Ready?"

"Yes!"

"You already know the spell, so we don't have to worry about the pronunciation."

She nodded, grateful the spell would be something she already knew.

He closed his eyes and held his wand in front of him once more. "Float itera." He lifted into the air and looked down at her.

Caroline gasped. "Wow!"

"Give it a try!" He lowered back down to the sand.

"You made that look so easy!" she said as she took hold of her wand like before.

"And so will you." His smile and words gave her confidence.

She closed her eyes and saw herself lifting much like he had. "Float itera." She slowly lifted into the night sky, the cold sand no longer under her feet. She opened her eyes, seeing Dutch a few feet below her with a large smile. "I did it!"

The spell released her.

He moved to grab her as she dropped to the sand, hard.

"Oof!" she cried as she landed on her left leg awkwardly.

"You okay?" he asked with a quavering voice.

Pain shot up her leg and into her hip. She dropped her wand as she bit her lip. The pain intensified.

He was at her side with worry. "Are you all right?"

"I think I landed wrong."

"Can you get up?" he asked, grabbing her hands.

"I think so," she said, her voice tight.

He pulled her to her feet.

"Can't you do that spell Jewel does?" she asked, bending over as the pain shot up her back.

His hand strongly held her hand. "I don't know how."

"Maybe I should be learning that."

Words George had told her once before came to mind. *You're not hurt. You just want attention. It's nauseating how needy you are.*

She didn't want to keep giving his words power. She stood through the pain.

"Let's try again!" She picked up her wand, dusting the sand off.

"Are you sure?" Dutch asked.

"Yes!" She held her wand like before. *I will not be needy.*

****

The next morning, Caroline woke up with so much pain. Stiffly, she stood from her bed. Somehow, even her neck hurt, but still the pain near her hip was the worst. Lifting her pajama pant, she saw that her left leg was a bit swollen. *Maybe I can tell Jewel I fell down the stairs last night.*

After the training—that had gone quite well—she and Dutch had agreed to keep the night a secret. She would simply tell Jewel—only if she asked—that she slept wrong.

She limped into the kitchen, wearing white pants and a soft green blouse. She hoped the pants would hide the swelling as she tried to hide her limp. The sweet smell of pancakes lingered in the air as she painfully climbed the two steps into the kitchen.

Jewel hummed as she waved her wand over an empty dish. Crunchy bacon filled it.

"Good morning!" Caroline called as she moved as fast as her leg would allow her to. The faster she sat down, the less Jewel could see her limp.

Her grandmother set a big plate of pancakes down next to the bacon in the middle of the table. "Did you sleep well?" she asked with a smile. She looked over at Caroline as Caroline reached her chair. Her smile faded.

Dutch walked into the room as he did every morning: with a big smile. "Hey girls!"

"What happened? Why are you limping?" she asked Caroline with a puzzled face.

"Okay. Bye!" he called, turning around to leave.

"Stop!" she called out to him. She pointed at the doorway he had just appeared in. "Dutch, come back."

He made his way back into the room.

"What was that about?"

Caroline turned to meet his eyes. Fear was written on his face. *What a horrible liar!*

"Nothing…" He moved into the room and sat at the table.

Jewel's eyes lingered on him before she looked back at Caroline. "What happened?"

"I'm fine. Really." Caroline sat, masking all the pain she felt from such a simple movement.

Jewel put a hand to her shoulder, making her tense from the pain. "What did you do?!" she asked, sounding alarmed.

"I'll be fine!"

"You can't even look up at me!"

Caroline tried to look up at her, but the pain in her neck made that movement impossible. Though she saw the worry in her eyes. "I fell down the stairs."

Jewel lowered herself to meet her eyes. "When?" The distress was clear in her voice.

Dutch slammed his hand into his face. "Stop lying to your grandmother!"

Jewel looked at him with a flash of anger. "You're lying?!" Her eyes fell back on Caroline.

"He told me too!"

She stood, her eyes back on Dutch. "What the hell is going on?!" she asked as her voice raised.

"Well… She learned how to, um, fly last night," he said.

Jewel's eyebrows shot up. "Dutch!"

"She did a great job. Only fell once!" He gave her an awkward smile.

She lowered herself next to Caroline once more. "Why didn't you ask me to heal you?" she asked, her voice soft.

"I didn't want to be needy," Caroline said.

Gently, Jewel put a hand to her neck. "Needy when you can hardly walk? Come on, Caroline."

Caroline closed her eyes and took a deep breath in as the pain eased. In a second, the pain in her body disappeared as if it had never been there. "Wow!" She put her hand to her leg. "That is amazing."

Jewel sat next to her. "Whoever made you think you are needy is a fool."

"George," she mumbled.

Dutch sighed from where he sat. "Go figure."

Jewel smiled. "Stop giving that man any power."

She nodded, wanting to do so.

Jewel's eyes landed on him. "And Dutch, you knew I didn't want her to learn to fly just yet."

"I'm sorry," he said. He grabbed two big pancakes and placed them on his plate. "But it was her fault she got hurt. Child thinks she can open her eyes and interrupt her concentration on the first try."

Caroline laughed. "Excuse me! You didn't tell me that I could fall so easily."

He passed her the pancakes. "I'm just grateful you didn't break your neck."

"OH MY GOODNESS!" Jewel cried.

Dutch turned to her. "I wouldn't have let that happen!" He pointed his fork at her as she rolled her eyes with a smile.

"I could have broken my neck?" Caroline asked as he simply passed her the pitcher of orange juice.

"No…"

She took the pitcher with a dry mouth. For some reason, getting hurt was not even an idea in her head. She poured orange juice into her glass. *I need to learn that healing spell one day.*

Chapter 28

Caroline sat on the crowded beach with Sal. He had come over shortly after breakfast and invited her to the beach to surf. Her red one-piece swimsuit was growing hot under the bright sun.

It was the warmest day since she had arrived so far, making the beach a popular place to be. All around them, people ate, talked, swam, and played in the sand.

She glanced over at him as he prepared the surfboard she was going to use. "I'm not too sure about this."

There were already a few people out in the water, surfing much better than she knew she would be able to. The last thing she wanted was to look like a fool in front of Sal.

"If you want, we can share a board." He smiled over his shoulder at her.

"You can do that?"

"Sure! My board is ready, so we don't have to waste any more time prepping this newer one." He glanced at the brown shiny board he had been working on.

"All right. Let's do that!"

He picked up the orange board and tucked it under his arm as if it weighed nothing. And maybe it did. But she still found it impressive. She followed him to the ocean, where the waves grew in feet. The wind was strong, causing her ponytail to move wildly behind her.

As they entered the ocean, Sal put the board down on the water. He held it strongly as the waves moved it. "Get on!" he called.

She moved to sit on the front of it. She feared drowning; she always had. But she pushed that thought away as she tucked her knees under her. *Sal won't let anything happen to me.*

He pushed her out deeper into the water. Each wave felt like a challenge to climb. He laughed as a big wave came close. "Hold on tight."

She closed her eyes and held on tight as the water crashed past her. Soaked, she looked back at him. "Are we far enough?" She looked past him and to the beach; it was farther away then she had thought.

"We should be!" he called as he jumped on behind her. The board rocked with the movement.

A wave grew far enough away for them to get ready.

"This is it!" Sal laughed and crouched down behind her. "Use your arms and turn us to the beach!"

She lay flat and did just as he asked. The wave pushed them faster.

"Keeping going!"

The wave grew behind them, and before she knew it, the best feeling entered her stomach. She let out a *whoop* as Sal stood behind her.

"You're doing it!" he called as he rode the wave.

She gently moved into a crouch, and he took her arm, pulling her to her feet. His hands grabbed her waist.

"This is amazing!" she yelled as the wave disappeared close to the beach.

Sal leaned off, taking her with him. They splashed into the water.

****

After two hours of swimming, surfing, and sneaking in small kisses, Caroline and Sal sat on the beach, their legs covered in sand.

"I didn't think I would enjoy that as much as I did." She turned to face him better.

"Your screams were cute." He smiled as she gently punched his arm.

"They were not!"

"They were."

She laughed till a figure in the corner of her vision caught her eye. Her eyes moved to the street. Achilles stood there, watching them.

"What's wrong?" Sal asked.

When she said nothing, he followed her gaze. He waved at Achilles, who now walked over toward them.

Dread filled her soul.

"Hello, Mr. Remis!" he called as he stood, dusting sand off from his legs.

"Achilles is just fine." His voice held a beat of joy.

She stood, sucking in a nervous breath. She was surprised Achilles was acting as if finding her in his house had never happened. Gladly, she went along with it.

"I didn't see you around town today," Sal said once Achilles was in front of them.

"I took a little trip." Achilles' eyes landed on Caroline, and her mouth grew dry.

"What brings you out here, sir?"

"Well, I was walking this way, and I saw your grandmother. She was rushing off to the hospital," he said, sounding concerned.

She took a step closer to Sal.

Worry made Sal grow tense. "What?"

"Your grandpa…" Achilles said. "He was holding his chest in great pain."

His eyes went wide. "Oh my God!" The panic in his voice was clear. He glanced around the beach. His eyes landed on the surfboards and then on Caroline. "I have to go!" He moved to leave.

"Wait!" She reached out to grab his arm, but he moved out of reach. "Let me go with you!"

He met her eyes, seeming to consider this. She moved to pick up a surfboard.

"Sal, you need to get to them now," Achilles said. "Maybe you can still meet them before they leave."

He looked at Caroline. "I'm sorry. I have to go."

He then raced off the beach, toward where his bike rested. She watched as he unhooked the bike trailer he had used to get the surfboards on the beach.

"I'll come get everything later!" he called before speeding away.

God, if he only knew who he left me with.

Caroline looked up at Achilles, who stared down at her with a thin smile.

"Nothing is wrong with his grandfather," he stated in a calm voice.

"You're sick," she spat, trying to sound as brave as she could. She moved to walk past him, her home within view.

He tightly took hold of her arm, stopping her. "I'm not done talking with you."

Their eyes locked.

"Well, I am." She pulled her arm free.

Rolling his eyes, he pulled a letter out from the pocket of his gray vest.

"What is that?" she asked, taking a step away from him.

"Relax, girl. It's just a letter for you." He held it out to her.

She kept her hands down by her sides. Fear built up in her chest. But still, she snapped, "I am not taking anything from you!"

"Take it!" he demanded. His purple eyes were hard. "It won't hurt you."

She slowly took it. The letter shook in her hands. "What is this?"

is lips curled into a smile. "Something I'm very proud of." H

She watched as he bent over and picked up a clam shell. It was an odd shade of pink and brown. He held it up with his thumb and forefinger.

"To remember this day." With a small chuckle, he turned to leave. "Do read the letter," he called over his shoulder.

Why didn't he hurt me? She looked down at the letter, and her heart pounded. *Why would he give me a letter?* Millions of ideas came to mind, but none made sense. Nothing that had happened had made sense.

She glanced back the way he had gone, not daring to move until he was out of her sight. As soon as he was, she ran home.

Chapter 29

"He just gave this to you?" Dutch asked and looked over at Caroline, who stood beside the kitchen table, still in her wet swimsuit.

The house was cold. Yet she shook from her nerves that made her stomach flip on itself. The letter in question sat on the tabletop.

"Yes," she said, wringing her hands. "He told me to read it." She looked over at her grandmother, who had been washing the dishes with magic but now stood with a pale expression.

"Should we open it?" he asked, sounding unsure.

She took a shaky breath. "I'm too nervous to read it," she said honestly.

"I-I can read it," Jewel said as she grabbed the letter.

Caroline and Dutch watched as she peeled back the seal and opened it. The air was thick enough to cut. She pulled out a folded piece of paper. As the light shined on it, Achilles' handwriting showed through the paper. Caroline forced her eyes on her, watching as her eyes moved left to right.

Jewel gasped and covered her mouth with her hand. "Oh my God…"

"What?" Caroline asked in a panic.

Dutch glanced from her to Jewel. "What is it?!"

Her heart pounded so loud that she could feel every beat in her ears.

Tears built in Jewel's eyes. "Oh Caroline…"

She needed to know what Achilles had given her, what words lay before her. Before she could think better of it, she took the paper from Jewel's hands. Her eyes read over his words.

Thanks to your indiscretion, I learned where your uncles have been hiding all these years. About three days ago, I went to your Uncle Edmund's house, and they were having a little party. Luckily, everyone was there: George, Robert, and all your cousins. There was so much happiness. To make this long story short…let's just say you no longer have uncles! Or a family.

I killed them all.

Don't worry. The pain of their loss won't last long because you are next.

Caroline's body grew numb. Chills ran up her spine, and her mind spun.

No. None of this is real.

Nothing written before her could be true. Edmund was all right. He was happy back in Washington. Norna was alive. Robert was fine. Everyone was fine.

They had to be.

Jewel put her hand on her shoulder. "Honey…" she said softly. Tears formed in her eyes.

"This…this is a lie!" Caroline snapped as she looked up from the letter. Her eyes found Jewel's as Dutch took the letter from her hand. "Edmund is fine!"

"Caroline…"

How foolish she had been. All those times when she had the chance to call him and chose not to.

And now he was gone. Never again would she see Uncle Edmund, hug him, or tell him how much she loved him. That even though he had hurt her, she still loved him.

Her legs felt weak, and her mind spun. Aunt Mary was gone. All her cousins… Norna.

"Norna can't be dead…" she heard herself say.

They were all gone. The room spun around her. Her legs were too weak to hold her up. She didn't even know how it happened, but she found herself in a chair.

Dutch put his hand on her shoulder. "Are you all right, youngin?" he asked in the softest voice.

But she stayed numb.

"Caroline?" Jewel asked, getting on her knees in front of her granddaughter and taking her hands into her own.

"He's gone," Caroline muttered. "They're all gone. My whole family." A sob escaped her as Jewel wrapped her arms around her. She rested her head on Jewel's chest, her cries painful and loud as her grandmother's hold tightened.

No. This was all a lie! Achilles was *lying*. The magic books would show her the truth.

Caroline pulled out of the hold. "You can go into a book!"

Jewel looked at her sadly. "I can't."

"Yes, you can!"

"I don't have a book about your uncles."

"Jewel, please!"

"I would if I could."

"NO!" Caroline sobbed. Her whole body shook. "You have to go in and tell me Achilles is lying!"

Jewel's eyes filled with tears. "Caroline…" She took hold of her arm tightly, her eyes pleading with her.

But Caroline's mind persisted. Achilles had lied, and Jewel had to go into the books before. Jewel had to have something about Edmund. Jewel had a book for so much. How could there be none about him?

"You must!" she said.

"Caroline…"

"Please!"

"*Sweetie*," she said louder.

Caroline's eyes met hers.

"I can't go into a book we don't have."

Caroline shook her head. Any hope she had left faded away.

Jewel hugged her. "I'm so sorry!"

Her sobs filled the house for what seemed like hours. She didn't know how long Jewel and Dutch held her, but the pain was still there even after her tears dried.

Chapter 30

"NOOOO!" six-year-old Caroline screamed, sitting up in her bed. Her happy dream had turned into a nightmare, one that felt so real.

She scanned the dark room. Norna's bed was empty. She sobbed, looking around for something to comfort her.

As she cried, her Uncle Edmund soon filled the doorway. "I'm here."

He flipped on the lights. Concern was written on his face. Her sobs continued as he crossed the space to her.

"Love, you're safe. I'm here."

She had lived with him for only a few months. But in that time, she had woken up many nights in such state. At times, Norna was enough to calm her, but most nights, he would wake to the sound of her sobs.

He sat at the foot of her bed, and she crawled out from under the sheets and made her way to him.

"What's wrong?" He slid his hands under her arms and lifted her into his lap.

"I had a bad dream," she said, rubbing away her tears with the back of her hand. She took in a shaky breath.

He sadly smiled at her as he wrapped his arms around

her small body. "This is the eighth nightmare this month," he said as he rubbed circles on her back.

"Where Norna?"

"She's at a friend's house tonight. Remember?" When she said nothing, he asked, "Do you want to tell me about your dream, sweetie?" He turned her in his lap to see her face.

Her watery eyes met his. "I am home. A man in a mask came. Then Mama and Daddy… He taked them…"

"Again?" Edmund asked, looking at her with sad eyes.

"Yeah. I hate it, Ed Moon," she said as tears rolled down her face. "I miss them." Her voice was so small.

"Me too." After a beat, he asked, "You know what might make it better?"

"What?" A faint smile formed on her mouth.

"Some hot chocolate!" He held her tighter as he stood. He spun once with her, and she laughed. "Shh! We don't want to wake up the rest of the house."

He made his way out of the room. They both laughed quietly as they walked toward the kitchen. His large body warmed her up as she rested her head on his chest. He was like a big teddy bear: warm and full of never-ending love. Once in the kitchen, he sat her down on one of the dining room chairs and went to make their hot chocolate.

She turned in her green chair to watch him make their favorite nighttime drink. Her hands grabbed onto the back of the chair as she rested her chin on them. "Can I have marshmallows?"

"Marshmallows? At three a.m.? Sure thing, sunshine." He got the bag of marshmallows out from one of the soft green cabinets.

Soon, they both sat at the table, enjoying their warm drink. The light from the living room cast enough light where they sat.

"Caroline, I think I have a milk mustache," Edmund said, pointing at the chocolate milk that sat on his lip. One marshmallow was also stuck there.

She laughed as the marshmallow fell back into his cup, making a small splash. "You silly." She took another sip of her hot chocolate. The mug was far too large for her little hands, but somehow, she made it work well enough.

They both sat in silence for a little while as they finished their drinks.

"That was tasty," Edmund said, patting his belly.

Caroline did the same, copying his moves. A big yawn escaped her mouth.

"I think someone is sleepy," he said, taking her cup. "We can't leave any evidence in the sink."

She watched as he cleaned the mugs in the sink by the window and left them next to the sink to dry.

"I'm not sleepy," she said as he picked her up. Another yawn escaped her mouth.

He carried her back up to her room.

"Ed Moon, I don't want to go back to bed," Caroline said as her uncle placed her under her blankets. She grew anxious. Under these sheets was where the nightmares happened. Where the man with the mask haunted her dreams. "I don't want to!"

He slid in next to her, making sure he covered both him and her under the blanket. "Why not?" he asked.

She cozied herself next to him, feeling safer with him. "Because that when *he* comes," she muttered with fear in her soft voice.

"Who, sweetie?"

"The man in the mask. I don't like him. He scare me."

Edmund ran his fingers through her brown hair, his eyebrows together in thought. Something like fear showed on his face, which she didn't understand. Maybe he was also scared of the man.

"I know, but he is only in your head," he said as his eyes found hers once more. "He can't hurt you. I won't let him."

She heard the truth in his words.

He brushed her hair away from her face. "What if we talk about what you want to dream about instead?"

She jumped onto her feet with a smile. "I want to dream about ponies and princesses!" She jumped on the bed as she went on. "Oh, and Santa too!" Her giggles filled the room.

He laughed as he grabbed her arm, letting her jump a few more times before pulling her back under the sheets. "All right. We can do that!"

He waved his hand over her head. Glitter softly fell and landed on her nose and her cheeks. She didn't understand where he got the glitter from, but she found she couldn't give it another thought as her eyelids grew heavy.

He gave her a kiss on her forehead. "Go to sleep. I promise you're going to have the best of dreams."

She found it hard to keep her eyes open as she smiled. "All right."

After a while, she felt him climb out from under the covers. He turned off the lights, leaving the night-light on by her bed.

"I love you, Uncle Ed Moon."

"I love you too. If you need me, I'm down the hall."

****

Now, a fourteen-year-old Caroline sat broken and incomplete, and no amount of hot chocolate could fix it. She lay in bed, awake. The sound of birds outside her window let her know she hadn't slept at all. That somehow the world was still spinning while hers had stopped.

She remembered her beautiful Aunt Mary baking cakes and other treats and how she always let her and Norna lick the spoons. *Did she suffer?*

Tears built up in her eyes. She could see her and Norna laughing and talking far past their bedtimes. *Did he kill her first?*

Robert came to mind, how happy he had been when he thought he was going to be a father. *Did he die before Elizabeth?*

Edmund's laughter and his voice came to mind next. She imagined that he would have fought for his family. That he would rather die than let anything happen to his wife and kids. *Had he died, keeping them safe?*

Then it dawned on her: *I am the last member of my father's family.*

Achilles would come for her next. It was only a matter of time now.

She turned over and looked out at the ocean. The sky was brightening as the sun peeked over the horizon. *I have the power to stop this.*

She could no longer just let her loved ones die by Achilles' wicked hand. She was a Smith. She had the power to stop this. To stop him. Anyone she loved would never be harmed by him again. Her days were not limited by him. *His* were.

She sat up and left to find Jewel's spell book.

Chapter 31

Caroline had been dressed and ready for the day hours before Jewel walked downstairs for breakfast. Her yellow skirt and white blouse seemed too bright after yesterday, but she still looked up from her book and weakly smiled at Jewel from where she sat.

"How are you doing, love?" Jewel said with a sad tone. In a simple pink dress, she walked into the kitchen. "You're never up before me."

"I haven't cried this much in years. I don't think he'll ever know how much I loved him, and that breaks my heart," Caroline said, trying not to cry as tears filled her vision once more.

She was done crying. It would get her nowhere.

"He knew, Caroline," Jewel said.

"How?"

"I spoke to him a few days ago."

Chills covered Caroline's skin. "You spoke to him?"

Jewel nodded as she sat across from her. She looked at the spell book she had open in front of her but said nothing of it. "When you were training the other day, he called."

Caroline's mouth grew dry.

"He was worried about you."

"How did he know I was here?"

Jewel shrugged. "I don't know. But he was worried about how you were settling in and if you were happy."

Unwanted tears filled her vision once more.

"The call dropped before I was able to get you."

"He wanted to talk with me?" Caroline's voice was no louder than a whisper.

Jewel nodded. "What are you looking at?" she asked, pointing at the spell book.

She glanced back down at the book, finding her voice. "I was looking for spells I wanted to learn."

A knock at the door made them both jump. She watched as Jewel stood and walked into the other room.

Dutch's voice filled the house. "Hey."

A click from a kiss came from the other room. Caroline's eyebrows moved together. Maybe she needed to sleep more than she thought.

"How is she?" he asked.

"She's doing better than yesterday," Jewel said.

She stood, lingering in the kitchen doorway as they spoke.

"I couldn't stop thinking about her all night," he said. "I just feel so horrible."

"Me too. But she seems to be handling it better than I thought."

Dutch caught sight of her, and a smile formed on his face. "Hey, youngin!" he said, walking over to her. "I got you something." He handed her a bear. Its limbs dangled down by its sides.

She smiled at it. "Thank you." She stepped into the living room.

"I also got you this." He handed her a little box.

She took it and pulled it open to reveal a golden heart locket. "Dutch…" She took the lovely necklace out of its box.

Jewel walked closer to see and gasped. "It's beautiful!"

"Where did you get it?" she asked, looking up at him.

He smiled at her with kind eyes. "I got it at one of the little shops around town. It's not really gold, but it sure does look like it. Open it." He took the bear from her so she could.

She opened the locket to find a photo of him, Jewel, and herself within. They all had bright, wide smiles. She recalled taking the photo at the carnival, which seemed like a lifetime ago. It warmed her heart to see them all together and happy. "I love it…"

"You have lost so much in your short life."

Her eyes found his.

"But there will always be people out there who love you. Family or not. You have us. And I might not be family, but I will carry you in my heart. And I will fight to keep you safe."

She wrapped her arms around him. "Thank you," she whispered as he hugged her tighter, resting his head on top of hers.

"No matter what, you will always have me and your grandmother. I promise."

As a tear rolled down her face, she hugged him tighter.

Chapter 32

hours later, Jewel rolled out the chalkboard from wherever she kept it, making Caroline jump from the noise. Dutch pulled out the fire extinguisher and sat on the couch.

"Do we still really need that?" Caroline asked as she sat in the chair by the sofa.

He held the extinguisher closer to his chest. "This is just for my own comfort."

Jewel laughed. "Dutch, I think she is not going to burn anything. We are past that."

"You can never be too sure," he mumbled.

She walked over to her granddaughter with a small smile. "Ignore him. You're doing amazing."

Caroline stood. "Thank you."

"I want to give you this." She snapped her fingers, and a shoebox appeared in her waiting palm. "Open it."

Caroline took the box. Removing the lid, she gasped. Inside was a wand with lovely golden designs spinning around it. "Is this real?"

"Yes. We thought you were ready."

Carefully, she pulled it out of the box.

"It was your mother's first wand."

She noticed it was a bit heavier than the wand she had been using. She looked closer at it and observed all the details engraved into it. "It has my mom's name!" She ran her finger over her mother's engraved name in the wood.

"She would be proud to see you use it," Jewel said as she looked at her granddaughter with pride.

"Thank you!"

"You are strong enough to hold it now. None of us are in danger."

Caroline smiled as she held the wand with more confidence.

"All right. The first thing I want to show you with your new wand is how to teleport."

"Finally!"

Dutch laughed. "You've been waiting?" he asked.

"I have!"

Jewel smiled. "It's easy. Think about Dutch. Nothing but him when you say the spell."

The coffee table was the only thing between them.

Caroline nodded. "Teleportsheam!"

With a flick of her wand, she stood next to him. He gasped and wrapped her in a side hug as she beamed. The fire extinguisher dropped to the floor.

"On her first try!" he said.

A knock came from the front door.

Jewel waved her hand at the chalkboard, and it disappeared. She then moved to the front door and peeked through the small window next to it. "It's Sal," she called to Caroline as Caroline hid her wand in the pocket of her dress.

Jewel waved her hand, removing the protection spell she had placed on the house days ago to keep anyone unwanted out. Like Achilles. She opened the door. "Hello!"

"Hi!" Sal said. "I was wondering if I could see Caroline."

Caroline stepped into view. He was dressed in light-colored jeans and a dark leather jacket, which made her wonder if he was uncomfortable in the heat.

"You look beautiful," he said as his eyes scanned her outfit.

Her cheeks warmed.

"I wanted to know if you wanted to go for a walk down the beach?"

She glanced at Jewel, who nodded.

"Sure." She walked out the door and smiled back at Jewel before she shut the door. "This is a nice surprise."

"Well, I wanted to talk to you about yesterday."

As they made their way onto the beach, she looked at him. "Did I do something wrong?"

He looked over at her. "No! When I got home after Achilles said something was happening, I found both my grandparents reading. Perfectly fine."

Before she could think better of it, she blurted, "He lied to you."

His eyebrows came together. "I know, but why would he do that?"

As she looked into his eyes, she knew it would be so much easier just to share everything with him. To have someone to talk with when her situation grew hard.

Anxiety bubbled in her. Would he stop seeing her? Or would Jewel get mad if she told him? What if she shared it with him? Would that really be a bad idea?

"Have you been crying?" he asked, taking her off guard.

"You can tell?" she asked, putting a hand to her face.

"What happened, Caroline?" he asked as he stopped walking.

She turned to face him, but her eyes scanned the water behind him. "My three uncles died."

His face paled. "I'm so sorry!"

She met his eyes.

"What happened? What do you mean all three of them died? Like in one day?" After a beat, he added, "I'm sorry. That was insensitive to ask."

She took his hand. "You're fine." What could she tell him? She scanned the ocean once more, trying to find a good lie. "Someone killed them."

His eyes widened. "Oh my God! When did this happen?"

"I found out yesterday after you left."

He took hold of her arms, his eyes bright with concern. "Are you all right? This must be so hard for you."

Tears built in her eyes.

"Let's sit down."

She followed him to a sand dune and sat next to him. The sand was cold. His arm wrapped around her shoulders as a few unwanted tears rolled down her face.

She didn't want to lie to him anymore. The words came out fast. "Achilles… He's the one who murdered them."

"What?" he asked, angling himself to meet her eyes.

She sighed inwardly before building up some confidence to go on.

"What do you mean Achilles killed them?! Are we talking about the same person?!"

Worry built in her. If he was so shaken with the news of Achilles' true personality, what would he think of the rest?

"You're pulling my leg. There is no way Achilles could—"

"I come from a family of magic!"

His eyebrows came together.

"I found out a week after arriving here. I have magic and so does my family. That is one reason why Achilles killed my uncles and their families."

His wide eyes stayed locked onto hers. "Did you hit your head?" he asked with a shaky voice.

"No. I'm serious, Sal. About everything."

He slowly turned away from her, his face unreadable.

"I've wanted to tell you for the longest time. It was odd keeping such a large part of myself from you."

He rested his forehead on his hands, his elbows on his knees. She moved to rest a hand on his back but thought better of it. He wasn't running away as she had, which was a good sign, but she didn't want to push it.

"Sal?" she asked after a beat.

"I'm sorry," he said. "This is just a lot to take in. And a part of me feels like you're lying." He met her eyes. "But I don't know why you would."

"I promise I'm not lying." Glancing around, she saw only a few families on the beach, and they were nothing but dots in the distance. Pulling her wand out of her pocket, she flicked it. "Teleportsheam." She reappeared a few feet away from where they sat.

His eyes grew wider. She giggled as he rubbed them before looking at her once more.

"You were being honest?" His eyes landed on her wand. "Crap! You do have magic!"

She nodded.

He took a deep breath in. "So, Achilles is after you? Why?"

She flicked her wand and was at his side once more. "Yeah. He also has powers."

Somehow, his eyes widened more.

"He is very powerful and very dangerous. He killed my uncles, aunts, and my cousins. I'm the only Smith left, and he wants me next."

Sal took her hand. "I'm so sorry."

"Why do you believe me?"

He scanned the ocean. "I didn't believe you till you showed me! I thought you were another wild girl I fell for."

"Another?"

"The point is I thought you had lost your mind, but then you"—he waved his free hand in front of him—"just appeared like that. How could I not believe you?"

"Can you keep this a secret?"

"You have my word."

She sighed with a smile. "Thank you, Sal. You have no idea how much this means to me."

"If you ever need me for anything—even just to talk about all this—I'm here for you."

"Thank you."

Chapter 33

After dinner, Caroline traind until she could teleport to each room of the house.

Storm clouds had rolled in. A clap of distant thunder made them jump.

"I'm going to head home," Dutch said as he pulled out his wand. "Jump in the shower before the storm gets here."

Jewel nodded with a smile. "Good night, Dutch."

He winked at her. "See you tomorrow." With that, he teleported away.

"Did he just wink at you?" Caroline asked.

Blush darkened Jewel's cheeks. "Let's go get ready for bed."

"Do I get to call him grandpa now?" she asked with a laugh.

"I'm not encouraging this behavior."

As they walked up the steps, Jewel snapped her fingers. The main level fell into darkness as the lights turned off. The only light came from Caroline's room, the door fully open letting her see the steps.

"He's so wonderful with you," Caroline said.

They came up the steps and moved toward her room. She flopped onto her bed as Jewel spoke.

"He is. He's a good person."

She smiled as Jewel sat at the foot of the bed.

Her smile faded as her mind sharply reminded her of what had happened the day before. *Edmund is dead.* Tears built in her eyes, rolling down her face before she could stop them.

"You all right?" Jewel asked, reaching for her hand.

She nodded, her face still wet with tears. "I remember… everything."

During the day, it had been easy to pretend that Edmund and her family were alive in Washington. That they just didn't call her like they normally did.

Rain tapped on the roof as if the world itself was crying with her.

"Come here." Jewel opened her arms for a hug, and Caroline moved toward her and let herself melt into her touch, sobbing. "I promise," she whispered with her head resting atop hers. "I promise this will get easier."

Caroline didn't know how, but she trusted Jewel. Maybe one day, she could think back on her family with a smile. But for now, she accepted the tears and the pain she would hold for months.

She didn't know how long they stayed there, holding each other. Eventually, the rain grew louder, and her tears dried.

"Better?" Jewel asked softly as she pulled away.

She nodded and dried her face with the back of her hand. A loud clap of thunder banged, making them both jump.

"Well, I guess showering is out of the question tonight." She pulled her wand out of her pocket and flicked it. In a flash, they were both in pajamas.

"Love you," Caroline said as she climbed under the sheets.

Jewel stood and tucked her in. "I love you so much. Now, get some sleep. We have a full day of training ahead of us."

She smiled. "I can't wait."

Her eyes closed as Jewel leaned over and kissed her forehead.

****

Caroline's eyes snapped open as a loud bang of thunder filled her ears. The rain slammed onto the roof, loud and present. The sound was peaceful, and her bed was warm. She found it hard to keep her eyes open. She rolled over.

A flash of lightning washed over her, followed by a bang of thunder. Her heart beat hard, waking her up. She looked over at the clock; it read 4:08 a.m.

Another flash of lightning brightened her room, and she covered herself with her comforter as another clap of thunder filled her ears. She felt unsafe. Though it was foolish to feel that way; she was surrounded by locked windows and doors. She was safe. But for unknown reasons, she couldn't convince herself of the fact.

"Come on, Caroline!" she muttered, staying hidden under the safety of her comforter. Like a child. "You're fine…"

Closing her eyes, she tried to focus on the sounds of the rain and the loud crashes of the waves. But a sound of movement from downstairs overpowered everything else.

Removing the blanket, she sat up. With wide eyes, she looked at her door that Jewel had left ajar. Another bang from the storm made her jump. Her heart in her ears. She could still hear movement coming from downstairs. No light could be seen coming up the steps, but her mind still concluded it was Jewel.

She got up from her bed and put on her slippers, wanting to see what her grandmother was doing. To seek comfort from her anxieties.

She walked out of her room. Lightning filled the hall.

She peeked into Jewel's room and went cold. It appeared her grandmother was lying in bed. The blankets lifted and fell with each breath she took.

Then who is downstairs?

More noises came from downstairs, making Caroline turn to face the dark steps.

Maybe Dutch forgot something... Or perhaps the storm was playing tricks on her.

She made her way down the steps. Her eyes stained to see with all the lights off. Slowly and carefully, she made her way to the base of the stairs.

She walked into something solid and unmoving. Air rushed out of her lungs. As her eyes adjusted, she made out a figure before her. "D-Dutch...?"

Lightning lit up the space enough for her to see Dutch was not in front of her.

Instead, half a black mask looked back at her.

A hand covered her mouth before she could scream.

"Well," Achilles said in a calm voice, "I didn't expect you to come looking for me."

A wave of fear washed over her. Every muscle in her body tensed. They had a spell up to keep him out! How had he... No! When Sal had left, Jewel didn't redo the spell.

Adrenaline flowed through her, making her body move before she truly thought it over. She kicked Achilles hard, her leg finding the place between his legs. He yelled out as he dropped to the floor.

Two at a time, she ran up the steps. "Jewel! Wake up!" She dashed into her grandmother's room and locked the door behind her.

Jewel tore from her bed, seeming disoriented. "What? What is it?!"

Caroline turned on the lights and raced to her

grandmother. Her whole body shook. "He's here!" Her voice was so full of panic that she didn't even recognize it. Her chest hurt, finding it hard to breathe.

"Who?!" Jewel asked.

"Achilles! Achilles is here!"

She paled. "What?!"

Tears ran down Caroline's face as she heard him marching up the steps.

"How did he get in?!" Jewel asked.

"The spell! When Sal—"

"OH MY GOODNESS!"

How could they have forgotten something so important?

The sound of Achilles running his nails over the other side of the locked door echoed. "Hiding just like always."

"What do we do?!" Caroline asked.

Jewel waved her hand, and both Caroline's wand and her own appeared in her hands. Caroline took her wand with a shaky hand.

"I can easily teleport inside that room and murder you both," his voice called from behind the door. "Or you can come out and die trying to fight."

Jewel pointed her wand at the door. "Don't let him get in your head," she said. "Stay here." She flicked her wand and teleported out of the room.

Caroline jumped about a mile out of her skin as she heard Jewel yell from the other side of the door.

"Fire itera!" Achilles yelled.

Spell names echoed within the house. Louder than the storm.

"Waicl!" he yelled.

Caroline's skin covered in chills as Jewel cried out in pain.

"Ready to die?"

No! Caroline unlocked the door and ripped it open. She flicked her wand at him. "Gepsic!"

He jerked away from Jewel—who was on her hands and knees—and hit the far wall. As he stood tall, he smiled. "The final Smith." He flicked his wand with force. "Plaguonyx!"

As the spell crossed the space to Caroline, Jewel jumped in front of her. "No!" she yelled. She waved her wand, sending the spell away from them.

"You fight well, Jewel," he said as he brushed a strand of hair from his face. "But Caroline is always hiding behind you like a scared dog."

Jewel shot fire his way, but he waved it away with ease. He moved his free hand in a pulling motion, taking her wand from her hold. She gasped. Quickly, he waved his wand once more, lifting her off the floor. With force, he sent her across the room and to the stairs.

"Jewel!" Caroline shouted.

Jewel slammed her head on the banister before rolling down the steps. Her body hit each step.

"Jewel, no!" Caroline yelled, horrified.

"Well, now that she's out of the way"—Achilles laughed as she looked back at him—"I can finally kill you."

Anger bubbled within her as her vision went red. "You're going to regret that!"

"Oh, I'm so scared," he mocked. "The *child* is mad."

She lifted her wand. In her mind, she shouted the spell, not wanting to give him the advantage. *Teleportsheam.* She teleported herself behind him and kicked his back, pushing him forward.

He turned toward her. "Hucabufs!" he called as he waved his wand.

She lowered herself, and the spell missed. *Fire itera.*

A ball of fire hit him, his mask burning on his face. He yelled as he clawed it off. His face was red with irritation.

"How dare you!" He threw the mask at her.

It hit her shoulder, but she hardly felt it. *Stone-soul.*

The spell missed as he flicked his wand at her. Lightning came from his wand in a bright flash. She moved but not fast enough. The electricity only hit her side, but it was still strong enough to suck the air out of her lungs. Crumbling to the floor, she gasped in agony.

"Ready to die, you pest?!" he hissed as he made his way to her.

Through her pain, she pointed her wand at him. *Teleportsheam.*

He disappeared, and she was alone.

She dropped her head to the floor, winded and weak. "Jewel?" she called as she turned her head toward the steps. A sob formed in her throat.

There was no answer.

"Jewel?" She forced herself to stand, holding her ribs to subside the discomfort, and limped to the steps.

As a flash of lightning lit the house, she saw Jewel. A scream escaped her throat. Jewel was crumbled at the bottom of the steps. Pale and so very still. Blood stained Jewel's face as her eyes stared off at nothing.

"No!" she choked out.

A hand grabbed a fistful of her hair, pulling her down to the floor.

"You senseless girl!" Achilles yelled. "You think you can get rid of me that easily?!"

She kicked him with all her might, hitting his chest and sending him back into a wall with a bang. He grunted. A picture fell off the wall, and the glass shattered.

She stood, pointing her wand at him. *Gepsic.*

He gasped in pain as the spell hit him. "Float itera!" he called, jerking his wand up and taking her with it.

She bumped into the ceiling before he flung her back to the floor. She caught herself with her arms, but her head banged on the floor hard enough that her ears rang for a moment.

Achilles grabbed her shoulder, turning her to her back.

"Let me go!" she yelled.

His hands went to her throat, and he squeezed, cutting all air from her lungs. His wand dug into her skin. She clawed at her neck, desperate to take a breath. Her legs kicked helplessly as he bared his teeth and pushed harder. Black spots formed in her vision. He smiled as a choking sound came from her.

She put her wand to his side as her face turned a light shade of blue. *Gepsic.*

He jerked back in pain, dropping his wand. Coughing and dizzy, she forced herself to stand. She moved to where his wand had fallen, stood on it, and put all her weight onto it. Snapping it in two.

"Just like your father!" he choked. "You will meet his fate!"

She stood over him and pointed her wand at him with fire in her eyes. "Stay down! I won't let you hurt me or anyone I love again."

"You're not in a position to decide what happens!"

He lifted his hands to her, and a strange power emerged from them. She gasped and ran out of its path. He grumbled as he followed her with the odd power. She ripped the porch door open and escaped.

But it was a dead end.

Rain poured down in sheets, soaking her. The waves roared as lightning flashed out over the ocean.

"Nowhere to run now!" Achilles said as he joined her. His white shirt was soaked.

She lifted her wand to him. "Leave me alone!"

"You think you have enough power to withstand me? No. You will join your father tonight."

Help. She needed help. *Teleportsheam.*

She appeared by Dutch's front door. "Dutch!" she yelled.

Achilles appeared behind her. "Gepsic!"

Somehow, without his wand, he zapped her, filling her body with the worst pain. Her legs gave out from underneath her, and she slammed into the wet asphalt. Pain exploded from her forehead.

"It ends now!"

Car lights filled the streets. Just before the headlights could hit him, Achilles disappeared. The car drove past, seeming to not see Caroline lying on the side of the road. Her body shook with her sobs, the agony too much to handle.

Her head pounded with each beat of her heart. Her body was weak and beaten.

Darkness filled her vision, and she let it take her.

****

A loud clap of thunder made Caroline's eyes open. Her body throbbed as she slowly stood. The rain had stopped, and birds sang around her. The sky that was poking through the passing clouds was a deep reddish pink.

How long did I black out?

She didn't give it another thought as she limped to Dutch's door. With a shaky hand, she teleported inside his house.

"Dutch!" She dropped her wand and bent over. Her ribs shouted in pain. She put a hand to her chest as the discomfort spread there.

Dutch came running down the stairs, still in his pajamas. "What happened? Are you okay?"

"You have to help Jewel!" She coughed.

He rushed to her, his eyes scanning her.

Her nightgown had been ripped. Rainwater dripped off her. Bumps and dirt covered her. Blood smeared down the side of her face from her forehead.

He grabbed her arms as his eyes landed on her forehead.

"Dutch, I think she's d-dead," she cried.

His eyes met hers. "What?! What you mean?!"

"Achilles came and..." Tears streamed down her face. "She d-didn't wake up!"

Tears filled his eyes as he raced next door.

Chapter 34

The next week was the worst Caroline had lived through. Each day seemed eternal, but once the week ended, the days blended. The hospital's black-and-white checkered floor and white walls grew familiar after the first seven days. Seven days of sitting in a room full of other people suffering around her.

The only person she cared about was Jewel, who still wouldn't wake.

She sat in a chair next to her grandmother, pinned between Jewel's bed and the patient next to her. Her grandmother lay still. She was as pale as the white sheets folded up to her chest.

Caroline scanned over her still form. An IV had been placed into the back of her hand and her neck, the saline slowly dripping from the pole behind Caroline. On the other side of the bed was a machine Caroline didn't quite understand. A tube came from its side, leading to an odd tube that had been placed in her mouth. Forcing her to breathe. Something she couldn't do on her own.

Dutch walked up to the bed and rested his hands on the metal bar at the foot of the bed. "How are your ribs feeling?" he asked, looking at Caroline.

She shrugged. "They'll be fine." Her voice was small.

Seven days ago, she had been treated for three broken ribs and a minor concussion. Ten stitches had been needed for the cut on her forehead. It all seemed so insignificant.

A doctor walked up behind Dutch. He was a very tall Indian man with soft black hair, but she couldn't recall his name. She didn't know if it was the concussion or the number of doctors they had met that made her forget.

"Can I speak with you both?" he asked.

In silence, they followed him into a small office with white walls and sat.

"How are you feeling, Miss Smith?" He flipped through a folder on his desk.

"I'm all right," she said.

Dutch glanced at her. She had been having a hard time getting around the house with her ribs, but that was not something she wanted to talk about. She wanted to know how Jewel was doing.

He smiled. "Glad to hear it."

Dutch cleared his throat. "Has there been any improvement on Julia?"

Her full name sounded odd coming from him.

The doctor took a deep breath in. "Miss Walker has not improved as we had hoped. We had thought she would have awakened days ago. After some tests, we have reasons for her state."

Dutch tensed in his chair. "Will she breathe on her own again?"

The doctor folded his hands on top of the desk. "She has suffered from a traumatic brain injury."

The words hung heavy in the room.

"The impact to her head from the car crash is very severe."

When they had come to the hospital, Dutch had lied, stating both Jewel and Caroline had gotten in a car accident. No one questioned their injuries.

"She may never heal."

Dutch put a hand to his face.

"But she'll wake up?" Caroline heard herself ask.

"*If* she wakes," the doctor said, "the symptoms you could see from her include long-term memory loss, no social desire, and trouble thinking of solutions."

Tears rolled down Dutch's face. Caroline moved her chair closer to him as her own tears fell. She rested her head on his shoulder, ignoring the pain in her ribs.

"I'm sorry. Don't lose faith but prepare for the worst. Her heart is weak, and her body has gone through a lot."

****

Three days passed before Jewel started breathing on her own again. And two days crawled by before she woke up.

Caroline stood next to her bed, holding her hand. Her eyes were closed, but her thumb rubbed the back of Caroline's hand.

The same doctor from before spoke to Caroline and Dutch. "Because of the severity of the injury, I would like to keep an eye on her here for a few more days."

He nodded.

"Once we see her staying stable for seventy-two hours, she can return home."

By the end of the week, Dutch happily took Jewel home. As he got her comfortable in her own bed, Caroline brought some of the things she had at Dutch's house back since she had been living with him for the past two weeks. She had enjoyed her time with him, but she was ready for things to go somewhat back to before.

As she walked past Jewel's room and to her own, Jewel spoke in a weak voice.

"Where am I?"

She froze, holding her dresses tighter in her arms.

Dutch answered softly. "You're home, love. You're safe here."

She sucked in a shaky breath as she went into her room.

A few days later, Caroline sat on the edge of Jewel's bed. The doctor had given her small exercises to work on.

"All right. Last time." She smiled kindly as Jewel looked at her.

Her eyes seem to hold a slight vacancy to them; Caroline could never look into them for long. It seemed like Caroline had lost her even though she lay right in front of her.

"Raise your arms."

She raised her own arms over her head, watching as Jewel—for the third time—lifted her arms an inch off her lap. The bruise from the IV was still dark on her skin. She lowered her arms, and Jewel did the same.

"Are you hungry?" She glanced at the clock on the wall. It was a few hours past dinner time, but Jewel hadn't eaten much.

Jewel said nothing.

"I'll go ask Dutch what pills you need now."

Standing, she moved to the dresser across from the foot of the bed. Dutch had brought up the record player; the soft music was something Jewel still showed she enjoyed. As she lowered the needle on the record, soft music filled the room.

"Be right back."

She glanced at her grandma. Jewel's eyes were closed. Sucking in a breath, she made her way down the steps.

"Dutch," Caroline called out. She found him in the magic room, where he had been working the past few days. "She—"

Her eyes fell to the mess on the table. More than ten books lay open around him. His hair was a bit messy, and his face looked overwhelmed by black circles. He stared at all the open books in front of him.

"I can't do the spell," he said in a quivering voice.

"What?"

Since Jewel had come home, they had put all their hope to heal Jewel on the healing spell. Something she had always made look so easy.

"What's wrong?" Caroline asked, making her way to his side.

Tears built in his eyes. "I don't know how to do it," he muttered, looking at her. "It's right here." He slammed his fist onto the book. "But I just can't do it."

"Why not?" Her voice was small.

"I don't understand it! It's been days, and I—" Tears rolled down his face.

"Dutch…" Her own eyes blurred with tears. "What are we going to do if we can't figure this out? W-what if we can't help her?"

He pulled her into a hug. "I'll figure this out. I promise."

They both stayed there until they had no more tears left to cry.

****

Once the sun went down, and the world around Caroline slept, she quietly entered Jewel's room.

She hadn't slept. Her quiet sobs left her lying in the dark for hours. Wiping tears off her cheeks, she walked to the other side of Jewel's bed and crawled in next to her.

Dutch had told her not to cry in front of Jewel. That she wouldn't understand. That it would only distress her. But as she lay next to her, scanning over her still form, tears spilled from her eyes. She tried not to make a sound.

She missed her uncles, she missed Norna, and most of all she missed her grandma's presence in the house.

Jewel woke when Caroline breathed in loudly to hold back a sob. Pain throbbed in Caroline's ribs. She looked over at her.

"I'm s-sorry," Caroline whispered.

Slowly, Jewel wiped a tear away from Caroline's cheek and smiled.

"I miss you." She took Jewel's hand in her own and kissed the back of it.

"Love you…" Jewel said weakly as she wrapped her fingers around her hand.

****

As the morning shifted into the afternoon, a knock sounded at the door. Caroline peeked through the window to see who it was. With the protection spell back up, she knew it could not be Achilles, but the thought still crossed her mind.

She spotted three familiar faces: Elena, Hector, and their daughter stood, holding a box of donuts and flowers. They were all dressed so well, their dresses nor his tie not holding one wrinkle.

Slight embarrassment bubbled in Caroline. She had worn the same jeans for a few days now, and her hair had been pulled out of her face and into a knotted ponytail.

Glancing at the paper Dutch had left by the door with the spell for the house, she read the spell and waved her hand before opening the door. The bright blue sky hurt her eyes, and the ocean was equally as bright. *The world is still in motion.* It hardly felt like it.

"Hello, dear," Elena spoke with a soft voice. "We heard what happened. And we brought these for you." She handed her the box of donuts.

"I don't know what to say," she said as she took the box.

Hector passed her the flowers. "Jewel is in our prayers," he said, picking up his daughter, who rested her head on his shoulder.

Their daughter's eyes lingered on the dark circles Caroline knew she had on her face.

"How are you recovering?" Elena asked.

The cut on her forehead wasn't pretty. Self-consciously, she reached for it with her hand but stopped when she recalled the flowers she held. "My ribs hurt when I breathe."

In her mind, it sounded so silly to complain about something so insignificant when Jewel was upstairs, unsure of where she was.

"Remember, caring for yourself is just as important as caring for your grandma."

It was just broken ribs. Over time, she would heal. Jewel was stuck this way forever.

"If you need anything, come to us, okay?" Elena gave her a small smile.

"Thank you," she said as they walked down the porch steps. After she shut the door and put the box and flowers down, she redid the spell.

Caroline opened the box of donuts. The fresh smell made her mouth water. Memories of her and Jewel eating donuts together filled her mind. She picked up the biggest glazed one and took a bite.

As she finished her second donut, another knock came at the door. Cleaning her hands on her jeans, she saw Sal in the window. Tears filled her eyes as she removed the spell. After she opened the door, she threw herself into his arms and sobbed.

Gently, he held her as she buried her head into his neck. "It's going to be all right," he whispered.

Her body shook in his hold. "She forgot w-who Dutch…was this morning."

His hand went to the back of her head. "I'm so sorry, Caroline."

As her tears subsided, they sat on the porch steps.

"Are you okay?" he asked, looking into her eyes. "That cut looks like you haven't been taking care of it."

She sighed. "Why does everyone keep asking me if I'm okay?"

Nothing had happened to her. Not really. It was not worth worrying about with what had happened to Jewel.

"Because we care about you, Caroline." He took her hand in his. "I care about you."

She sucked in a breath, ignoring the pain that followed. "I'll clean the cut later."

She watched as people played in the ocean and walked down to the beach. Smiling and happy. She looked away with bitterness.

"I was happy," she whispered as a tear fell into her lap. "Even with everything happening, I was happy. I loved that I got to live with her."

He said nothing.

"It hurts me that she's stuck like that. When I brought her breakfast, I could tell she didn't know w-who I was for a beat."

His hand went to her back.

"I should have hugged her more. I should have started calling her grandma! I don't even know why I called her Jewel."

Sal rested his head on her shoulder. His comfort was everything. She looked up at the sky.

"She's still here," he said. "She's different, but she's still upstairs."

"It's not the same…"

On the beach, two labs chased after a ball that their

owner had thrown. One chocolate, one black. Both tails wagging.

"When I moved here, she took the time to get me new clothes. She would cook for me every morning and night. With magic, but still. She made sure I was okay and always had something funny to say to make me smile. I never thought I would feel so loved again, and now it's all gone. She's gone."

"I'm sorry, Caroline."

****

The next hour, a few familiar faces stopped by. Scott came and gave Caroline flowers for Jewel, along with a plate of cookies for her as he wished her a speedy recovery. Patti came over with lunch. As Dutch and her ate, she helped clean the house. When she and Sal went home, the mayor's assistant came over with a huge bouquet of roses. She was a short woman, making the bouquet seem larger than it was.

"Thank you," Caroline said as the assistant handed her the flowers.

"The mayor wanted me to tell you that the town is having a candlelight vigil this evening for your grandmother."

Caroline's mouth formed into a small smile.

"The whole community has her in their prayers."

Before she could answer, she spotted Achilles with yellow carnations mixed with a few black roses in his hands. Her eyes locked onto his. Her rage grew with each step he took closer to the house.

How. Dare. He.

She focused on the assistant. "T-thank you so much. I'll let Dutch know."

The assistant nodded before heading on her way.

Achilles then climbed up the steps. "Dear Caroline," he said with a hand to his chest. His eyes fell on her forehead,

233

and a smile twisted on his lips. "I am so sorry to hear about your grandma."

He handed her the flowers, but she threw them to the floor. A mess of pollen and petals exploded by his feet.

"I don't want your flowers!" she hissed through a clenched jaw.

He laughed. "I must say you put up quite a fight the other night." He glanced at their surroundings. "Though I am surprised *she* is alive. With how hard she hit her head, I really thought I killed her."

She balled her fist.

"Must be losing my touch."

"I am done!" Her fists were so tight that her knuckles turned white. "Come near me again, and I swear to God—"

"You really think you can best me in a fight?"

"I'm still alive! You didn't achieve anything!"

He raised his eyebrow.

Her voice then lowered. "Now, leave me alone!" She kicked his leg, making him jump back.

"Don't get too arrogant. I will succeed in ending your life."

She entered the house and slammed the door.

Quickly, she put the protection spell up, and from the window, she watched him walk down the steps and down the street. The breeze picked up, and the broken flowers blew away.

Chapter 35

"You're doing great!" Dutch said later that day as he carefully cut the stitches on Caroline's forehead.

She sat on the bathroom sink's counter, holding her breath. "Achilles brought Grandma flowers."

He met her eyes with shock. "When?"

"This afternoon."

He shook his head and put the scissors down next to her.

"He's acting like he's not the reason for all this."

"He's such a manipulator. Has this whole town wrapped around his finger."

He picked up a pair of tweezers and gently worked the stitches out. She closed her eyes, trying to ignore the tugging sensation.

"You doing all right?" he asked as she squeezed her eyes shut.

"Feels weird."

His other hand held her head as he pulled the stitch out completely. "It looks good. It's not red or swollen."

She opened her eyes.

He moved to the sink, running water over a rag. Softly, he cleaned the cut before saying, "Look how well it's healing."

She twisted to look at herself in the mirror behind her, her ribs protesting the movement. She hardly recognized herself. Her skin was pale, the dark circles under her eyes stood out, her eyes were red and puffy from crying, and her hair was dirty. She then glanced up at her forehead, seeing a closed cut. Dutch was right; it was healing well.

His hand went to her back. "Little by little, we'll push that night behind us."

She doubted it but smiled anyway. "Can I read over the healing spell?" She turned back to face him. "I can't put that night behind me. Not until she's okay."

He nodded. "I have no doubt that you can find a way to do it."

She hopped off the sink, and he moved to let her pass as he cleaned up their small mess.

"The spell book is on the coffee table," he called.

As she sat on the sofa, she pulled the book into her lap. It naturally flipped open to the healing spell. She closed her eyes and took a deep breath before slowly letting it out. *I will understand this.*

****

As the sunset shined in through the window, Caroline sat with Jewel's spell book on the coffee table. The book was still open as she rested her head in her hands.

The healing spell didn't make sense! The wording was odd, the text was faded, and the instructions were unclear. Pulling her green trousers up, she looked at where Jewel had healed her that night on the beach. No mark remained. Nothing showed that she had been hurt. *Why didn't Grandma teach me the spell?*

A knock at the front door pulled her out of her thoughts.

Dutch came down the steps with Jewel's full dinner

plate. "Can you see who that is, youngin?" he asked as he disappeared into the kitchen.

She closed the book with a slam, walked over toward the door, and peeked through the window. The bright sun made the three people outside nothing more than shadows. Until the one closest to the door met her eyes through the glass.

It can't be!

With a frantic wave of her hand, she removed the protection spell and opened the door.

She stepped back as her eyes locked with Edmund's. Her body shook, and she spoke through the knot in her throat. "Is it really you?"

"Yeah, it's me," he said, entering the house and smiling.

She sobbed as she jumped into his arms.

Tightly, he wrapped his arms around her. "I was so worried about you," he said, sounding as if he was trying to hold back his own tears.

"I thought you were dead!" She raised her head as George shut the door behind Robert. "I thought you all were dead."

Robert wiped a tear from her face. "We're all right now."

Edmund pulled her out of the hug. "You've gotten so big!" Pride filled his eyes. "You're much taller." He smiled and pulled her into another hug.

"You look the same," she said.

And he did, minus the bruise on his jaw.

As he let her go, she scanned over her other two uncles. Robert had something wrapped around his arm, reaching past his elbow. And George's hand was wrapped in the same white cloth.

"Achilles..." she muttered. "He gave me a letter..."

"Who?" Robert asked.

"The masked man. He told me he killed you. All of you."

Edmund rested a hand on her shoulder. As she looked

up into his brown eyes, it all seemed too surreal. That he was with her. That he was all right.

"He did attack us," he said. "And…it was really bad. Burned the hell out of us."

Her eyes fell on the white cloths they had wrapped around their arms.

"But we got away," George added.

She swallowed under his gaze. "So, everyone else is all right?" she asked with concern in her voice.

"He hurt each of us, and he unfortunately killed some of our friends we had over," Robert said.

"Everyone is okay now," Edmund added. "Mary broke her leg, but she's getting around better."

She swallowed.

"All the boys got a bit beat up but are doing better and—"

"And Norna?"

"Thankfully, she somehow got away without a scratch." His eyes landed on the cut on her forehead. "What happened?"

Self-consciously, she put her hand to the cut. "Achilles attacked me."

His eyebrows moved together in concern. "I wish we could have come sooner."

Before she could ask, George said, "It took us a while to ensure everyone was all right. That no one's condition would grow worse."

"Where's Jewel?" Edmund asked as he walked into the living room. He looked at Dutch, who stood in the doorway to the kitchen. "And who are you?"

Dutch's face beamed.

Caroline moved next to him. "Edmund, George, and Robert, this is my loyal friend, Dutch. He has magic just like us."

Dutch shook their hands, but his eyes hardened on George.

As he took Edmund's hand, Edmund asked, "And Jewel?"

"Achilles tried to kill her," he answered in a soft voice. "He left her with mild brain damage."

The silence in the room grew heavy.

"She's upstairs." He looked down. "She's just not the same person anymore."

Edmund pulled Caroline closer to him, into a soft hug. "I'm so sorry. She is such a bright and unique person. It has to be hard to have lost that."

Tears filled her eyes. She blinked them away, not wanting to cry again in front of George.

"May I go see her?"

Dutch smiled sadly. "First door to your left."

Edmund patted Caroline's back before turning and heading up the steps.

"Now that we are here and that you guys know who the masked man is," George said, "I think it's best we form some sort of plan to get rid of this deranged man."

Dutch gestured for the two brothers to come into the kitchen and sit.

Caroline sat along with everyone else.

As he sat, Dutch asked, "Has Achilles always been after you guys? And if so, why?"

Robert shrugged. "He took our parents away from us at a young age. As the oldest, George took us under his wing and hid us from him."

"He also killed our grandparents long before I was born," George added. "Something happened between our two families, but I've never known what."

Caroline swallowed. "For some reason, he wants to be mayor here—"

"Excuse me. We're talking," George snapped, looking at her with hard eyes.

Her mouth went dry. "But I can help," she said.

He laughed. "You? Help? Please, Caroline." He rolled his eyes. "Let the adults talk."

She crumbled, just like she did back at his house. And she hated it.

"George, is it?" Dutch asked, making her uncle's eyes look away from her. "She has told me all about you and what you've told her."

George stiffen.

"And I insist you treat her with respect in my home."

She looked at Dutch with watery eyes. For years, she had wanted someone to put George in his place, and the fact he dared to do it overjoyed her.

Robert looked him over, seeming confused.

"If not," Dutch continued, "I'll stick my foot so far up your a—"

"I get it!" George mumbled as he rolled his eyes.

It was overwhelmingly perfect to see George coward under Dutch.

After a beat, Robert spoke. "What were you saying, Caroline?"

She sucked in a breath. "He's running for mayor for some reason."

"That's odd."

"That's why he's here."

Edmund walked into the room with a soft smile. "She smiled when she saw me," he said, sitting next to Caroline. "Didn't talk, but I could tell she was happy to see me."

Dutch beamed at the news.

"I think I have an idea on how to kill Achilles," George said, making everyone glance at him. "Hear me out."

Chapter 36

With Caroline's uncles, it seemed like the house had shrunk three times. Almost every room had someone sleeping within it. Edmund slept on the sofa in the living room to keep an eye on the front door, even with the spell up. George and Robert slept in a guest room on the second floor, and Dutch slept in the guest room next to Jewel's room, where he had been staying since she had returned home.

Caroline slept with more peace than she had all week, just knowing Edmund was all right and downstairs. It was amazing to see him again, to feel loved and cared for. As if a day hadn't gone by since the last time she had seen him.

As she rolled over in her sleep, the spell book she had opened in her lap dropped to the floor with a very jarring bang. She jumped awake with a drumming heart.

Her room held a soft light from the night-light Dutch had gotten her. It sat on her dresser, giving her enough light to see the book that had fallen. Standing, she picked up the spell book and placed it on her dresser. *Maybe tomorrow I can ask for Edmund's help with it.*

After sliding her slippers on, she made her way down to the kitchen.

The hallway was well lit now. She and Dutch had put lights all around the house. The dark house had caused anxiety after Achilles.

As she passed the living room, she crept, trying not to wake Edmund. Once in the kitchen, she opened one of the cupboards to get a cup. She also pulled out a small pot to heat up the milk and a little bag to make hot chocolate.

"Who's there?" Edmund called out.

She jumped at his sudden voice. "It's me," she whispered.

Dressed in a blue pajama set, he walked into the kitchen. He turned on the light, causing them both to squint at the brightness till their eyes adjusted. "What are you doing up?" Half asleep with his hair messy, he sat at the table.

"I woke up kind of nervous. Wanted something to calm my nerves."

He looked around to see what she was doing. A smile formed on his face as his eyes landed on the pot. "Are you making…hot chocolate?" he asked, meeting her eyes.

"Yes." She ripped open the bag.

"You just committed a crime in front of me!" he called out, standing. He removed the bag from her hand. "That is not how you do it. You need real chocolate!"

Caroline smiled as she grabbed a chocolate bar that was sitting on the counter. "I'll use real chocolate if you make it." She passed him the bar.

"Deal."

Soon, they both sat at the table with hot chocolate.

"You've changed," Edmund said after they took their first sip.

"What do you mean?" she asked.

"You are more mature. I don't know. You're just different from the last time I saw you."

She did *feel* different from when she had lived in

Washington. But how could she not change? She took another sip. "I feel happy here."

He looked at her sadly. "Were you not happy back home? With me?"

Caroline knew the reason for everything that had happened, but her heart still ached at the memory of him moving her out. "Well…"

"Well?" He put his mug down.

"I was happy when I was with you," she said, looking down into her cup.

"But…?"

She sighed. "Moving out really hurt me."

"Jewel was telling me that," he muttered.

"What?" she asked, sitting taller.

"Before. We talked for a little bit before you two got hurt."

She leaned back in her chair. "I understand why you had to. But it hurt me so much. George and Mia were so horrible to me!"

"I'm so sorry, Caroline."

"Do you know how much it hurt to watch your car pull away from the house? I thought after what happened with Robert and the baby, I would move back in with you."

Tears built in his eyes.

"Y-you were like a father to me, and you left, and I felt so unloved." She took a breath in, trying to steady her voice. "I never understood what I did wrong. Why you never reached out to me. Or why I never saw you again." She understood now, but her heart still hurt. "I missed all my cousins, especially Norna. I saw her like a sister. And with no explanation, I lost her too."

A tear rolled down his cheek.

"You could have told me what was happening. You

should have. I could have handled it. It would have been easier than feeling like I was not worth loving."

"George and Mia treated you badly?" he asked in a whisper. There was pain in his face, but she went on.

"She would hit me when George was at work, and he would make me feel worthless with the things he would say."

His face dropped. "No… Please tell me that's not true."

"I wish it wasn't."

He moved to her side and kneeled to be at her height. His eyes filled with tears once more. "I'm so sorry." He took her hand in his. "I let you down. I should have come to see you; I should have risked it to ensure you were in a good home." His tear-filled eyes made her own eyes water. "I hope you can forgive me!" His voice was thick with emotions.

She wiped away a tear that rolled down his face. "Of course, I forgive you."

He hugged her tight, while she rested her head on his shoulder. "I love you very much, sweet girl." He ran his fingers through her hair, much like he did when she was younger. After a beat, he asked, "Would it be wrong to kill George in his sleep?"

She laughed under her breath. "Just a little bit."

As he let her go, he glanced at the clock on the wall. "This whole mess has kept you two girls apart long enough."

Caroline's heartbeat faster.

"What do you say? Let's teleport over to Norna. You can even stay the night." A smile formed on his face. "Like old times."

Tears stung in her eyes. She missed the old times more than she cared to admit. To waking up to the sound of him and Mary talking in the kitchen. To being in bed and talking with Norna late into the night as if they hadn't spent the whole day together. "I would love that!"

He snapped his fingers, and his wand appeared in his waiting hand.

Caroline stood ready to leave when a thought stopped her: Dutch.

In the weeks since Jewel had gotten injured, Dutch had stepped up in her life. He had made and taken her to doctor appointments. He had ensured everything she needed for school was signed, so when classes started in a few weeks, she would be enrolled. Somehow, someone who was nothing but a stranger months ago had grown into someone close to a father.

And if she left, he would wake up and worry, and with everything they had been through, she didn't want to be the cause of more stress.

"Wait," she said. "I can't leave without Dutch knowing."

Edmund's eyebrows came together as he scanned the kitchen. "Then we'll leave him a note."

She nodded, opened the junk drawer by the sink, and handed him a notepad and pen. He put the pen down once he was satisfied with the note. He then moved to the refrigerator and set the note there with tape.

"Ready?" he asked as he turned to face her.

She nodded as she took his hand.

With a flick of his wand, they teleported somewhere she didn't recognize. But the smell was familiar. Somehow, it smelled like home.

Scanning the new space, she knew this was not the house she had grown up in. The living room she stood in was small. The walls were a mint green, making the brown carpet clash. There was a desk with an old fan and a brown chair next to it. A large bookshelf sat in the corner of the room with a record player on one of its shelves. Music lightly came from it. A window peeked from behind a brown curtain, the moon bright enough for her to see rain falling.

"This is where we're hiding," he said as he watched her look around.

Before Caroline could say anything, Mary's voice came from the other room. "Edmund?" She entered the room in a white nightgown and with a crutch under her right arm. "What are you—" Her eyes landed on Caroline. She gasped as tears built in her eyes.

Caroline smiled at her as tears of her own threatened to fall.

"Oh, lovebug!" she cried out, limping to Caroline.

Caroline's old nickname caused a wave of emotions within her. She moved to her aunt and wrapped her in a hug.

"My dear, you have grown so much." Her aunt's voice was thick with tears.

Edmund smiled as Mary held her tighter.

"I've missed you," Caroline whispered as her aunt pulled back and cupped her face with her free hand.

"Are you all right?" Her aunt's blue eyes landed on her forehead.

"I am. What about your leg?"

Edmund moved out of the room and called for Norna.

"Nothing that will slow me down." Mary laughed. "I'm due in a few months, so it better heal fast."

Caroline glanced down at her aunt's baby bump with a smile. "You think it's another boy?"

"Is it silly to wish it's a girl?"

In a pink pajama set, Norna walked into the doorway and froze with tears in her eyes. Caroline met her eyes with a grin.

Her cousin had grown as well. She was much taller, and her dirty blonde hair seemed blonder since the last time she had seen her.

A sob came from her mouth as she crossed the room. Caroline wrapped her arms around her, her own face soaked with tears.

"I missed you so much," Norna whispered. She pulled back and locked eyes with her. As if she didn't believe she was really here.

Caroline laughed through her tears, not truly believing it either, before she hugged her once more.

****

"So, is it true you live on the East Coast?" Norna asked an hour later.

She and Caroline both sat by the fireplace on the living room floor as Mary and Edmund spoke in the other room.

"I do," Caroline said. "The weather is a lot different there." She hadn't even walked out of the house yet, but she could feel that wherever they were hiding was cold.

"Don't even get me started on the weather." Norna laughed before leaning in and whispering. "Where Dad hid us is *freezing*. I've never been to Alaska before. We're in some town named Willow—"

"Don't tell me more," she said, resting a hand on her knee.

"Why?"

"What if something happens, and Achilles gets that information from me?"

Her cousin nodded. "So, is that what that maniac is called?"

"Yeah."

"He showed up and hurt us. Even killed Mum's friends. It was really scary."

Caroline could see the fear in her eyes. "He's a horrible person."

"Yes, and he was so strong. It makes me happy to see

only this cut on your face." Her brown eyes moved up to her forehead. "In fact, it's quite impressive you only walked away with that."

"And some broken ribs."

Laughter bubbled from Norna, the sound taking Caroline back to her childhood. But she put a hand over her mouth as her eyes went wide. "I swear I'm not laughing about that! It's just… I hugged you so tightly!"

Caroline chuckled. "It's all right. I was so excited that I hardly cared."

"But still!"

As they laughed, Edmund peeked into the room with a smile. "It sure feels beautiful to hear that sound again."

Caroline smiled at him.

For the rest of the night, they talked and laughed till their eyelids grew heavy.

Chapter 37

It almost rained for a whole week, keeping everyone inside. As the sky stayed dark, Caroline worked on her magic every day and night.

The idea of having all her uncles train her had seemed exciting at first, but having them around made training a bit harder. Each had a different way of doing it. Robert made her stretch beforehand, for reasons she was unsure of. Edmund would not explain spells enough, leaving her confused. George didn't even bother to give his input. But he had no problem letting her know what she was doing wrong.

She trained with Dutch most of the day, which she enjoyed.

But once everyone went to bed, Caroline kept working.

As the waves and the rain filled her ears, she turned on her nightstand's lamp to read under its light. She opened Jewel's spell book, hoping that she would finally grasp the spell to heal her grandmother. It seemed impossible, but she would not give up.

She couldn't.

She reread the spell she knew by heart. With her wand in hand, she cleared her mind and whispered, "Guerir."

Her forehead tingled. She sat up with a pounding heart

and moved to the mirror over the dresser. In awe, she watched as the cut slowly disappeared from her skin.

Her mouth went dry. Running, she made her way to Dutch's room and flung the door open. "Dutch!"

He was sleeping in the bed with his back to the door.

She grabbed his arm and shoulder, shaking him. "Dutch, you have to wake up!"

He jerked awake. Sitting up, he grabbed her arm. "What? What?"

Their eyes locked in the dark room.

"Are you all right? Is Jewel—"

"Dutch, I did it!" Her voice shook as his eyebrows came together. "I did the healing spell!"

He sat up taller as she reached over and turned on the bedside table's light. Its yellow glow caused him to blink a few times before he looked up at her. "It's gone!" He grabbed her upper arms, pulled her to sit by him, and scanned her forehead again. All signs of the cut were gone.

"Dutch, I did it."

His thumb lightly brushed over where the cut had been. "You can heal her…"

She nodded.

Together, they made their way to Jewel's room. Caroline opened the door softly, not wanting to wake her. Only the smallest amount of light came from his room as they left both doors open. Caroline stood next to where she slept. *This has to work.* Dutch watched her as he wrung his hands.

She rested her wand on Jewel's head. "Guerir." She closed her eyes. Praying. Hoping this was it. That her grandmother would wake up and be perfect once more. That her grandmother's mind would be as strong as it had been before.

But when she opened her eyes, Jewel still looked the same: pale, thin, and still.

"Grandma?" she asked, no louder than a whisper. She removed her wand and shook her grandmother gently.

Dutch moved closer as Jewel opened her eyes.

Yet her eyes still held a distant look within them. She glanced around the room, seeming lost. Her eyes looked through both of them, and Caroline's eyes filled with tears.

"It didn't work," he whispered as he gently pulled Caroline back.

Her grandmother's voice was weak. "Where am I?"

He lowered himself to his knees next to her, his hand gently brushing her hair back. "You're safe. Go back to sleep, Jewel."

Jewel looked at him, and her eyebrows moved together in confusion. As if she didn't know who he was.

Caroline stepped out of the room. Tears rolled down her face as disappointment grew within her. Her cut was gone, so why hadn't it worked? What did she do wrong?

Dutch stepped out of the room and closed the door behind him.

"Let me try it again," she stated, moving to the door. "Maybe I did something wrong."

He grabbed her arms, stopping her. "She's really confused right now."

She locked eyes with him.

"We'll try again later."

A sob escaped her mouth, and he wrapped his arms around her.

****

"Okay. Try it again," Robert said as he watched Caroline try a new spell: heatlingn.

The spell was meant to make her skin unbearably hot to the touch. But no matter how many times she had tried it in the past hour, her skin didn't grow warm enough.

251

She was dressed in a white and blue striped short jumper. The skirt—that she could remove if she pleased—held to her waist by a few white buttons. A part of her feared the spell would light her outfit aflame if she did it wrong.

"She's never going to be able to do it," George muttered.

She swallowed as she glanced at where he sat at the bottom of the steps, his chin resting in his palm.

"George, that's an unnecessary comment," Edmund snapped, his eyes hardening in his direction.

A weak smile formed on her lips. Since telling him about George, he had not let any of his harsh comments pass.

"Proud of you," he said, meeting her eyes.

She smiled at him.

"Let's work on teleporting now," Robert said.

She looked back at him. "I already know how."

"I know, but it never hurts to keep working on spells we know."

She nodded and cleared her mind. She thought of the table in the kitchen and flicked her wand. "Teleportsheam." In a blink, she stood in the kitchen, facing the table by the windows.

"Can you go any farther than that?" George asked with a roll of his eyes.

She looked up at the ceiling and sighed. *I hate you.*

"Caroline, come back," Dutch's voice called from the other room.

She walked out into the living room. "Yes, I can go farther. I didn't think you wanted me too."

"The farther away you go, the better." The harshness in George's voice hurt.

This was far more than just about training.

"You sent me across the country, George!" she snapped.

He looked at her with raised eyebrows. As if she was challenging him.

"How much farther do you need me?"

"This isn't about that. You need to get better to fight Achilles." He stood, towering over her.

"George," Edmund warned.

Her mind filled with thoughts of Achilles. Of their fight and how she had walked away alive. Something the man before her didn't validate.

"George," Dutch snapped.

George looked back at where the other man stood.

"She's doing her best."

"Well, her best is not good enough! It never has been." Dutch stood.

Holding her wand tighter, she flicked it. "Teleportsheam!"

A dark and cold room surrounded her. Her heart beat hard in her ears. Glancing around, she saw that she was facing a galley kitchen. Red tiles made the walls, and white counters shined with the light from the open refrigerator. A man stood, looking into it. As he turned around, their eyes locked.

Caroline gasped, taking a step back.

"Well, isn't this a nice surprise?" Achilles said with a calm voice. "What are you doing here?"

Her body filled with chills. She looked at her wand, wondering why it had betrayed her like this. But she knew why. This was her own doing. She had held him in her mind while doing the spell, and it had brought her straight to him.

"Nice to see you here." He set down the sandwich he held in his hands. He was dressed in gray khakis with a white button-up shirt. A black tie rested around his neck, undone.

She held her wand tight. "Teleport—"

He waved his hand, pulling her wand from her hand. "There will be none of that," he said with a wicked smile.

She moved to run to where she knew the front door was, but something wrapped around her ankle, tripping her. Her knees slammed into the ground. The removable skirt snapped free from the harsh movement.

"Do stay," he said, holding out a wand of his own.

Pain squeezed at her waist as she tried to free herself. But it was no use. Everything felt so tight. His spell—whatever it was—held her strongly.

"What are you going to do?" she asked as he walked up to her. "I thought you were too proud to let your tricks kill me."

He smiled. He crouched on the balls of his feet and grabbed a fistful of her hair, making her look at him. She bit back a cry.

"Any last words?"

"Heatlingn!"

Her skin grew hot, pricking at her skin. Achilles jerked back from her with a sharp gasp. His hand was red and irritated. His spell released, and she stood.

She didn't know where her wand was, and she was not going to waste time trying to summon it. Instead, she raced to the door. A lightning spell zipped by her, missing her by inches. As she reached the door, she pulled it open, ready to scream for help.

But the door slammed shut as Achilles waved a hand at it. The handle disappeared, and the door was stuck shut with his magic.

"No!" she screamed as he grabbed her arm.

His nails scratched into her bare arm. He shoved her into his hidden room.

"Let me go!" she yelled.

"You will die here!" he hissed as he shoved her to the floor.

Desperate, she held a hand open. *Wand to my hand!* Her

wand shot out of his pocket and into her waiting hand. "Teleportsheam!"

He grabbed her wand, ripping the magic away from her. The spell hit something on his desk instead. His hand smacked her face, sending her into a ball on the floor.

"There will be no help, Caroline." He pointed his wand at her.

Her eyes filled with tears.

"But first, I want to see you suffer before I end your pitiful life."

Her eyes widened, and her mouth dried.

"Gepsic."

Her jaw tightened as the agony intensified. As he continued to send his magic into her, a scream ripped from her mouth.

Chapter 38

Dutch came back in from looking for Caroline outside—empty-handed.

"Caroline?" Edmund asked as he came back down the steps.

Robert came in from the back door.

She was still nowhere to be seen.

"You caused this!" Dutch snapped at George, who sat on the sofa.

"Excuse me?" George asked as he stood to face him.

"You pushed her! And now she's missing! Who knows where she went to get away from you!"

Edmund's hard eyes looked at his older brother with anger.

"I only told her the truth." George crossed his arms over his chest. "The brat will show up at some point."

Dutch's heart rate picked up, and his fists balled at his sides. "Don't you dare talk about her like that!"

The other man's eyes narrowed. "I'm not going to get into an argument with you about someone who's not worth it."

He saw red. "Your brothers might put up with this, but I'm not."

"What does that mean?" George asked.

Dutch reeled his fist back and slammed it into the other man's face. "That is what that means!"

George stumbled back. Dutch sucked in a breath as the other man dropped to his back side. As he hissed up at him, blood showed on his teeth.

Robert laughed under his breath, and Edmund looked at something on the floor.

"Teleport back to wherever you came from!" Dutch pointed at George. "You're not welcome here."

"Dutch! What is this?" Edmund called, making him look over at him. He held a seashell sculpture.

Dutch moved to his side. He remembered Caroline mentioning that Achilles had odd sculptures in his house. Just like this one. Fear bubbled in him. "She's with Achilles!"

His mind ran a million miles an hour. They had been talking of him when she had teleported. Was it possible that she hadn't cleared her mind enough before doing the spell?

"She is at his house?!" Edmund asked, looking shocked.

Panic overtook him as he put a hand to his head.

"Damn you! Look what you caused!" Robert snapped at George, who stood. "We have to go help her," Dutch said. He could not leave Jewel alone, but he also couldn't just leave Caroline alone with Achilles. Without a second thought, he teleported to someone who could help.

He appeared in Sal's room.

Sal—completely unaware of his arrival—sat at his desk, reading a book with a dog sitting on his lap. He petted his little head. Only music from his record player filled the room before the dog spotted Dutch and barked. The dog jumped off his lap and moved toward Dutch.

"What are you—" He turned and spotted Dutch. "AAAHHHH!" he yelled as he fell off the chair.

"Sorry, kid!" Dutch helped him up before he teleported both of them back to Jewel's house.

"What the heck was that?!" he asked, looking around Jewel's house. "Why?" He looked over at Dutch.

"You need to watch Jewel!" Dutch said. "Caroline is in danger and needs our help."

He nodded. "Go!"

Dutch and the three men teleported off.

Chapter 39

Caroline slowly woke up. Her head pounded with each beat of her heart. She didn't know when she had lost consciousness, but a fuzzy part of her memory played back the pain and then Achilles slamming her head into the frame of a mirror.

Something around her wrists pained her. Glancing down with unfocused eyes, she saw that she was tied to a chair. The bright lights around her hurt her eyes. *I need to get out of here.*

As she hung her head between her shoulders, blood dripped onto her lap, staining her jumper. Where the blood was coming from, she was unsure. She looked to her right and saw her reflection in the mirror.

Blood stained her hairline, dripping down her face. Her lip was cut, adding to the mess of the blood. Through the glass, she spotted Achilles watching her.

"I wanted you to be conscious," he said as he stepped closer to her. The tie he had around his neck was gone. "So you could suffer more."

She turned her head to face him. "Why are you even doing this?" she asked, her voice cracking.

He pulled a knife out from his pocket, and her eyes widened.

"Why?" He laughed, rolling his eyes.

"Why do you hate me? My family?"

"Shut up!" he said, raising his voice.

He grabbed her face. His fingers dug into her skin as she cried out. The knife was held inches from her cheek. She pulled away from him as much as she could. The back of her chair dug into her back.

"I want to enjoy this."

He smiled as he dug the side of the blade into her skin. Just enough to draw blood.

"Your family ruined my whole life," he whispered.

She saw the pain in his eyes. "I don't k-know what my family did to you." Her voice shook as he moved the blade to her leg. "I didn't do anything."

"You're a Smith. That's enough to kill you."

He slashed the blade across her thigh. She cried out, and he cleaned the blade with his shirt, staining it.

"They took everything from me," he spat.

She saw a look in him that she knew too well. A look of pain as one thought of their loved ones who were taken away. She found it weird to have that in common with him.

"I was just a boy when I lost my mother." His jaw clenched. "Your family could've prevented it, but they didn't. She died, and it's all the Smith's fault."

He walked up to her and put the knife to her neck. She swallowed the knot in her throat as tears spilled down her face.

"If your family had helped," he hissed, "she would've been with me for the time she should've been. You and your family must pay for what was taken from me."

"It's a horrible feeling."

His eyes filled with rage, and the knife dug into her skin, pricking it. "Don't you dare try to act like you understand me!"

"I'm sorry for what my family did to you back then."

He lowered the blade.

"But please be a better person and stop this."

"Stop talking!" He pushed the back of her chair.

She fell to the floor with a gasp. Her head bounced off the stone floor, and stars exploded in her vision. Her ears rang as the room spun.

Everything faded into nothing.

****

Achilles threw the knife to the floor. He was done. Once she woke up, he would kill her slowly.

"Gepsic!"

Pain blasted in his shoulder. He yelled as he stumbled a few feet and hit his desk. Books and paper fell off with the harsh movement.

He turned to find Edmund, George, Robert, and Dutch standing within the room. All wands pointed at him. His mouth grew dry at the sight of the brothers. Alive.

"I killed you all!" he snapped as he pointed his wand at them.

"You failed," George said as he flicked his wand. "Fire itera!"

He moved as the fire passed him, hitting the wall. "Gunfoly!" he yelled with a hard flick of his wand.

As the brothers sent more spells at him, he saw Dutch remove the rope around Caroline out the corner of his eye. "NO!"

She needed to die! He would not let them take her.

He flicked his wand with anger. The three Smiths went stiff. As he lifted his wand, their feet lifted from the floor. He held them there.

Dutch held a limp Caroline in his arms, panic written over his face. "Achilles, stop this!"

Achilles held his wand up, keeping each brother frozen in the air.

"She's just a child!"

Achilles flicked his wand, making each brother slam into the wall and drop to the floor. "Child or not, Smith blood flows through her!" He pointed his wand at her.

Her head hung in the crook of Dutch's elbow.

"And for that, she must die!"

A punch to the side of the head knocked Achilles off his feet. Pain shot through his skull as he staggered.

"You'll have to kill me before you so much as touch her again!" Edmund spat as he kicked him in the ribs.

A snap sent a wave of discomfort through him.

Robert flicked his wand at him. "Gepsic!"

Achilles dropped to the floor, screaming through the pain.

The three brothers stood around him, each sending pain down from their wands. No. No, he would not die by their hands. He was stronger than that.

Through the agony, he slammed his hands together, sending the three of them into the wall. "You all will die!" he hissed as he stood. With a hard flick of his wand, he trapped each brother in a force field.

****

Dutch shielded Caroline's head as books dropped from the shelves around them. She weakly opened her eyes; the soreness in her head made them ache. As he pulled away, he met her eyes.

"D-Dutch," she whispered, half assuming she was dreaming.

He was not with her. No. He was back at home. Safe.

She reached up and touched his face.

He was *real.*

"Look who finally rejoined us!" Achilles said as he flicked his wand.

Caroline was yanked from Dutch's arms.

"No!" he yelled as he reached for her.

Weak and dizzy, she stood in Achilles' hold. His arm wrapped tight around her shoulders, and he held his wand to her neck.

Dutch flicked his wand at him, but he waved the spell off with ease and removed Dutch's wand from him before trapping him within a force field. Caroline watched in fear as Dutch slammed his fist against the force field.

"Once I'm done with her!" Achilles put the wand to her temple.

Her breath was erratic. Everyone was trapped. No one could help her. Edmund pushed on his force field, but it was no help. It seemed he was yelling, but she could not hear him. She heard none of them as they pushed and kicked at the force fields around them.

"I'll come back and kill you!"

She tried to push away from him, but his hold tightened.

"Teleportsheam!" he yelled, taking her away from her family.

Chapter 40

A wave of panic hit Caroline as she realized she didn't know where she was. But now, she couldn't breathe.

Water surrounded her. She opened her mouth out of fear, and a strong taste of salt burned her throat. The water stung her eyes, and her lungs begged for air.

Instinct kicked in, and she swam up. Her head broke the surface as she took a large gasp of air. Her bangs covered her eyes. Swimming in place, she turned and was face-to-face with Achilles, who growled. He put his hands around her throat before pushing her back under the water.

Water filled her mouth as he squeezed her throat. Salt water burned her nose. A stabbing pain seized her chest as he slammed his knee into her stomach, making her breathe in more water. Desperate, she reached up to him, clawing at her neck to remove his hands. Her lungs burned. And his hold only tightened.

I'm going to die.

She didn't want to die this way.

Her vision grew blurry. Weakly, she grabbed his hands around her neck. *Heatlingn.* Her skin grew hot, to the point where he had to release her. His wand floated by her, and she took it. *Teleportsheam.*

Black dots filled the corners of her vision as she lay on her hands and knees. Now on the beach, she coughed and gasped, and her lungs spasmed. Her throat burned. The water she had breathed came up her throat. She puked it out onto the sand, blinking away her fading vision. Sand stuck to her wet skin as she coughed.

A kick hit her side, and her ribs cried out. She dropped onto the sand with a scream.

"Stop escaping from my grasp!" Achilles yelled. "You are only causing yourself more pain!" He snapped his fingers, and his wand jerked out of her hold and into his.

"I forgive you for what you did to my family." She coughed as she forced herself to stand. Her legs were weak.

He grimaced. "I will never forgive what your family did to my mother!"

He flicked his wand at her, shooting a fast spell her way. Without a wand, she rushed to move away from his magic.

She had seen Jewel use her magic without a wand before and hoped something in her understood how to do it. "Fire itera!" she called, waving her hand in his direction. She gasped as a short flame came from her hand and hit him. Her eyes widened, and he hissed.

"Just like your father!" He aimed his wand at her foot.

The sand moved, knocking her off her feet.

"But I will ensure your ending is not like his!"

She held her hand out. "Wand to my hand!"

Out of his pocket, her wand zoomed to her waiting hand.

"Gepsic!" he yelled as she flicked her wand, and the spell disappeared.

He waved his wand in a downward movement, sending her sinking into the sand. Her wand shot out of her hand as her arms were pulled into the sand. She pulled with all her might, but she was trapped. The cold sand surrounded her. Everything up past her elbows was exposed for him.

Achilles calmly walked to where her wand had fallen. He put his entire weight on her mother's wand, snapping it in two.

"No!" Caroline cried.

What was left of her mother was now gone, broken by the same man who had taken her mother from her.

"Stone-soul," he said.

Not even her hair moved with the wind as he froze her in place. All she could move was her eyes as she looked around for anything that could help her.

"This ends now, child." He pointed his wand at her for the final blow. A wicked smile stretched across his face.

But strong magic—that looked like a ball of fire—hit him, making him fall to the sand. Hard.

Caroline sucked in a breath. Before she could even wonder what had happened, something hit her, making her unfreeze and come out of the sand.

She looked at where Achilles had fallen. He stood and pointed a wand at her. Another ball of fire hit him.

Chapter 41

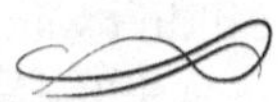

"Get away from my granddaughter!" Jewel hissed as she teleported closer.

Caroline stared at her with tears building in her eyes. The healing spell had worked!

Achilles' eyes held shock, but he quickly masked it as he stood taller. "Well, Jewel, I must say you are stronger than I had thought."

"Back away, Achilles!" Caroline moved next to her grandmother as she balled up a fist. She'd rather die than let the man before her hurt Jewel again.

"You should have stayed in that bed!" he hissed as he pointed his wand at her. "Because now I have to kill you!" He flicked his wand. "Gunfoly."

Jewel spun her wand and sent the spell flying right back at him. As he waved it away, she shot a fire spell at him. He yelled, his tone filled with pain and frustration.

He flicked his wand at Caroline, teleporting her deep into the sand where the waves broke. The wet sand held to her waist as she fought to remove herself from the sand. A wave covered her completely. The salt burned as it traveled up her nose and into her mouth once more.

A hand took hold of hers. As the wave pulled back, she saw Sal try to pull her out of the sand. But she stayed put.

"Sal!"

"I got you!"

Another wave washed over her. It pulled away, and she coughed. Before she could even try to push her way out, another wave came.

"No!" Sal gasped.

Nothing he was doing helped.

Fear gripped her. She didn't want to lose her grandmother again, and she didn't want Achilles to hurt Sal. Not when all she could do was watch as each wave stole air from her lungs.

After what seemed like a lifetime, the wave pulled back. She gasped for air as he pulled hard.

"Jewel, help her!" he yelled.

Another wave crashed over her. Yet she was teleported out of the waves and the sand. She lay on her stomach, coughing as air made its way back into her lungs.

Sal rushed to her side.

"You need to get out of here!" she said.

"I'm not leaving you!"

Looking toward Jewel, she saw Achilles flick his wand at her.

"Waicl!" Dark smoke came from his wand.

"No!" she screamed.

Jewel flicked her wand at him, and in a second, he was teleported in front of her. The spell blasted him in the chest.

She backed away as he slowly looked down at his chest. Fear flashed in his eyes as he dropped his wand. A shaky hand went to his chest.

With her heart beating wildly, Caroline watched from where she lay, her mouth ajar. Sal held her as he too watched with fear.

Achilles looked down at where the spell had hit him, back at Caroline, and then at Jewel. Slowly, small pieces of what looked like dust came off him and floated around him.

"You think you have bested me?!" he snapped as he looked at Caroline. His arm slowly deteriorated, and more dust floated around him. "This is not the last of me!"

Sal gasped.

Parts of his face faded; more dust moved around him. "You are a fool!"

Caroline's mouth grew dry, and her body shook. Sal's hold tightened.

"I will come back. And I will kill you!"

With a flash of bright light, he was gone. A handful of dry colorless leaves appeared before gracefully falling to the sand. The dust that had come off him traveled down the beach and turned off to where she knew his house was at.

"What just happened?" Sal asked.

"Are you okay?!" Jewel asked, moving to her.

Caroline looked up at her grandmother, and a sob came from her mouth. She lowered her chin to the sand.

Her grandmother was all right. She was here, and she was all right.

Jewel kneeled next to her. "Did he hurt you?"

Caroline pushed herself up and into her grandma's arms. She melted into her hold. Jewel held her tight as she cried into her chest.

"You're okay!" She closed her eyes. She never wanted to let go. "I was so worried I had lost you!"

"I'm okay now." Jewel rocked her softly, the waves roaring behind them. "I'm okay." She then pulled out of the hug and helped her to her feet. She scanned over her granddaughter, her eyes lingering on the spots Achilles had cut her. She gently put her hands on her granddaughter's face, and slowly, the cuts, the blood, and the pain disappeared.

"How can you do that so easily?" Caroline asked through her tears. "You make it seem so easy when it's not!"

Jewel laughed as she healed the deep cut on her leg. "It might be hard, but you did it."

"But you didn't heal right away!"

She cupped her granddaughter's face as tears built in her green eyes. They were so filled with life that it overwhelmed Caroline in the best way.

"It didn't matter how long it took. You got me out of that." A tear rolled down Jewel's face. "Thank you for giving me a second chance at life."

Caroline wrapped her arms around Jewel, and Jewel tightly held her close. Her ribs protested the squeezing. "Can you fix my ribs? A few broke that night."

In a second, the pain was gone.

As Jewel let her go, she picked up what was left of her mother's wand. "Thank you, Sal."

He moved to them as she smiled.

She then picked up Achilles' wand, tossed it into the air, and flicked her own wand at it. It blew up.

"Do you think he's dead?" Caroline asked, looking the way the dust had gone.

"Where did his body go?" Sal asked.

Jewel sucked in a breath as her eyes glanced at the leaves that had been left. "I really don't know."

Dutch appeared a few feet away from them. His eyes landed on Caroline and relief filled his face.

"Dutch!" Jewel said, making him turn to see her.

His eyes widened as tears formed. "Oh my God." He stumbled to her before wrapping his arms around her. "I missed you so much." His voice was thick with emotions.

He pulled back enough to place his lips to hers. She ran her hands through his messy hair.

Edmund, Robert, and George teleported to the beach. Caroline smiled at the sight. They were all right. Robert put a hand to his chest at the sight of her, and Edmund ran to her. A faint smile flickered on George's face.

"Are you all right? Did he hurt you?!" Edmund asked as he hugged her so tightly that he lifted her off the sand. "Everything is okay now."

She sighed as she watched Jewel smile at Dutch and he kiss her hands tenderly.

Dutch patted Sal's arm. "Thank you for keeping my girls safe."

"Is he dead?" Robert asked as he walked up beside Edmund.

"I believe so."

His final words rocked her. What did he mean?

Edmund set her down and put his hand to his chest. "My children will grow up safe."

Jewel took Dutch's hand in her own as she walked over to Caroline. "Let's go home."

Caroline smiled, wanting nothing more than to safely return home with everyone she loved by her side.

Epilogue

Caroline hung silver tinsel on the Christmas tree she had Dutch put up in the living room. It stood proudly by the windows, allowing anyone walking down the beach to see the tree—that was up almost four weeks early. The sun coming through the windows danced off the tinsel beautifully. She could hardly wait to see it at night.

Her red dress moved around her legs as she moved to the other side of the tree. The black ribbon that wrapped around her waist held static and would annoyingly pull some of the tinsel off the tree and onto her dress.

The house was full of joy and conversations. She could hear Jewel, Mary, and Elizabeth laughing in the kitchen as they worked on Thanksgiving dinner. The smell of the turkey in the oven made her stomach growl. All morning, the house had had that mouthwatering smell.

Christmas music lightly played off the record player by the front door. Bing Crosby's soothing voice sang "White Christmas" as she hung another strand of tinsel.

Through the window, she saw her cousins—Edmund's sons—out in the yard with a football. The television was on, adding to the sounds around her. Edmund, who was holding his three-month-old son sat on the sofa with Robert, Norna, and Dutch watching the parade with much interest.

"Caroline, remember how that balloon would scare you as a kid?" Norna laughed from where she sat next to her dad, his arm over her shoulders.

Caroline put the box of tinsel down and looked at the television. The Hobo Clown, with its green round body, floated down a street in New York City.

"Yeah, I remember," she mumbled.

Robert laughed. "Why?" he asked as Dutch smiled at her.

Her ears turned pink. "I don't know."

Edmund's shoulders shook. "She would start crying. I'd have to pick her up and remove her from the room to calm her down."

Caroline went back to her decorating as Dutch laughed.

"Here. Let me help you." He picked up the box filled with tinsel. "I don't agree with the tree being up this soon. No one else in the world does this today. But by the time you'll be done, it'll be Halloween."

She had forced Jewel and him to get a Christmas tree weeks before they normally would, excited to celebrate the holiday with her grandma and wanting to start celebrating as soon as possible. He had to teleport to a tree farm that had not opened yet to get it. Jewel had been horrified even though he had insisted he had left money.

He grabbed a handful of tinsel and threw it on the tree.

"One at a time, Dutch!" She laughed as she removed his fistful.

"That's why it is taking so long." He grabbed another fistful and dropped it on her head.

Norna laughed from the sofa. Caroline sighed with a smile as the tinsel hung from her hair.

Jewel walked into the room as she wiped her hands clean on her brown cobbler apron. Her orange dress somehow still held a stain from helping in the kitchen. She eyed the Christmas tree. "You know that stuff goes *on* the tree, right? The one you stole, Dutch."

He smiled as he turned to her. "For the last time, I didn't steal the tree. She wanted a Christmas tree. I got her a Christmas tree."

Edmund looked over at them with a raised eyebrow. "You stole the tree?"

He sucked in a breath. "Smells amazing. You girls are working hard."

She removed some tinsel from Caroline's hair and hung it on the tree. "Mary and Elizabeth are doing most of the work." She lowered her voice. "You know I can't cook to save my life."

He smiled and quickly left a kiss on her lips.

She glanced at Caroline. "How did you get him to help you with the tree?" She pulled more tinsel from her hair. "He never helps with the tree."

Caroline shrugged with a giggle.

She turned to where everyone sat in the living room. "Dinner is ready!"

Everyone crowded into the kitchen as Edmund called in his sons. With so many people over, the young boys sat around the coffee table while everyone else tightly fit around the kitchen table. The newest Smith member slept in Caroline's room.

The biggest turkey Caroline had ever seen sat in the middle of the table. It was a mouthwatering golden brown with so much stuffing packed inside that it slid out onto the platter. There was also a bowl of green beans, gravy, mashed potatoes, and cranberry sauce. Though almost no one touched the cranberry sauce. Only Norna added some to her full plate.

"Gross, Norna," Caroline whispered next to her. "You're from Washington. You disgrace your ancestors by putting that on your plate."

She filled her fork with the jiggly red sauce and poured it into her mouth.

Caroline laughed as she lightly pushed her shoulder. "Gross!"

"Leave me alone. It's good!"

Once everyone had their plates full, Jewel snapped her fingers, and the wine bottle lifted and filled everyone's glasses. Edmund covered Norna's and Caroline's glasses with his hands as the bottle hovered by.

Norna laughed. "Ah, boo!"

When he lifted his hands, punch filled their glasses.

Jewel stood, holding a wine glass in her hand. "Before we start eating, I just want to say how wonderful it is to have the house full this Thanksgiving."

Dutch smiled as he looked up at her. His tie matched the color of her dress perfectly.

"The past ten years have been just me and Dutch. It was lonely. And now, as I look around the table…" She swallowed as tears burned in her eyes. "I wasn't meant to be here this year. I would have been up in my bed, unaware of the day." Her voice grew thick as she looked across the table at Caroline. "What you did for me, I am so grateful."

Norna put a hand on Caroline's back as a tear rolled down Caroline's face.

"I am so grateful that you came into my life, Caroline." A tear rolled down her cheek. "You brought an aliveness to this lonely house."

Caroline glanced around the table with a smile. Mary held Edmund's hand. Robert's hand lay on top of Elizabeth's on the table as she rested her head on his shoulder.

"You brought love and family back to this house," Jewel said. "I love you."

"I love you too," Caroline said with a smile.

She lifted her glass up. "To family!"

Everyone grabbed their glass and held it up. "To family!"

"Dig in, everyone!" she called as she sat once more.

Norna poked Caroline as she took another bite of the cranberry sauce. "Yum," she mumbled.

Caroline winced. "Norna, please stop!"

Her cousin filled her fork with it once more before dropping it onto her plate.

"No!" She laughed.

"Just try it."

Snapping her fingers, she turned the sauce into more green beans.

"Wow! How'd you do that?"

Caroline looked across the table at Jewel laughing at something Dutch had said. "I have great teachers."

****

The dungeon's lowest level was cold and dirty. Moisture hung in the air, leaving the stony floor slippery. The dirty stones that made the walls—forty-eight thousand two hundred and seventy-three of them to be exact—pulled away any warmth from anyone unfortunate enough to be locked away under the castle above.

A man—who didn't recall his name—sat with a knee propped up under his chin. For hours, he sat in this position and mumbled to himself. The chains around his wrists dug into his skin. Some dry and fresh blood stained his irritated skin. Red and angry sores dotted the space by the metal.

The space was dim. The only light weakly made its way from the bars atop the door to his cell. He glanced up at the door. If he had to guess, it was late afternoon by the color and reach of the light. Another day had passed as slowly and sorrowfully as the one before.

His eyes moved to the stone wall next to the door, where he scratched until it left a line to mark the day that had passed.

On unstable thin legs, he stood. The chains hissed and tapped as he moved toward the wall.

"Then I can… Know I should," he mumbled as he ran a pale and shaking hand over the markings.

The wall was full of them, but he knew it had been longer since his freedom had been taken from him. Before the prison riot, he had been locked away for twelve months or less. He didn't remember.

"November?"

His eyebrows moved together as he ran a hand through his knotted beard. Some grays had worked their way into his brown hair, which was nerve-racking. Time was passing. The marks on the wall showed as much, but he could feel it in his body too.

"It's…N-November," he mumbled.

More than three thousand lines marked the wall. As he glanced at each line, a smile formed on his lips. One of those markings was the day he lost his wife. She was free, wherever she went.

He coughed as he moved back to his spot by the wall. He dropped to his boney knees, and a cough escaped him once more. His stomach hurt in a form he had grown used to. Hunger. Ignoring the discomfort, he closed his eyes and put his shaky hands together in front of him.

His name had long since faded, as did so many other things. But one name had stayed in his mind, shining with hope like a candle in a dark room.

"Caroline…will find me."

Opening his eyes, he slowly pulled his hands away from each other as a ball of light formed between his palms. He pinched his tongue with his teeth. In a world without magic, he worked endlessly to regain his powers. To make his voice heard.

As the light grew bigger, he pulled his hands apart and kept his mind on Caroline. He could still see her in his mind: her brown hair tied in ribbons, her strong brown eyes, the way her little hand would reach for his, how one of her socks would roll down no matter what…

As his mind failed him more and more, she stayed. Every detail of her burned into his mind, pushing him to work on his magic. To work his way back to her.

His hands shook uncontrollably, so he closed his eyes and took in a breath. "She needs me."

Mumbling, he put more force into the spell he was casting. If he was doing the spell right, his voice should be traveling somewhere outside these walls around him—to wherever Caroline might be.

"Caroline will find me."

A cough burned his lungs, causing the spell to fade. Each breath burned. Weakness built within him. Wherever he was locked away didn't hold the same magic from his home. There was something different here. Something that made even the smallest spell drain him.

As he leaned on the wall where his chains were nailed to, tears rolled down his dirty face. One day, she would hear him, and one day, all the draining spells would pay off. He just had to keep pushing through.

He glanced at the door. "One day."

Footsteps came from the other side of the door. Dread waved through him. The man with the odd hair would come and kick, cut, and punch him whenever he pleased. Pushing his knees to his chest, he tried to make himself as small as he could.

The footsteps grew louder before the sound of a key in the keyhole filled the space. Panic flooded him. He whispered his fear under his breath. As the door creaked open, someone much taller stepped into his cell.

Achilles.

A thin smile formed on Achilles' face, but there was no joy in it. Only rage.

"No!" the man cried as he pushed himself back into the wall. The stones poked at his spine.

It had been many marks on the wall since he had seen the masked man. Too many. Enough that he had believed he would never see him again.

"Don't h-hurt me!"

Achilles walked up to him with slow intimidating steps. "Your Caroline."

The chains pulled at his wrists as he cowered in the corner.

"She brought me back to you."

No, this man couldn't know who Caroline was. She was his! "What did you do…" Tears rolled down his face. Had he killed her? Was his Caroline gone?

Achilles cracked his knuckles. "Don't worry. Your Caroline has more luck than you ever did." He stood in front of him, his eyes glaring with hate. "But that luck will run out soon. And when it does, I'll throw her body in here with you."

His hands went to his head as his body shook violently.

Achilles kicked him in the ribs. Hard. A crack filled the space as he gasped.

"Just know." Achilles kicked him again, and pain zapped

through him. "I don't want you to die yet." He pulled out a wand and flicked it at him.

Somehow, this wicked man held the power in this world.

Screaming, the man balled up on the floor. His heart beat painfully. As if it would give up on him at any moment.

"I want you to suffer, Smith."

The magic stopped, and he sucked in a breath. "Caroline!"

Achilles laughed. "She's not coming!" His foot slammed into his ribs once more. He flicked his wand down at him again, and the man screamed till his voice went hoarse, and his vision grew dark.

Caroline! She will find me.

Seaside Magic
THE WORLD OF THE MIRROR
VIANLIX-CHRISTINE SCHNEIDER

Prologue

1943
In a Magical World

Merlin's eyes passed over the village people who had gathered around the table. They were dressed in their best for him, their king.

The castle never seemed more alive than when a banquet was held. From the large windows lining the wall, sunlight softly spilled in. Sounds of laughter and conversations around the long table filled the great hall. Lunch sat under food domes in front of each seat, and smoked lamb and fresh salad held a strong scent that made Merlin's mouth water.

He stood tall at the end of the table with confidence and a kind smile. He had a dark skin tone, and his dark brown hair was always neat no matter what time of day. He dressed fairly humble in a nice white shirt and a beautiful burgundy vest, along with cream trousers and shiny black boots. Maybe that was why the village people loved him so: he never acted as if he was better than them, and he treated everyone the same.

Looking around the room, he scanned the crowd one last time as everyone took their seats. *She had promised not to be late this time*, he thought with a sigh. He picked up his gold chalice that was filled with ale and tapped his wand against its side. Three taps was all it took for the room to fall silent.

"I am truly enthusiastic that we can share this afternoon with each other," Merlin said. "As usual, I have opened my doors to you, my people. Without you, this kingdom would not be what it is today. So, let us drink, eat, and enjoy our time together."

Every day, he held a banquet at the castle for his people. He always looked forward to it, planning meals with the cooks to make sure everything was perfect. For some banquets, he had a singer or a jester perform.

"I want to—"

His eyes moved to the large wooden doors as they opened halfway. The guards standing nearby turned to see who came in before moving aside. Zuly and Athena made their way into the room without a sound.

Zuly slowly closed the door behind them. He was pale with a slick black man bun and always held himself with confidence. He was still a fairly young man even though he was the captain of the guards.

Merlin smiled at Athena as she arrived at last. Her story had always broken his heart. While walking through the village's outskirts with Zuly four years ago, many screams had filled the calm morning air. A home was burning at an alarming rate, and everyone had desperately tried to control the fire with their magic, but it was past the point of control. No one else had dared to go in to save those who were still inside. Without a second thought, Merlin had raced inside to find a young Athena choking on the smoke. Her parents had been lost in the flames, but he took her to safety.

Quickly, Merlin's and Zuly's roles in her life had become something like a father and an older brother respectively.

Merlin gave her a place to stay in one of his many rooms at the castle and gave her dresses like she was a princess. Mostly because he treated her like his own. Zuly gave her piggyback rides around the castle, her laughter filling the halls. In that first week, Merlin had noticed just how strong her powers were and started to train her. She became his loyal apprentice.

Merlin's smile faded as he saw mischievous grins on both Zuly's and Athena's faces. "One moment," he said to the crowd as he set his chalice down. He walked over to his captain and his young apprentice.

"Sorry she is late, my King," Zuly said with a bow.

Merlin brushed it off with a smile. "Not to worry. I am just glad you both made it. Do I dare ask what you both were up to?"

"Zuly said it was okay," Athena said, her right dimple showing. She smiled up at her master before rushing to her seat next to his.

"Do not worry, Merlin," Zuly added. "I did not let her do anything you would not want her to do. I just let her drop off water to Christopher, the new guard, with her magic."

The other man smiled. "I see no harm in that. It is a hot day out after all."

Zuly shook his head with a grin. "Well, I shall leave you to enjoy your meal. I will make sure everything is running well, my King." He placed his fist across his chest and bowed.

"Please, you can eat here with us tonight."

He gave his king a surprised look. "I am not sure how it would look if I was not doing my job. I—"

"I do not care what they might think of such a thing. Come and have dinner with us, my good friend." Merlin gestured to the empty seat across from Athena, who looked back at the two men.

Zuly stayed where he was.

"I know you must be hungry," Merlin added as he rested his hand on his friend's back.

He smiled. "The food does smell great."

"Good. The guards can take care of themselves for one night."

They made their way to the empty seats. Zuly sat as Merlin picked up his chalice once more.

"Sorry about the wait," he said, speaking to everyone. "I will make this shorter than I had planned. Thank you for coming. Bless tonight and this meal."

"Merlin the Great!" everyone called out, lifting their glasses before the room fell into conversation once more.

Zuly looked across the table to see Athena lift the food dome wearily. "It is just lamb, Athena. You will be fine."

Merlin looked over, having forgotten that she disliked the meal. He picked up his wand and tapped her plate with it.

"Thank you," she said with grateful eyes as the lamb and salad turned into chicken and cold pasta.

"How have you been, Zuly?" he asked, turning to his friend as he cut a large piece of meat. "I feel as if I had not seen you much of late."

Zuly looked down at his food. "I-I have been busy training the new men."

"I hope they are doing better than the last time I stopped by to see them," Merlin said kindly.

"Just a bit." He shook his head. "They are messy, but I know they will be much better soon. I can only hope."

"You are training them. They will be fine."

After chewing a bit of chicken, Athena looked up at the two of them. "When do you believe they will be ready?"

"Soon, I hope," Zuly said.

They ate in silence for a few minutes.

"Merlin, did you see the jester when he came in?" Zuly asked, keeping his voice low.

"No. What happened?" Merlin asked after taking a sip of ale.

"When he came in through the main gate, some child told him that he was not funny."

Athena smiled.

"Not again," Merlin said lightly as he put his hand to his head.

Zuly laughed. "It gets better. He yelled at the kid until he cried, declaring he was the funniest man in the land. It was sad to watch, but I cannot lie. I found it hard not to laugh."

Merlin shook his head. "Only you would find that funny. Making a poor child cry is not amusing."

"Oh, you should have seen it," said Athena, obviously hiding her laughter. "I do not think he is that funny either." She lowered her voice. "But I would never dream of saying that to his face."

Zuly reached across the table and took a piece of chicken from her plate. "For the next banquet, I think we should stick with music. At least a singer has never made anyone cry."

The three of them laughed, but Zuly stopped short and took a deep breath. Merlin watched, knowing that his friend could smell anything for miles.

"Something is not right," Zuly whispered.

The castle shook hard, and the room fell quiet.

"What was that?" Athena asked, looking wide-eyed from Merlin to Zuly.

Merlin grabbed his wand. "I do not know. Zuly, come with me." He cleaned his lips with his napkin as he stood. "Do not worry," he told the crowd as they looked to him for reinsurance. "Enjoy your meal. We shall be back soon." He moved over to Athena and spoke in a low tone. "I will come get you if I need your help."

Once out of the great hall, Merlin turned to Zuly. "Something is not right. I can feel it."

They both paused, waiting for the shaking to come back or for a strange sound.

"What do you think it could be?" Zuly asked, resting his hand over the wand on his belt.

The castle shook again.

A guard ran over to them, seeming flushed. He bowed to Merlin before addressing his captain. "Sir, there is an intruder in the castle."

"What do you mean?" Merlin asked before Zuly could speak.

"A man broke in. So far, we do not know how. He has killed anyone who has gotten in his way. He is going towards the gem."

"What?!" Merlin gasped, feeling faint. "Who is he?!"

"I do not know, but he has strong magic."

He turned to Zuly, who looked much paler than normal. The gem was the reason everyone in this land had magic, some stronger than others. In the sunlight at the highest point of the castle, it had never moved in the history of the kingdom. If gone, magic would disappear, leaving everyone powerless.

"Zuly, do whatever you can. I need to get Athena," Merlin said.

"What about the villagers?"

Merlin looked at the guard. "Please advise them to teleport away from the castle immediately. Stay safe!"

Both Zuly and the guard bowed before Zuly left, and the guard stayed. Merlin took a deep breath and opened the great hall's door with the guard following close behind.

Merlin and Athena made eye contact. He gestured for her to come.

****

The sun's rays came in through the stained-glass window of Merlin's office. It filled the room with various colors. Many books, wands, and other items that any magical person might need filled this large room. A light ink smell lingered in the heavy air. On a normal day, this room was filled with life and magic. Merlin could sit behind his large oak desk for hours, ignoring the world. This room was his favorite, the one place that was truly *his*.

A room filled with wonder that was now empty.

It stayed calm until the heavy wooden door opened with a loud creek, and Merlin ran in. "Hurry!" His heart beat fast in his chest. "We do not have much time!"

His apprentice ran in after him, her face a light color of red from trying to keep up. "Yes, master!" She bent over, resting her hands on her knees, as she breathed heavy.

He looked around the room, his hands pushing objects all over. He searched for anything that could help them. His mind rushed as he looked through the mess of books and papers on his desk.

The castle shook once again, throwing them off-balance. Dust and pebbles fell from the ceiling and landed on Merlin and Athena as they shared a look of panic.

"What do we do, Merlin?" she asked.

He pulled a wand out from a bag by the window before turning to look through a spell book. He noticed how both of her hands fidgeted with her dress' hem. Her green eyes darted everywhere.

Never in all his life had someone broken into the castle with such bad intentions. But he could not let fear take over his young apprentice. "Athena," he said, "we are going to be fine!"

She released the hem, letting it drop back down, she moved her hands to her long, light orange hair that was done into a neat braid. She nodded to him.

Before he could tell her anything more, the castle shook again, much stronger this time. It knocked her off her feet. She landed on her side, catching herself with her hands. He grabbed onto the desk, making himself sturdy as everything shook around him. More dust and small stones fell. Athena coughed.

Merlin needed to do something fast. Once the shaking was not as bad, he let go of the desk and helped her back to her feet.

"Are you all right?" she asked with a shaky voice.

"Athena, we cannot let that man take the gem. We must do whatever it takes to keep it out of his hands."

She nodded as he handed her a wand. The shaking stopped, but the great wizard knew it was only temporary.

"What spell are we to do?" she asked.

"We should try Hucabufs and see if that one works. Stay close to me!" he said, hoping she would listen. She had never disobeyed him before, but he wanted her to understand that she must do as he said.

She nodded.

Zuly ran to the doorway, out of breath. "Your Highness!"

Merlin and Athena turned to look at him. His uniform that had been so neat a few minutes ago was now in disarray. The front metals had flipped over, his dark brown boots were scuffed, and his hair stuck to his forehead with sweat.

"The intruder has killed all my men! He made it to the gem!"

Merlin's eyes went wide. "What?!" he yelled out, not

daring to believe it. *How can that be? They were trained by the best!*

"If you are going to do something, I think it should be now."

Merlin closed his eyes. The time of action was now; he only wished that no one had died. He met Zuly's panicked eyes, a rare emotion from him. "We are going now!" he said, taking Athena by the shoulder. "If things get bad, I will teleport you away from the danger."

"No! I want to stay with you!" she protested, holding her wand tightly.

"No, you must not! Athena, you will do as I ask. You must stay away till I come and get you," he said, meeting her eyes before looking up to Zuly. "If needed, Zuly will get you. You will not be alone again. I promise." He guided her out the door, passing their captain as they made their way up to the tower.

"Your Highness," Zuly called, making the pair pause to look back at him. "I will take this man by surprise. Distract him, so I can come in when he least expects it."

Merlin nodded. "Good plan, my friend."

"Stay safe, you two," he said, looking from Athena to Merlin.

"You as well!" she said, smiling at him before Merlin put his heavy hand on her shoulder once again.

"Stay safe, Zuly. I will see you after," he said, and they turned to head up to the gem.

Once they traveled up the tower, they found the man they were looking for. But the strong winds seemed like they might just knock them off the side if they were careless.

"There he is! The great wizard and his pet!" the man said over the wind as he turned around to face them. A white mask covered his face. "I thought you were just going to let me take the gem, but I see you *do* want to fight me for it. The great king of this land…" He raised his eyebrow, it peeking over the mask. "Should I feel honored you graced me with your presence?"

Merlin gripped his wand as he stared at this man. Athena looked up and copied her master, standing the same way he did.

"I do not know who you are, but I know what you want!" Merlin said in a stern voice, his eyebrows drawn. "I cannot let you have it!"

The man laughed, giving Merlin chills. "You will not let me?" he asked, mocking Merlin's voice. "Let me tell you something." He stepped closer to the gem that sat between them. The gem was large, the size of a nightstand. "When I, Achilles Remis, want something, I always get it."

"Back away from the gem!" Merlin called out sternly as anger filled his body. He did not want to talk to this man any longer than he needed to. His wand pointed at him.

Achilles brought out his own wand. "I'm not leaving here without this gem." He lifted it and shot a strong power toward Merlin.

Merlin launched in front of Athena and flicked his wand back toward the man.

Achilles laughed as he flicked his wand, moving the spell away. "Be careful, King. Or your pet might get a boo-boo."

Merlin shot a strong lightning spell toward the man. It hit his arm. With a yell, Merlin created a strong wind that sent Achilles back a few feet. Achilles flicked his wand, making Merlin lose his footing. He tumbled back till the back of his feet touched the air, having no more flooring to stand on.

"Merlin!" Athena yelled as he disappeared over the edge.

Merlin held onto the tower's edge with his fingertips. His wand dug into his palm. He was getting ready to teleport back up when Athena's head popped up from above him. She lay on her belly, reaching her left arm toward him.

"Merlin!" she yelled as she reached her arm farther down.

"Athena, you need to teleport out of here!" he yelled, fearing for her safety.

"No! I will not leave you!"

"Athena!" he yelled as she grabbed his hand. He saw the man in the mask come up behind her. "Athena, look out!"

She let go of Merlin, standing to face Achilles. "Stay away from me!" She used her wand to lift herself into the air and shot her powers down to him.

Since Achilles was busy fighting her, Merlin let go of the edge and used his wand to teleport. Pushing away his frustration, he stood back in the tower as she lowered herself down next to him.

Achilles laughed as he looked at the pair. "For such a powerful wizard, you sure let this child fight your battles for you."

Merlin knew that he was trying to get under his skin, but he was not going to let him. He and Athena were a team. He flicked his wand toward him, making him jump out of the way and move next to the tower's stairs. Away from the gem. Just like he wanted.

"Sorry, old man, but the powers of this land are mine!" Achilles hissed.

Merlin could tell that Achilles was getting blinded by his own anger, which he could use to his advantage. He stood between the man and the gem, and Athena followed him, not pointing her wand away from Achilles. Merlin hit the man again with pure power.

At the same time, Zuly came up the steps with his body low. He held his sword in one hand and his wand in the other. They made eye contact before Merlin looked back at Achilles, not wanting him to know that Zuly would attack from behind. He noticed Zuly's stare and poked Athena's back with his finger, so she'd look away from Zuly.

"Ready to die?" Achilles asked as he looked at the pair in front of him.

Merlin held his breath, waiting for Zuly to make the final blow. Zuly's eyes were set, but something on his face looked off to Merlin. Like he was overthinking it. *Do it!* He seemed like he was frozen with his sword up, ready to run it through the other man.

But then he lowered his sword and brought his wand up, pointing it away from the man's back. He turned to where Athena stood. Her eyes went wide. A second later, his spell flew toward her so fast that she did not have time to move or fight back. Merlin watched in horror as the spell hit the middle of her chest, making her scream. A scream he would never forget.

She dropped to the stone floor like a lifeless doll, one hand over her chest and the other reaching for him. Her eyes weakly opened as she looked toward him. She lifted her outstretched arm before her eyes closed again, and her arm dropped back down to the ground. Her wand rolled out of her hand.

"NO!" Merlin yelled, dropping to her lifeless side. His heart sank. He took her small hand in his while running his other hand down her innocent pale face. "Zuly, how could you?!"

Achilles and Zuly now stood next to each other, side by side.

Zuly's face had no remorse. "I let him into this world!" he said with pride, holding his wand tightly.

Merlin felt like an ice dagger stabbed his heart.

"Now, I serve him and only him. I do not listen to your orders anymore!"

"How could you?!" Merlin yelled, letting go of her hand as he stood. He did not want to leave her, but his anger pushed him. He and Zuly had been there for each other many times. How could he just turn on him so easily? How long had his trusted friend wanted this to happen? "Zuly," he muttered, "I trusted you. *She* trusted you." He pointed at Athena, but Zuly's face stayed hard like a stone.

"I have been planning this for longer than you could ever know. You were wrong to trust me."

Before any other words could be shared, Achilles flicked his wand, hitting Merlin with a spell that pushed him back hard. He fell out of the tower once more. He tried to grab the edge again, but this time, he missed.

His nails felt like they were ripping off as they clawed at the tower's side. While in the air, he used his magic to slow his fall before landing on the ground below. He landed harder than he would have liked, and pain shot through his body.

Everything had happened so fast that his mind still tried to take it all in.

The worst pain in his life swelled inside as his powers drained. It felt like his life force was being pulled from his soul. His whole body weakened. He dropped to the ground, resting his forehead on the cold stone and finding no strength to keep his head up. He breathed in heavy, knowing Achilles had just removed the gem.

"My kingdom!" he cried, looking to his land that no longer had the bright colors it used to moments ago.

In a matter of seconds, the land had turned into a nightmare. The trees' green leaves changed to the darkest grays, browns, and blacks. The grass around him also became a dark brown color. The sky darkened along with the clouds. The moat around the castle turned black like tar. It looked like something right out of his darkest nightmares.

"No," he whispered. "What have I done?"

His mind went back to Athena. Her endless joy and contagious smile were now gone forever. He would mourn her till his last breath!

But it was also no longer safe. He would continue the fight—to get the gem back—but his body seemed as if it would give up on him. He had to get off the castle grounds.

He grabbed his wand that he had dropped and hoped it had one more spell left in it. "Teleportsheam." It took everything in him, but he removed himself from his castle and landed in the middle of the woods.

He dropped to the ground with a rushing mind and a broken heart as he let out a sob.

Chapter 1

1954

Night was falling on the small, peaceful town of Duck, North Carolina. The warm sun had shone on the town all day, but now it lowered as the moon rose in the cool air. As the pink sunset turned into a night sky full of bright stars, lights from each shop and house turned on. Behind each light was a life, someone with their own story. It was always such a lovely sight to take in, something so peaceful.

But for fifteen-year-old Caroline Smith, these lights meant she was late. *Extremely* late. She had promised her grandmother to be home before the town lights turned on and long before the sun went down. But here she was, biking through town with Sal by her side. He tried to keep up with her fast pace on his own bike.

Tonight, she had to be home for dinner. It would be a late dinner, but Jewel, her grandmother, had insisted that they have a grand meal to celebrate. Today marked the one-year anniversary of when Caroline had moved in with her grandmother and her whole magical journey had started. The path was a hard one, but she wouldn't give it up for anything. Learning magic was a gift she held dearly to her heart. She loved the family she had found in Duck.

As she biked faster, her legs burned, and she took a deep breath, breathing in the salty air. Her brown hair flowed behind her in a low ponytail. Sal now trailed her, breathing heavy. He had started out as her friend when she got to Duck but had soon become so much more.

"Keep up!" she called, looking back as he started to fall behind.

"Why…can't…we…just…teleport?!"

"Because," she called back, "I get to spend more time with you this way!"

The house she called home was in the back of the neighborhood with the big blue ocean in front. Throughout the whole day, she could hear the waves breaking on the shore. It was one of the many things she loved about the house. She didn't even know if she could sleep without the sounds of the waves anymore.

Once she made it home, she put her bike away. Sal stood next to his bike, looking at her. She looked back as she fixed her ponytail. His hair was surprisingly neat, and his face was a light shade of pink from the bike ride.

She smiled. "What?" she asked as he smiled back at her.

"Oh, nothing. It's just that you've never biked that fast before." He put his bike's kickstand down and walked up to her.

She laughed, taking his hand in hers. "I told you I was late."

"I told you we could have gone to see the lighthouse another day."

"I know, but I've been here for a year, and I hadn't seen one up close yet," she said, recalling the view from the lighthouse. She had felt as if she was on top of the world.

"Well, go eat your dinner. I don't want Jewel to get mad that I kept you." He slowly approached her and kissed her lips. They shared a smile as he kissed her hand. He turned to get back on his bike.

"Good night," she said as she watched him leave, smiling the whole time. *Gosh, he's so handsome.* She looked down at where he had kissed her hand.

She took a second to look at the beach and hear the waves crashing on the shore. Though it was late, a few families were still out on the beach, talking and laughing. She looked up to see all the stars appearing one by one in the darkening sky before closing her eyes to take in the waves' crashes one more time.

One newer sound that had become present was gleeful screams as little crabs came out from the sand for the night. The long winter had seemed so quiet without that sound. This year already seemed to have more crabs than the year before. Those who visited Duck stayed out a bit later to watch them crawl out. Dutch tried to stay off the beach instead since he hated the idea of crabs crawling around him.

She walked up the few steps to the front door. Lights were on in the living room, along with lights in the kitchen where Jewel had been cooking for what seemed like an entire day. She had started when Caroline had woken up at seven a.m. and had insisted that she wanted no help. But she only knew how to cook with her magic. She would use her wand to make amazing meals in seconds. Without magic, it took her twice as long and was twice as messy.

Caroline opened the door. "I'm home!" As she walked in, she heard the radio. A smell filled her nose, but she couldn't tell what it was or if it was good.

Jewel popped her head around the corner. She had a big smile on her face along with what looked like mashed potato on her right cheek and a green bean stuck in her brown curly hair.

"You have a green bean in your hair," Caroline pointed out as she walked past her and into the kitchen.

Jewel stopped smiling and patted her head. "Oh boy." She pulled out the green bean and threw it into the trash.

"Do you need help, Grandma?" Caroline asked as she saw the mess. More mashed potatoes lay out of the pot than in it. A mess of seasoning bottles were on the counter, some open and spilling out onto the floor. She looked down and noticed that some bottles had rolled off the counter. She picked them up, not wanting Jewel to fall over them.

"I'm almost done cooking," Jewel said, walking back over to the stove and pulling a wooden spoon out from the mash potatoes. She pulled with force since the potatoes acted like a sticky paste.

"You made my favorite?" Caroline asked as she saw what looked like meatloaf on the table.

"Yep!" Jewel said. "That's why I made it today." As she spoke, she never looked up from what she was doing. She stayed focused as she put butter in the pot with her tongue sticking out the corner of her mouth.

"Hey, youngin!" Dutch called out from behind Caroline, making her turn to see him sitting where he sat every night at the table for dinner.

"Hi, oldie," she said.

He had lived next door long before Caroline was even born. Jewel and Dutch had been friends for even longer, but this past year, their friendship had become something more, something sweeter. Jewel liked to say they were sweethearts, but Caroline knew they would get married one day. When he looked at Jewel, Caroline saw love in his eyes. It was beautiful to see, and she hoped that she and Sal would have that type of love for each other one day.

"What did you do today?" he asked, pulling out a chair for her to sit next to him.

She took the seat, folding her hands on the table. "Well, Sal wanted to do something fun today, so he took me to see a lighthouse."

Jewel turned back and smiled. "Was this the lighthouse you had been asking me to take you to?"

"Yes. We should go together one day. The view was amazing." A part of her was glad that it had been Sal who took her. The thought of them holding hands at the lighthouse had been lovely. "Do you need help, Grandma?"

"No, sweetie. I'm done," Jewel said, cleaning her hands. "But you can help me set the table."

The dinner was better than Caroline had thought it would be. Jewel even looked surprised by how good it tasted. The only thing Caroline didn't like was the mashed potatoes; they were gummy somehow and tasted like school glue. Though no one dared to say it, it was clear that no one liked them because they were the only things that remained on their plates.

Once they finished eating and cleaning up, Dutch suggested they play charades together. He and Jewel moved the coffee table out of the living room, so they had more room to play. Caroline turned on the record player, putting Nat King Cole on low. The music lightly filled their ears.

Jewel pulled out the cards, holding them facedown. "All right. Who wants to go first?" she asked, sitting on the sofa.

"I think the girl who changed our lives a year ago should go first," Dutch said as he winked at Caroline with his light blue eyes.

Caroline smiled and took one of the cards from Jewel's hand. It read *seagull!* She knew this card would be easy since she had seen them fly every day. She stood in the middle of the room, facing Jewel and Dutch. She flapped her arms up and down as if she was flying. She thought it was clear, but it was not.

"Plane! Fanning a fire! Flaring!" he called out loudly.

Caroline jumped, flaring her wrists hard. She tucked her arms in like a bird on land, walking around the way she had seen them on the beach. She even bobbed her head as she moved.

"Kid, what the heck are you?" he asked as Jewel laughed.

"Caroline, stop," she said. "You're going to hurt yourself. Time is up."

Caroline stopped and looked at Dutch. "How did you not know what I was?" she asked, sounding a bit irritated.

"How could I?"

"It was a seagull!"

Jewel laughed even harder. "No, it was not!"

Caroline made her way to the sofa with her arms crossed. "Whatever. Whose turn is it?"

As they played for a bit longer, no one really kept points. They were all just having fun and learning that Caroline was no good at this game, which frustrated her. She sat on the sofa with her arms crossed as Dutch picked up the last card.

He smiled. "Okay. Here we go," he said as he put it back. He moved to stand right in front of Jewel as he reached into his back pocket, pulling out a small box. "Jewel," he said as he got down on one knee, "will you marry me?"

"What..." Jewel muttered as she put her hand to her chest. A smile grew on her lips. She covered her mouth with her hands as the diamond sparkled back at her. "Dutch..."

Caroline smiled as she looked between Dutch and Jewel. She knew he had wanted to ask Jewel this question for what had felt like the longest time. A few months ago, he had told her all about the idea after he had picked her up from school. He had wasted no time to ask her if she was fine with it.

She had stopped walking and looked up at him with the biggest smile. "Are you kidding me?! Of course!" She gave him a hug. "Oh, I am so happy for you both! When are you going to ask her?"

"I'm happy too. One reason I wanted to pick you up today was because I want you to help me pick the ring," he had said as they started walking to the car again.

"This is so exciting! You're going to be my grandpa!" She could not stop smiling. "When can I start calling you grandpa?!"

Dutch smiled as he opened the door to his Bristol 401 for her. "I would like that but not until I ask your grandma. I don't want her to have any idea it's coming."

Each day that went by, Caroline had waited for him to ask Jewel the big question. She would look across the table at them and wonder if today was the day. And at last, the day had come!

As she watched the pair, excitement coursed through her. She looked at her grandmother and waited for her answer.

"I'm sorry, Dutch," Jewel said shyly.

Caroline froze. *What?*

Dutch's smile fell. "Jewel?" he whispered.

"Dutch, we have only been going steady for almost a year."

Hurt was written all over his face. "But we've known each other for years, longer than I even know."

"I know, but—"

He stopped her, raising his hand. "I-I don't get it." He stood. "I love you, and I've stayed by your side when you needed me the most. So what if it's only been a year? We have been through more than anyone has."

She sighed, looking away from him.

Caroline no longer smiled as she looked back at Jewel.

She had thought Jewel would be jumping and hugging him. Not this.

"Dutch, it's too soon."

"I don't understand why—"

Jewel raised her hand to stop him, making both him and Caroline look at her in shock. "I think you should go home."

Caroline's body went numb.

Dutch looked as if his heart had been broken into two pieces. "What? Jewel…"

Jewel walked away and then slowly turned back to him. "Please go."

His arms dropped to his sides.

"Grandma?" Caroline called softly.

But she left the room and headed up the stairs.

"Good night, Caroline," he muttered before turning toward the front door.

"Wait!" Caroline said, moving fast to get in front of him. She put her hands up to stop him from leaving. "She'll come around."

He didn't look her in the eyes.

She followed his gaze to the ring box still in his hand. "I'm sorry," she mumbled as the weight of the night fell on her. She looked up to find tears building in his eyes, making her heart break.

"Good night, youngin." He sighed, resting his hand on her shoulder before he headed out the door.

About the Author

After graduating from high school in 2020, Vianlix-Christine's goal was to start a career on Broadway. But the pandemic hit, and like most of the world, she became stuck at home, wondering what would happen with her dreams and career. Her first book, *Seaside Magic*, took her out of the world for a few hours a day and brought with it joy and blessings as a new career started. Vianlix-Christine lives in Virginia with her supportive family, along with her two dogs, Hershey and Oreo.

Acknowledgments

I would like to thank you, my readers. For picking up this book and going on a journey with *Seaside Magic*. I also want to thank my dad (Scott, whom I named Scott after) who has believed in me, in everything I have done. I love you to pieces. You're really the most supportive and loving dad out there. Thank you to my mom for helping make my dreams a reality. There are not enough words to say how much I love you. Thank you to my grandpa, who used to tell me to never outgrow my imagination, and to my grandma for reading this story first and being the first to believe in it. To my brother for bearing with me when I had endless questions about the story and plot that confused us both and for not thinking I was nuts when I told you I wanted to write this story. And mostly I want to thank Abby Saul for helping me with every process and showing me this was not impossible; Robin LeeAnn, my editor who helped make my words beautiful sentences; and Lena Yang whose stunning art made the cover of this book. Your art is inspiring. Lastly, I want to thank anyone who has picked up a book, shared it with friends, and let authors take you out of the world for a while. From the bottom of my heart, thank you to everyone!!

Don't Miss the Next Book in the Seaside Magic Series!

More from Vianlix~Christine Schneider

9 798986 923963